W9-DEU-408

OLD GLORY

ALSO BY ROBERT HEDIN

POETRY

The Old Liberators: New and Selected Poems and Translations

Tornadoes

County O

At the Home-Altar

Snow Country

TRANSLATIONS

The Roads Have Come to an End Now:
Selected and Last Poems of Rolf Jacobsen
(with Robert Bly and Roger Greenwald)

The Bullfinch Rising from the Cherry Tree: Poems of Olav H. Hauge

The Dream Factory: A Children's Story by Bjørn Sortland
(with Emily Christianson)

Night Music: Poems of Rolf Jacobsen

In Lands Where Light Has Another Color: Poems of Rolf Jacobsen

EDITED COLLECTIONS

Perfect in Their Art: Poems on Boxing from Homer to Ali
(with Michael Waters)

Keys to the Interior: Twenty-Five Years of the Great River Review
(with Richard Broderick)

The Zeppelin Reader: Stories, Poems and Songs from the Age of Airships

The Great Machines: Poems and Songs of the American Railroad

The Great Land: Reflections on Alaska
(with Gary Holthaus)

Alaska: Reflections on Land and Spirit
(with Gary Holthaus)

In the Dreamlight: Twenty-one Alaskan Writers
(with David Stark)

OLD GLORY

GLORY

American War Poems from
the Revolutionary War to the War on Terrorism

Edited by Robert Hedin
with a Foreword by Walter Cronkite

A Karen & Michael Braziller Book
PERSEA BOOKS / NEW YORK

Persea Books, Inc.
853 Broadway
New York, NY 10003

Library of Congress Cataloging-in-Publication Data

Old Glory : American war poems from the Revolutionary War to the war on terrorism / edited by Robert Hedin ; with a foreword by Walter Cronkite.
    p. cm.
"A Karen & Michael Braziller Book."
Includes bibliographical references and index.
ISBN 0-89255-310-3 (original trade pbk. : alk. paper)
1. War poetry, American. 2. United States—History, Military—Poetry. I. Hedin, Robert, 1949– II. Title.

PS595.W36O43 2004
811.008'0358—dc22   2004001906

Designed by Rita Lascaro
Manufactured in the United States of America
First Edition

From the moment they left the gates the road was encumbered with huge gray motor-trucks, limousines, motorcycles, long trains of artillery, army kitchens, supply wagons, all the familiar elements of the procession he had so often watched unrolling itself endlessly east and west.... Nothing new in the sight— but something new in the faces! A look of having got beyond the accident of living, and accepted what lay over the edge, in the dim land of the final.

EDITH WHARTON

CONTENTS

WAR ON TERRORISM

FOREWORD

THE POEMS HEREIN ARE GRAPHIC DESCRIPTIONS of the heroism and horror of war and its political and cultural meaning. It is almost irresistible to plunge immediately into the magnificence of the poetry that came alive from the pens of untutored soldiers and master craftsmen. Their poems inform us as to how our wars were perceived by those contemporary to the action or by those who, with the passage of time, have contemplated their significance and meaning and have adorned them with history's verdict.

But, dear Reader, as strong as is that literary magnet, don't be so enthralled as to skip Robert Hedin's complementary prose. His dissection and analysis of our nation's armed conflicts supplement the poems and are important editorial commentary on each of these wars. They explore the cultural and political revolutions that caused them or resulted from them—the events that inspired the poets.

As I, enthralled, read this superb book I was forced to reflect, not kindly, on my own experience as a correspondent in the Second World War and Vietnam. I did my best to report on the merciless carnage of war, of our armies' victories and defeats, and close-ups of unimaginable gallantry and suffering and pain and selfless sacrifice.

When the wars ended and I was back home, friends and relatives were encouragingly complimentary. "Great stuff, Walt. I read every word you wrote." But then they added the discouraging sequel. "Tell me," they went on, "what was it *really* like?"

All those great dispatches of mine apparently failed in their purpose to tell what it was really like. I have solemnly pondered this in all these ensuing years. Now I know that the problem was not in my efforts at prose but in the fact that I chose the wrong field. It seems that the gift of telling what war is really like has been bestowed upon the poets.

Walter Cronkite
New York, 2004

ACKNOWLEDGMENTS

I AM INDEBTED TO MANY PEOPLE who helped in the preparation of this book: W. D. Ehrhart, Benjamin Hedin, Gregory Orfalea, Tammy Wadley, and Michael Waters. I am also grateful to the staff of the Red Wing Public Library for its help in researching the background of many of the poems. Above all, I wish to express my gratitude to those at Persea Books—Karen Braziller, Michael Braziller, Gabriel Fried, Rita Lascaro, and Enid Stubin—for their persistence, illuminations, professionalism, and their unfailing commitment to make this collection possible. Thank you all.—RH

INTRODUCTION

THE TRADITION OF WAR POETRY IN AMERICA IS YOUNG, at least when compared to other western countries. Little more than two centuries old, it is one of the latest descendants in a large family that can trace its bloodlines back more than 2,700 years to a common ancestor, Homer and his great war epic, the *Iliad*. Still, the American tradition has established a unique literary province, and as the poetry resulting from our nation's recent conflicts testifies, it is still very much in the making.

Old Glory is the first anthology of its kind—a unique historical record that traces the course of American war poetry from its nationalistic and patriotic roots in colonial times to the disillusionment that pervades much of contemporary poetry about war. Included are poems on legendary encounters—Gettysburg, Pearl Harbor, and September 11, to name only a few—and on individuals who have played defining roles in the creation of our nation's mythology—Paul Revere, Abraham Lincoln, Sitting Bull, and others. Add in lesser known figures and conflicts, and the result is a story of grand proportions, intricate and overlapping plots that resonate with stunning complexity, played out on a stage that stretches from Bunker Hill in Boston to the deserts of Iraq.

Of the 140 poets in this book, roughly half have seen action as combatants, from Philip Freneau to Ernest Hemingway to Yusef Komunyakaa. The rest served on the peripheries of battle in field hospitals, war relief efforts, or in various roles on the home front. The collection also offers a number of poems by pacifists, conscientious objectors, and other dissenting voices from the long tradition of American anti-war poetry. Together, they render the war experience from so many vantage points that a wide range of themes and attitudes emerges, going beyond the American experience to explore the nature of war itself. *Old Glory* can often be read as a dialogue. Individual poets—sometimes whole generations—talk back and forth in subtle and often spirited ways. They address the nature of honor and heroism while at the same time challenging, redefining and, in some cases, debunking as illusory some of war's most hallowed tenets.

But still the question: Why, when there exists a virtual cottage industry devoted to the publication of war literature—histories, biographies, memoirs, novels, and so on—should we listen to our poets? We should do so for the same reasons we have always turned to them. In moments of individual or national crisis, poets sweep away the many layers of illusion and uncover a deeper stratum of meanings that otherwise might be lost. Through the powerful and intimate tool of language, they give voice, shape, and texture to profoundly human truths that cannot always be found in conventional historical accounts, regimental histories, letters and diaries, or other annals of the battlefield—truths, in other words, that can be expressed in only one way, in the ordered, imaginative whole of a poem.

The poetry of the Revolutionary War is valued today more for its historical importance than for its literary merits. Heavily influenced by leading British poets of the time, such as Pope, Goldsmith, and Gray, it was, with few exceptions, a poetry of limited gifts that rarely strayed far from the traditional norms of heroic war poetry. These were mostly well-educated, aristocratic poets who understood the political and moral imperatives of the war and willingly embraced their roles as celebrants and mythmakers. They concentrated on exalting heroes and glorifying the exploits of battle, filling their poems with revolutionary fervor, idealism, and conventional patriotic sentiments. As a result, they kept the war's terrible realities at a distance. In reading their work, one is hard-pressed to find any loss of human life—only "the martyred patriot," to quote John Pierpont. Unlike later American war verse, their poetry offered few if any clues as to what the day-to-day life of the common soldier was like. Though imbued with noble attributes, he remained a part of the background, subordinated to the larger patriotic picture.

In their attempt to give birth to national heroes who could stand shoulder to shoulder with the great warriors of the past, poets fixed their attention on figures of high rank, those in military positions similar to the poets' own high social stations. John Paul Jones, Joseph Warren, and George Washington were invariably portrayed in inflated and heroic, if not divine, terms. Likewise, to galvanize the revolutionary spirit and lay claim to the American soil, such places as Trenton, Bunker Hill, and Eutaw Springs, all sites where Americans had shed their blood with valor, were consecrated as hallowed ground.

What poetry of artistic value that did arise from this period was written by those close to the action, such as Philip Freneau, America's first professional journalist. His poetry often achieves moments of genuine authority and authenticity not found in other work of the time. In "The British Prison Ship," for example, certainly one of the most anti-British poems ever written by an American, Freneau captures the horrifying conditions he experienced as a prisoner:

Down to the gloom we took our pensive way,
Along the decks the dying captives lay,
Some struck with madness, some with scurvy pained,
But still of putrid fevers most complained?
On the hard floors these wasted objects laid,
There tossed and tumbled in the dismal shade,
There no soft voice their bitter fate bemoaned.
And death trode stately, while the victims groaned . . .

Such stark, measured detail can describe virtually any prisoner-of-war camp—Andersonville, the Hanoi Hilton—then as now. It should also be noted that many of the poems about the revolution were written long after the conflict had concluded. "Paul Revere's Ride" by Henry Wadsworth Longfellow, a poem whose famous opening lines, galloping tetrameter rhythms, and dramatic conclusion have assured it a permanent place in the popular canon, was published in 1863, some eighty-eight years after the event that occasioned it and the same year as both the Emancipation Proclamation and the Gettysburg Address—a reminder to a country split by civil war of its common roots. "Black Samson of Brandywine" by Paul Laurence Dunbar, a poem about a legendary soldier who acts with great prowess, was composed more than a century after the battle of its title and served to emphasize the significant roles that African Americans had played in the making of our country. The rest of the era's poetry, overshadowed by the political tracts, pamphlets, and fiery sermons of the day, has slipped quietly, and not altogether unjustifiably, into history, a part of an unabashedly heroic expression of war that no longer strikes a chord with modern readers.

The same cannot be said of the poetry of the Civil War. To this day it commands our attention, in part because of the central role the war plays in our nation's history and also because the best of its poetry established its own identity, freed from what Emerson called "the courtly muses of Europe." Some of America's most popular poems date from this era. "Barbara Frietchie" by John Greenleaf Whittier, "Sheridan's Ride" by Thomas Buchanan Read, and "The High Tide at Gettysburg" by Will Henry Thompson, for example, all enjoyed wide readerships during the war and are routinely anthologized in textbooks. Others such as "The Battle Hymn of the Republic" by Julia Ward Howe and "John Brown's Body" (the authorship of which is uncertain), both marching songs of the Union Army, were quickly adopted into our nation's folkloric traditions and can still be found in songbooks today. The Civil War also witnessed the rise of war poetry by women—notably that of Emily Dickinson—as well as by those in the infantry, such as Sidney Lanier and Ambrose Bierce.

The heroic traditions were alive and well during this period. Celebrations, exhortations, and the typical honorific portrayals of high-ranking figures could be found in great numbers. But the kind of all-out zealotry that dominated so much earlier verse was tempered by the dark, underlying reality of the war's sheer ugliness and of brother killing brother, a reality that was simply too powerful for poets to avoid. It was this reality that gave rise to such sobering pieces as "Fredericksburg" by Thomas Bailey Aldrich and "The Battlefield" by Lloyd Mifflin, both of which concern the war's human toll. This reality also allowed Herman Melville and Walt Whitman, the two titans of Civil War poetry, to break with the past and to introduce a poetic sensibility that bordered on the modern.

Though both Melville and Whitman were forty-two years old and too old for soldiering when war broke out in 1861, they addressed the conflict in their poetry. Melville was a staunch Unionist who refused to celebrate the war but instead gave us poems that were dense and brooding and filled with brutal realism. In "The College Colonel," far example, he offers the portrait of a figure who has seen all his chivalric illusions die on the battlefield. A maimed hero unlike any previously depicted in American war poetry, he parades through town stunned by war's crushing realities, a personification of its physical and psychic toll. Likewise, in writing about the first battle of the ironclads in "A Utilitarian View of the *Monitor*'s Fight," Melville sees the end of the heroic age, the exploits of the individual soldier supplanted by mechanized weaponry:

> Yet this was battle, and intense—
> Beyond the strife of fleets heroic;
> Deadlier, closer, calm 'mid storm;
> No passion, all went on by crank,
> Pivot, and screw,
> And calculations of caloric.

Whitman's poetry, meanwhile, exhibits a much different ethos. In such poems as "Vigil Strange I Kept on the Field One Night" and "The Wound-Dresser," both arising from his experiences in the war-hospitals of Washington, D. C., he displays a genius not found in American war poetry up to this point. Full of empathy and devotion for the wounded on both sides of the conflict, he writes with profound intimacy and acts as a kind of conscience:

> Bearing the bandages, water and sponge,
> Straight and swift to my wounded I go,
> Where they lie on the ground after the battle brought in,
> Where their priceless blood reddens the grass the ground,

Or to the rows of the hospital tent, or under the roof'd hospital,
To the long rows of cots up and down each side I return,
To each and all one after another I draw near, not one do I miss,
An attendant follows holding a tray, he carries a refuse pail,
Soon to be fill'd with clotted rags and blood, emptied, and fill'd again.

Indeed, few poets before or after have so successfully rendered, with such tenderness and sympathy, the plight of the common soldier. His are some of the most poignant portrayals of suffering in American literature.

During the First World War, as Virginia Woolf writes, "human nature changed," and the world took a hard, brutal turn. What began for many as a romantic adventure quickly turned into what Hemingway called "the most colossal, murderous, mismanaged butchery that has ever taken place on earth." In all, almost ten million people were killed, and twenty million others died of disease and starvation. The Great War was a fulcrum. During its four years of conflict, the balance of power shifted. The Romanovs, Ottomans, Hohenzollerns, and Hapsburgs, all the empires and monarchies that had monopolized the control of Europe, crumbled. In their place were Soviet communism, Arab nationalism, and new countries such as Poland, Yugoslavia, and Czechoslovakia. The great centers of art and culture also changed: Berlin, Vienna, and Prague were replaced by London, Paris, and New York. All these factors provoked a decisive and permanent shift in the poet's outlook.

In reading the poetry of the First World War, one finds little if any glory, no exultation, and no embracing of nobility. All the traditional reasons for going to war—youthful enthusiasm, patriotic zealotry, the lure of a great cause, the deliverance from a dull and tedious peacetime—were swept away along the 470 miles of trenches and barbed wire that constituted the Western front. In their place lay a modernist stance of irony and defiance, disillusionment, and bitterness that constituted a new poetic style. The heroic tradition, so durable for so many years, proved to be woefully inadequate. Moreover, the increased size of armies and new technological weaponry, as well as the introduction of aerial and gas warfare, all conspired to diminish the role of the individual soldier. Indeed, more often than not, the soldier is depicted as one among many, a victim of circumstance. His death is never idealized. As John Peale Bishop writes in "In the Dordogne":

And each day one died or another
Died: each week we sent out thousands
That returned by hundreds
Wounded or gassed. And those that died
We buried close to the old wall

> Within a stone's throw of Périgord
> Under the tower of the troubadours.
>
> And because we had courage;
> Because there was courage and youth
> Ready to be wasted; because we endured
> And were prepared for all endurance;
> We thought something must come of it:
> That the Virgin would raise her child and smile;
> The trees gather up their gold and go;
> That courage would avail something
> And something we had never lost
> Be regained through wastage, by dying . . .

Many poets, not just Peale, felt their obligation was to destroy the myth of war, to depict its devastating reality in unadorned terms, and to expose its awful truths to civilians and other non-combatants who still carried some vague romantic notion of battle.

Only Alan Seeger preserved a sense of past traditions. There on the front-lines along the Aisne, in a landscape of "wrecked promise and abandoned hopes," he finds:

> There we drained deeper the deep cup of life,
> And on sublimer summits came to learn,
> After soft things, the terrible and stern,
> After sweet Love, the majesty of Strife . . .

Today Seeger's work appears almost juvenile in its outlook—the product of a last, young innocent proudly bearing the banner of the past into the savage machinery of modern warfare. Other poets—Cummings, Pound, MacLeish—were unable to muster such grandiose visions. Pound, in "Hugh Selwyn Mauberley," one of the most searing indictments of war, answers Seeger:

> Some quick to arm,
> some for adventure,
> some from fear of weakness,
> some from fear of censure,
> some for love of slaughter, in imagination,
> learning later . . .
> some in fear, learning love of slaughter;
> Died some, pro patria,

> non 'dulce' non 'et decor'. . .
> walked eye-deep in hell
> believing in old men's lies, then unbelieving
> came home, home to a lie . . .

An estimated fifty million people, most of them civilians, died in the Second World War. America alone lost 290,000, a relatively small figure when compared to Russia's 7,500,000 losses or the estimated six million who died in Nazi concentration camps. Yet no war before or after has inspired so much American poetry. In a sense, these were poets who were already prepared for battle, already schooled in the ghastliness they would find on the modern battlefield. They had few false expectations and even fewer illusions to lose.

Though some of the finest poems to come out of the war were written by poets far from the battle-lines—"Roosters" by Elizabeth Bishop, "In Distrust of Merits" by Marianne Moore, and "Memories of West Street and Lepke" by Robert Lowell—an abundance of poetry rose from the ranks of citizen-soldiers who had little or no awareness of a heroic tradition. Their journey through the war's inferno—from young, innocent initiates to hardened warriors—was laced with a desperate sense of isolation, of being cut off from their past and cast adrift in a strange, elemental world of attack and counterattack. As George Oppen writes in "Survival: Infantry":

> We crawled everywhere on the ground without seeing the earth again
>
> We were ashamed of our half life and our misery: we saw that
>   everything had died.
>
> And the letters came. People who addressed us thru our lives
> They left us gasping. And in tears
> In the same mud in the terrible ground

They wrote with a decided lack of fervency and patriotism and instead looked upon war as a job. They endured miseries, loneliness, and fatigue and fought not so much for peace or a noble cause as for the war's end. As a generation, they were skeptical, if not dismissive, of such time-honored martial concepts as glory and heroism. "Needless to catalogue heroes," writes Edwin Rolfe, "Hero's a word for peacetime. Battle / knows only three realities: enemy, rifle, life."

What this poetry lacks in zealotry, it makes up for in candor. It depicts modern war in highly unadorned, ignoble terms—a massive, indifferent machine in which the individual soldier is nothing more than an expendable part. Death's full weight and fury can be felt in virtually every poem. Nowhere is this more evident than in the poetry of the pilots, bombardiers, navigators, and others who played roles in the air campaigns of the Second World War. While the tragic enormity of trench warfare dominates the poetry of the First World War, the modern technology of aerial combat dominates that of the Second. Howard Nemerov, Randall Jarrell, Edward Field, and Harvey Shapiro all deal with the air war's brute destructiveness. As Randall Jarrell writes in the stark confession of "Losses":

> In bombers named for girls, we burned
> The cities we had learned about in school—
> Till our lives wore out; our bodies lay among
> The people we had killed and never seen.
> When we lasted long enough they gave us medals;
> When we died they said, "Our casualties were low."
> They said, "Here are the maps"; we burned the cities.

Though the poetry of the Second World War is the poetry of victors, it is also a deeply wounded, compassionate verse, undeniably elegiac. For many, the war became a lifelong subject, and they felt an obligation to return to it, to give shape and texture to an experience that had played a defining role in their lives. Years later, recalling the horrors he had endured as a young man in "The Pit," Lucien Stryk offers a grim reminder that victory and winning are not always synonymous terms: "Ask anyone who / Saw it, nobody won that war."

Fought on the heels of the Second World War, at the dawn of both the Atomic Age and the Cold War, the Korean conflict is our nation's "forgotten war." A wretched ordeal that lasted nearly as long the Second World War, it involved over a million Americans and cost 33,629 lives. Despite its length and bloody toll, the war failed to produce any significant body of verse. Of all our nation's modern wars, only the Spanish-American War, a conflict that lasted one year and involved far fewer troops, gave us less poetry.

Still, what poetry was produced is both striking and unerring in its depictions of warfare. Spare and often rough-cut, it comes to us in an undeniable voice of authenticity, as though it had been composed directly on the battlefield, in the brief peace between salvos, without the luxury of rumination or revision. As Rolando Hinojosa writes in "A Sheaf of Percussion Fire":

> Early this morning, we opened up on Them;
> Tit for tat, then,
> They opened up on Us, and there was Death,
> Out of breath,

Trying to keep the count. Death is badly in need of assistants,
But the young and able are busy for the moment.
So, resourceful Death makes do
With a Burroughs for Us and an abacus for Them.

The news that Hinojosa and others bear from Korea is candid and fueled by a sense of anger and cynicism. For them, the individual soldier has become nothing more than a lowly pawn on the vast, strategic chessboard of the Cold War. Poets of the Second World War rarely ask why America is fighting. Those of the Korean War repeatedly beg the question. Stripped of glamour and moral imperative, war has degenerated into a brute test of endurance.

Modern American wars tend to be fought in pairs; much like the First and Second World Wars, the Korean and Vietnam conflicts are linked. One ended in a stalemate, while the other was the first war America lost. None of our country's conflicts have generated a more vocal anti-war poetry than the Vietnam War. So pronounced is this anti-war sentiment that, for the first time, it overshadows much of what came directly from the battlefield. Moreover, as the war dragged on, many of the traditional delineations between anti-war poetry and war poetry began to break down. Anti-war poets at home and combat-poets in Vietnam began to share a similar outlook: the belief that this war was a tragic exercise in futility.

With few exceptions, poets at home depicted the conflict as lacking moral value—a corrupt endeavor made to indulge capitalist and expansionist interests, as well as the vanity of our leaders, political and military alike. In "Up Rising," one of the most incendiary poems to come from the war, Robert Duncan writes:

But the mania, the ravening eagle of America
    as Lawrence saw him "bird of men that are masters,
    lifting the rabbit-blood of the myriads up into—"
    into something terrible, gone beyond bounds, or
As Blake saw figures of fire and blood raging,
    —in what image?   the ominous roar in the air,
the omnipotent wings, the all-American boy in the cockpit
    loosing his flow of napalm, below in the jungles
        "any life at all or sign of life" his target, drawing now
            not with crayons in his secret room
the burning of homes and the torture of mothers and fathers
            and children,
        their hair a-flame, screaming in agony, but
in the line of duty, for the might and enduring fame
    of Johnson, for the victory of American will over its victims . . .

Much of the poetry sides with the victims of the war—the peasants of Vietnam, whose way of life is often depicted as pastoral or idyllic. During no other war has this identifying with the opposition occurred on such a scale. Such poems as "What Were They Like?" by Denise Levertov, "The Asians Dying" by W. S. Merwin, and "The Birds of Vietnam" by Hayden Carruth remind us that the war was Vietnam's tragedy, too. Poets offered a view of the war from inside out, countering the jingoistic propaganda of government officials and other proponents of the conflict.

The poetry of those who served in Vietnam bears ample evidence that, as John Balaban writes, the war "wasn't just a macho game." There were no great hordes of enemies as in the Korean War, nor traditional battle-lines like those of the two world wars. In poems like "Search and Destroy" by Dale Ritterbusch or "Caves" by Michael S. Harper, it was a war fought on the run, against a phantom enemy hard to locate and sometimes even harder to identify. Because events tended to unfold at random, in brief, explosive engagements, its plot was episodic and possessed no clear storyline like that of the Second World War— nothing to compare with the sequence of events that unfolded between Normandy and Berlin.

The soldier-poets rarely deal with the war's historical foundations or express an understanding of Vietnamese culture. For the most part, they remain outsiders looking in at an alien society, not knowing if they are aggressors or liberators, bearers of good or evil. Along with their rifles and grenades, they have imported Bob Hope and the Gold Diggers, Christmas bells, and other accoutrements to recast Vietnam in the American image. Michael Casey describes the Vietnamese reaction to this in "For the Old Man":

> The man clasped his hands
> In front of him
> And bowed to us
> Each in turn
> To Booboo, Albert, and me
> He kept it up too
> He wouldn't stop
> His whole body shaking
> Shivering with fright
> And somehow
> With his hands
> Clasped before him
> It seemed as if
> He was praying to us
> It made all of us

Americans
Feel strange

If there are benefits to this war, they cannot be found in its poetry. Honor, courage, and patriotism have been replaced by moral confliction, cynicism, and a sense of futility. Survival is the highest honor. But with it comes a haunting. As W. D. Ehrhart writes on behalf of his generation, "Vietnam. Not a day goes by without that word on my lips."

To date, the Gulf War of 1990–1991 and the current War on Terrorism have produced no soldier-poets. Perhaps the replacement of the military draft following the Vietnam War in favor of the present all-volunteer system explains this. Still, battlefields tend to create poets. That no verse of any real value has been produced by either of these conflicts is curious. Lacking the firsthand experience that has lent so much authority to American war poetry in the past, the poems of this period are largely an expression of watching.

The notion of distance has everything to do with the Gulf War, the first conflict in history to be broadcast live to worldwide audiences on television. Americans sat in the safety of their homes and were surfeited with dramatic footage of explosions lighting the landscape, with the video-game look and precision of "smart" bomb weaponry. We became voyeurs of events that took place thousands of miles away in Kuwait and Iraq. Unlike the gruesome images televised during the Vietnam War, these pictures arrived in our living rooms free of such realities, of anything that might result in protest. The Gulf War was delivered to us as theater. As part of a daily package of entertainment, it came complete with commercials and honorific images of high-ranking figures—General Norman Schwarzkopf, for example—transformed by television into celebrities. The common soldier was so thoroughly dominated by images of weapon-wizardry and of his military superiors that he was essentially forgotten, and once he was removed, the tenets of courage and heroism collapsed.

Largely due to the tragedy of the attack on the World Trade Center in New York City on September 11, 2001, the War on Terrorism has been treated in a different light, in traditional, pre-Vietnam images. The common soldier has been brought back to center stage; sacrifice, courage, and heroism have been resurrected. War, in other words, is once again dirty and bloody, a brutal business to be endured for a cause. Virtually every soldier, even those at home waiting to be deployed to the frontlines, has been depicted as a hero. Outfitted with all the equipment of modern war, he looks invincible.

None of this has been lost on poets. Allusions to television are found throughout the poetry of the Gulf War, while images of the September 11 attacks dominate the verse of the War on Terrorism. Despite how successful the military and television industries have been in marketing the opposing personalities of these two wars, our nation's poets have remained unconvinced. They have not embraced patriotic illusions. After September 11, when the government was again singing what C. K. Williams calls its "canticles of vengeance and battle prayers," many poets reacted with a countersong. Recalling the days of Vietnam, the poetry is unequivocally dissenting in spirit. Poets are writing like hardened veterans who already know the results—a resounding chorus against the mad cycles. Here is Shirley Kaufman in "Cyclamen":

> While the planes
> roar and practice over our heads,
> and we dutifully buy bottled water,
> tape for our sealed rooms,
>
> and check our gas masks.
> Caught in the same efficiency
> that kills. How many marches
> in the streets of peace?
>
> How many wars?

Old Glory is arranged chronologically by conflict. Each section is organized according to the sequence of historical events, the date of a poem's composition, or the year of its publication. Readers should bear in mind that the volume represents only a sampling of the vast amount of war poetry that has been produced in this country. Many of the selections have enjoyed popularity for years. Others are not so well known, and some will be introduced to readers for the first time.

Through the power of imagination, the poets of *Old Glory* have fashioned out of war's horror and human carnage some of the most enduring poetry in our culture, a poetry that preserves important aspects of our nation's history and helps to establish our national continuity. They guide us into a world in which the living and the dead—those who survived and those who were sacrificed— are forever linked. In so doing, they have forged a compassionate pact to remember, to document, and, in the end, to fulfill one of the poet's primary tasks—to give voice to those who have fallen silent. The result is a book, both haunting and memorable, that speaks from a great depth of time as well as from the immediacy of our own moment.

Robert Hedin
Red Wing, Minnesota

OLD GLORY

REVOLUTIONARY WAR
(1775–1783)

Paul Revere of Boston, in the Colony of Massachusetts Bay in New England; of Lawfull Age, doth testify and say, that I was sent for by Docr Joseph Warren, of said Boston, on the evening of the 18th of April [1775], about 10 oClock; when he desired me "to go to Lexington, and inform Mr Samuel Adams, and the Honl John Hancock Esqr that there was a number of Soldiers, composed of Light troops, & Grenadiers, marching to the bottom of the Common, where was a number of Boats to receive them; it was supposed, that they were going to Lexington, by way of Cambridge River, to take them or go to Concord, to distroy the Colony Stores." I proceeded immediately, and was put across Charles River, and landed near Charlestown Battery, went to town, and there got a Horse.

"MEMORANDUM," PAUL REVERE, 1783

HENRY WADSWORTH LONGFELLOW (1807–1882)

Henry Wadsworth Longfellow was born in Portland, Maine. Author of such poems as "The Wreck of the Hesperus" and "The Song of Hiawatha," he remains one of America's best-loved poets. Published in 1863, "Paul Revere's Ride" is his most popular work, despite its historical inaccuracies.

Paul Revere's Ride

Listen, my children, and you shall hear
Of the midnight ride of Paul Revere,
On the eighteenth of April, in Seventy-five;
Hardly a man is now alive
Who remembers that famous day and year.

He said to his friend, "If the British march
By land or sea from the town to-night,
Hang a lantern aloft in the belfry arch
Of the North Church tower as a signal light,—
One, if by land, and two, if by sea;
And I on the opposite shore will be,
Ready to ride and spread the alarm
Through every Middlesex village and farm,
For the country folk to be up and to arm."

Then he said, "Good-night!" and with muffled oar
Silently rowed to the Charlestown shore,
Just as the moon rose over the bay,
Where swinging wide at her moorings lay
The Somerset, British man-of-war;
A phantom ship, with each mast and spar
Across the moon like a prison bar,
And a huge black hulk, that was magnified
By its own reflection in the tide.

Meanwhile, his friend, through alley and street,
Wanders and watches with eager ears,
Till in the silence around him he hears
The muster of men at the barrack door,

The sound of arms, and the tramp of feet,
And the measured tread of the grenadiers,
Marching down to their boats on the shore.

Then he climbed the tower of the Old North Church,
By the wooden stairs, with stealthy tread,
To the belfry-chamber overhead,
And startled the pigeons from their perch
On the sombre rafters, that round him made
Masses and moving shapes of shade,—
By the trembling ladder, steep and tall,
To the highest window in the wall,
Where he paused to listen and look down
A moment on the roofs of the town,
And the moonlight flowing over all.

Beneath, in the churchyard, lay the dead,
In their night-encampment on the hill,
Wrapped in silence so deep and still
That he could hear, like a sentinel's tread,
The watchful night-wind, as it went
Creeping along from tent to tent,
And seeming to whisper, "All is well!"
A moment only he feels the spell
Of the place and the hour, and the secret dread
Of the lonely belfry and the dead;
For suddenly all his thoughts are bent
On a shadowy something far away,
Where the river widens to meet the bay,—
A line of black that bends and floats
On the rising tide, like a bridge of boats.

Meanwhile, impatient to mount and ride,
Booted and spurred, with a heavy stride
On the opposite shore walked Paul Revere.
Now he patted his horse's side,
Now gazed at the landscape far and near,
Then, impetuous, stamped the earth,
And turned and tightened his saddle-girth;
But mostly he watched with eager search

The belfry-tower of the Old North Church,
As it rose above the graves on the hill,
Lonely and spectral and sombre and still.
And lo! as he looks, on the belfry's height
A glimmer, and then a gleam of light!
He springs to the saddle, the bridle he turns,
But lingers and gazes, till full on his sight
A second lamp in the belfry burns!

A hurry of hoofs in a village street,
A shape in the moonlight, a bulk in the dark,
And beneath, from the pebbles, in passing, a spark
Struck out by a steed flying fearless and fleet:
That was all! And yet, through the gloom and the light,
The fate of a nation was riding that night;
And the spark struck out by that steed, in his flight,
Kindled the land into flame with its heat.

He has left the village and mounted the steep,
And beneath him, tranquil and broad and deep,
Is the Mystic, meeting the ocean tides;
And under the alders that skirt its edge,
Now soft on the sand, now loud on the ledge,
Is heard the tramp of his steed as he rides.

It was twelve by the village clock,
When he crossed the bridge into Medford town.
He heard the crowing of the cock,
And the barking of the farmer's dog,
And felt the damp of the river fog,
That rises after the sun goes down.

It was one by the village clock,
When he galloped into Lexington.
He saw the gilded weathercock
Swim in the moonlight as he passed,
And the meeting-house windows, blank and bare,
Gaze at him with a spectral glare,
As if they already stood aghast
At the bloody work they would look upon.

It was two by the village clock,
When he came to the bridge in Concord town.
He heard the bleating of the flock,
And the twitter of birds among the trees,
And felt the breath of the morning breeze
Blowing over the meadows brown.
And one was safe and asleep in his bed
Who at the bridge would be first to fall,
Who that day would be lying dead,
Pierced by a British musket-ball.

You know the rest. In the books you have read,
How the British Regulars fired and fled,—
How the farmers gave them ball for ball,
From behind each fence and farm-yard wall,
Chasing the red-coats down the lane,
Then crossing the fields to emerge again
Under the trees at the turn of the road,
And only pausing to fire and load.

So through the night rode Paul Revere;
And so through the night went his cry of alarm
To every Middlesex village and farm,—
A cry of defiance and not of fear,
A voice in the darkness, a knock at the door,
And a word that shall echo forevermore!
For, borne on the night-wind of the Past,
Through all our history, to the last,
In the hour of darkness and peril and need,
The people will waken and listen to hear
The hurrying hoof-beats of that steed,
And the midnight message of Paul Revere.

ANONYMOUS

There is no satisfactory explanation of how the term Yankee came to be applied to English settlers of Colonial America. Some believe it derives from the Dutch word Jankees, a combination of Jan and kees (cheese), thus signifying John Cheese. On April 18, 1775, while marching from Boston to do battle at Concord Bridge, the British stepped to this tune. Later, it became a popular marching song among American troops; its appeal had much to do with the term's subsequent wide usage.

Yankee Doodle

Father and I went down to camp,
Along with Captain Gooding;
And there we saw the men and boys,
As thick as hasty pudding.

Chorus:
Yankee doodle, keep it up,
Yankee doodle dandy;
Mind the music and the step,
And with the girls be handy.

There was Captain Washington
Upon a slapping stallion,
A-giving orders to his men,
I guess there was a million.

And then the feathers on his hat,
They looked so 'tarnal fin-a,
I wanted pockily to get
To give to my Jemima.

And then we saw a swamping gun,
Large as a log of maple;
Upon a deucèd little cart,
A load for father's cattle.

And every time they shoot it off,
It takes a horn of powder;
It makes a noise like father's gun,
Only a nation louder.

I went as nigh to one myself,
As 'Siah's underpinning;
And father went as nigh ag'in,
I thought the deuce was in him.

We saw a little barrel, too,
The heads were made of leather;
They knocked upon it with little clubs,
And called the folks together.

And there they'd fife away like fun,
And play on cornstalk fiddles,
And some had ribbons red as blood,
All bound around their middles.

The troopers, too, would gallop up
And fire right in our faces;
It scared me almost to death
To see them run such races.

Uncle Sam came there to change
Some pancakes and some onions,
For 'lasses cake to carry home
To give his wife and young ones.

But I can't tell half I see,
They kept up such a smother;
So I took my hat off, made a bow,
And scampered home to mother.

Cousin Simon grew so bold,
I thought he would have cocked it;
It scared me so I streaked it off,
And hung by father's pocket.

And there I saw a pumpkin shell,
As big as mother's basin;
And every time they touched it off,
They scampered like the nation.

Yankee doodle, keep it up,
Yankee doodle dandy;
Mind the music and the step,
And with the girls be handy.

PHILLIS WHEATLEY (1753?–1784)

Brought from Africa in 1761, Phillis Wheatley became the slave of Boston merchant John Wheatley, who educated her and encouraged her literary talent. After gaining her freedom in 1773 or 1774, she traveled to England, where she published Poems on Various Subjects, Religious and Moral, *the first book by a black American. A pioneering figure in African American literature, she nevertheless died poverty-stricken in a boarding house, her poems and letters largely forgotten. "To His Excellency General Washington" was written in October 1775, four months after George Washington was named commander-in-chief of the Continental Army.*

To His Excellency General Washington

Celestial choir! enthroned in realms of light,
    Columbia's scenes of glorious toils I write.
While freedom's cause her anxious breast alarms,
She flashes dreadful in refulgent arms.
See mother earth her offspring's fate bemoan,
And nations gaze at scenes before unknown!
See the bright beams of heaven's revolving light
Involved in sorrows and the veil of night!
    The goddess comes, she moves divinely fair,
Olive and laurel binds her golden hair:
Wherever shines this native of the skies,
Unnumbered charms and recent graces rise.
    Muse! bow propitious while my pen relates
How pour her armies through a thousand gates,
As when Eolus heaven's fair face deforms,
Enwrapped in tempest and a night of storms;
Astonished ocean feels the wild uproar,
The refluent surges beat the sounding shore;
Or thick as leaves in Autumn's golden reign,
Such, and so many, moves the warrior's train.
In bright array they seek the work of war,
Where high unfurled the ensign waves in air.
Shall I to Washington their praise recite?
Enough thou know'st them in the fields of fight.
Thee, first in peace and honors—we demand
The grace and glory of thy martial band.
Famed for thy valor, for thy virtues more,

Hear every tongue thy guardian aid implore!
    One century scarce performed its destined round,
When Gallic powers Columbia's fury found;
And so may you, whoever dares disgrace
The land of freedom's heaven-defended race!
Fixed are the eyes of nations on the scales,
For in their hopes Columbia's arm prevails.
Anon Britannia droops the pensive head,
While round increase the rising hills of dead.
Ah! cruel blindness to Columbia's state!
Lament thy thirst of boundless power too late.
    Proceed, great chief, with virtue on thy side,
Thy every action let the goddess guide.
A crown, a mansion, and a throne that shine,
With gold unfading, WASHINGTON! be thine.

JOHN PIERPONT (1785–1866)

John Pierpont was minister of various Unitarian churches, a Civil War chaplain, and a clerk in the United States Treasury Department. "Warren's Address to the American Soldiers" concerns Joseph Warren—Boston physician, Revolutionary patriot, and a major general in the Massachusetts Militia—who dispatched Paul Revere and William Dawes to warn Sam Adams and John Hancock of the British attack on Concord. Warren was killed in the battle of Bunker Hill on June 17, 1775, the first officer of rank to fall in the Revolutionary War.

Warren's Address to the American Soldiers

Stand! The ground's your own, my braves!
Will ye give it up to slaves?
Will ye look for greener graves?
  Hope ye mercy still?
What's the mercy despots feel?
Hear it in that battle-peal!
Read it on yon bristling steel!
  Ask it,—ye who will.

Fear ye foes who kill for hire?
Will ye to your homes retire?
Look behind you! they're a-fire!
  And before you, see
Who have done it! From the vale
On they come! And will ye quail?
Leaden rain and iron hail
  Let their welcome be!

In the God of battles trust!
Die we may, and die we must;
But, O, where can dust to dust
  Be consigned so well,
As where Heaven its dews shall shed
On the martyred patriot's bed,
And the rocks shall raise their head,
  Of his deeds to tell!

WILLIAM CULLEN BRYANT (1794–1878)

William Cullen Bryant was a lawyer and newspaper editor, as well as one of America's leading poets. "Song of Marion's Men," published in 1832, portrays American general Francis Marion, nicknamed the Swamp Fox, and his band of guerrilla soldiers, who eluded the British by hiding in the swamps of South Carolina.

Song of Marion's Men

Our band is few, but true and tried,
    Our leader frank and bold;
The British soldier trembles
    When Marion's name is told.
Our fortress is the good greenwood,
    Our tent the cypress-tree;
We know the forest round us,
    As seamen know the sea.
We know its walls of thorny vines,
    Its glades of reedy grass,
Its safe and silent islands
    Within the dark morass.

Woe to the English soldiery,
    That little dread us near!
On them shall light at midnight
    A strange and sudden fear:
When, waking to their tents on fire,
    They grasp their arms in vain,
And they who stand to face us
    Are beat to earth again.
And they who fly in terror deem
    A mighty host behind,
And hear the tramp of thousands
    Upon the hollow wind.

Then sweet the hour that brings release
    From danger and from toil;
We talk the battle over,
    And share the battle's spoil.
The woodland rings with laugh and shout,
    As if a hunt were up,
And woodland flowers are gathered
    To crown the soldier's cup.
With merry songs we mock the wind
    That in the pine-top grieves,
And slumber long and sweetly
    On beds of oaken leaves.

Well knows the fair and friendly moon
    The band that Marion leads—
The glitter of their rifles,
    The scampering of their steeds.
'Tis life to guide the fiery barb
    Across the moonlight plain;
'Tis life to feel the night-wind
    That lifts his tossing mane.
A moment in the British camp—
    A moment—and away
Back to the pathless forest,
    Before the peep of day.

PAUL LAURENCE DUNBAR (1872–1906)

Poet and novelist Paul Laurence Dunbar was born in Dayton, Ohio, the son of a former slave. Thought by many to be the first African American poet to achieve nationwide recognition, he wrote six volumes of poetry, his Complete Poems *still widely read today. In early 1777, over 500,000 free black men and slaves, representing all thirteen colonies, were recruited into the Continental Army and went on to fight with valor in many battles, including the battle of Brandywine (Pennsylvania) of Dunbar's poem.*

Black Samson of Brandywine

> *In the fight at Brandywine, Black Samson, a giant Negro, armed with a scythe, sweeps his way through the red ranks.*
>
> C. M. SKINNER'S "MYTHS AND LEGENDS OF OUR OWN LAND"

Gray are the pages of record,
    Dim are the volumes of eld;
Else had old Delaware told us
    More that her history held.
Told us with pride in the story,
    Honest and noble and fine,
More of the tale of my hero,
    Black Samson of Brandywine.

Sing of your chiefs and your nobles,
    Saxon and Celt and Gaul,
Breath of mine ever shall join you,
    Highly I honor them all.
Give to them all of their glory,
    But for this noble of mine,
Lend him a tithe of your tribute,
    Black Samson of Brandywine.

There in the heat of the battle,
    There in the stir of the fight,
Loomed he, an ebony giant,
    Black as the pinions of night.

Swinging his scythe like a mower
 Over a field of grain,
Needless the care of the gleaners,
 Where he had passed amain.

Straight through the human harvest,
 Cutting a bloody swath,
Woe to you, soldier of Briton!
 Death is abroad in his path.
Flee from the scythe of the reaper,
 Flee while the moment is thine,
None may with safety withstand him,
 Black Samson of Brandywine.

Was he a freeman or bondman?
 Was he a man or a thing?
What does it matter? His brav'ry
 Renders him royal—a king.
If he was only a chattel,
 Honor the ransom may pay
Of the royal, the loyal black giant
 Who fought for his country that day.

Noble and bright is the story,
 Worthy the touch of the lyre,
Sculptor or poet should find it
 Full of the stuff to inspire.
Beat it in brass and in copper,
 Tell it in storied line,
So that the world may remember
 Black Samson of Brandywine.

ANONYMOUS

Published in 1778, "The Yankee Man-of-War" deals with legendary American naval officer John Paul Jones, commander of the Ranger, *who made daring raids along the coast of the British Isles and, in 1778, captured the* Drake, *a British warship.*

The Yankee Man-of-War

'T is of a gallant Yankee ship that flew the stripes and stars,
And the whistling wind from the west-nor'-west blew through the pitch
    pine-spars;
With her starboard tacks aboard, my boys, she hung upon the gale;
On an autumn night we raised the light on the old Head of Kinsale.

It was a clear and cloudless night; and the wind blew steady and strong,
As gayly over the sparkling deep our good ship bowled along;
With the foaming seas beneath her bow the fiery waves she spread,
And bending low her bosom of snow, she buried her lee cat-head.

There was no talk of short'ning sail by him who walked the poop,
And under the press of her pond'ring jib, the boom bent like a hoop!
And the groaning water-ways told the strain that held her stout maintack,
But he only laughed as he glanced aloft at a white silvery track.

The mid-tide meets the Channel waves that flow from shore to shore,
And the mist hung heavy upon the land from Featherstone to Dunmore,
And that sterling light in Tusker Rock where the old bell tolls each hour,
And the beacons light that shone so bright was quench'd on Waterford Tower.

What looms upon our starboard bow? What hangs upon the breeze?
'T is time our good ship hauled her wind abreast the old Saltees,
For by her ponderous press of sail and by her consorts four
We saw our morning visitor was a British man-of-war.

Up spake our noble Captain then, as a shot ahead of us past—
"Haul snug your flowing courses! lay your topsail to the mast!"
Those Englishmen gave three loud hurrahs from the deck of their covered ark,
And we answered back by a solid broad-side from the decks of our patriot bark.

"Out boom! out booms!" our skipper cried, "out booms and give her sheet,"
And the swiftest keel that was ever launched shot ahead of the British fleet,
And amidst a thundering shower of shot, with stun'-sails hoisting away,
Down the North Channel Paul Jones did steer just at the break of day.

PHILIP FRENEAU (1752–1832)

Often called the "Poet of the American Revolution," Philip Freneau was a member of the Monmouth (New Jersey) Militia, a seaman on a blockade runner, and a journalist, as well as a translator under Thomas Jefferson at the State Department. His brutal treatment as a prisoner of war in 1780 led to "The British Prison Ship," published a year after his release and one of the most anti-British poems ever written by an American. A celebrant of the Revolution, he wrote numerous poems exalting heroes and glorifying the American cause. A good example of such lionization, "To the Memory of the Brave Americans" concerns Nathanael Greene, commander of the Carolina campaign, who, with his troops, engaged the British under General Cornwallis at Eutaw Springs, South Carolina, in 1781, a decisive battle that helped end the war.

from The British Prison Ship

Now towards the Hunter's gloomy sides we came,
A slaughter house, yet *hospital* in name;
For few came there, 'till ruined with *their* fees,
And half consumed, and dying of disease;—
But when too near, with labouring oars we plied
The *Mate*, with curses, drove us from the side;
That wretch who, banished from the navy crew,
Grown old in blood, did here his trade renew,
His rancorous tongue, when on his *charge* let loose,
Uttered reproaches, scandal, and abuse,
Gave all to hell, who dared his *king* disown,
And swore mankind were made for *George* alone.
A thousand times, to irritate our woe,
He wished us foundered in the gulph below;
A thousand times, he brandished high his stick,
And swore as often that we were not sick—
And yet so pale!—that we were thought by some
A freight of ghosts, from death's dominions come—
But calmed at length—for who can always rage,
Or the fierce war of boundless passion wage,
He pointed to the stairs that led below
To damps, disease, and varied shapes of woe—
Down to the gloom we took our pensive way,

Along the decks the dying captives lay,
Some struck with madness, some with scurvy pained,
But still of putrid fevers most complained!
On the hard floors these wasted objects laid,
There tossed and tumbled in the dismal shade,
There no soft voice their bitter fate bemoaned,
And death trode stately, while the victims groaned;
Of leaky decks I heard them long complain,
Drowned as they were in deluges of rain,
Denied the comforts of a dying bed,
And not a pillow to support the head—
How could they else but pine, and grieve, and sigh,
Detest a wretched life—and wish to die.
    Scarce had I mingled with this dismal band
When a thin victim seized me by the hand—
"And art thou come," (death heavy on his eyes)
"And art thou come to these abodes,—(he cries;)
"Why didst thou leave the *Scorpion's* dark retreat,
"And hither haste, a surer death to meet?
"Why didst thou leave thy damp infected cell?—
"If *that* was purgatory, this is hell—
"We, too, grown weary of that horrid shade
"Petitioned early for the doctor's aid;
"His aid denied, more deadly symptoms came,
"Weak, and yet weaker, glowed the vital flame;
"And when disease had worn us down so low
"That few could tell if we were ghosts, or no,
"And all asserted death would be our fate—
"Then to the doctor we were sent—too late.
"Here wastes away *Eurymedon* the brave,
"Here young *Palemon* finds a watery grave,
"Here loved *Alcander* now, alas! no more;
"Dies, far sequestered from his native shore;
"He late, perhaps, too eager for the fray,
"Chaced the proud Briton o'er the watery way,
"Till fortune, jealous, bade her clouds appear,
"Turned hostile to his fame, and brought him *here.*
    "Thus do our warriors, thus our heroes fall,
"Imprisoned here, sure ruin meets them all,
"Or, sent afar to Britain's barbarous shore,

"There pine in prisons, and return no more:
"Ah rest in peace, each injured, parted shade,
"By cruel hands in death's dark weeds arrayed,
"The days to come may to your memory raise
"Piles on these shores, to spread through earth your praise."

To the Memory of the Brave Americans

Under General Greene, in South Carolina,
who fell in the action of September 8, 1781

At Eutaw Springs the valiant died;
    Their limbs with dust are covered o'er—
Weep on, ye springs, your tearful tide;
    How many heroes are no more!

If in this wreck of ruin, they
    Can yet be thought to claim a tear,
O smite your gentle breast, and say
    The friends of freedom slumber here!

Thou, who shalt trace this bloody plain,
    If goodness rules thy generous breast,
Sigh for the wasted rural reign;
    Sigh for the shepherds, sunk to rest!

Stranger, their humble graves adorn;
    You too may fall, and ask a tear;
'Tis not the beauty of the morn
    That proves the evening shall be clear.—

They saw their injured country's woe;
    The flaming town, the wasted field;
Then rushed to meet the insulting foe;
    They took the spear—but left the shield.

Led by thy conquering genius, Greene,
    The Britons they compelled to fly;
None distant viewed the fatal plain,
    None grieved, in such a cause to die—

But, like the Parthian, famed of old,
    Who, flying, still their arrows threw,
These routed Britons, full as bold,
    Retreated, and retreating slew.

Now rest in peace, our patriot band;
    Though far from nature's limits thrown,
We trust they find a happier land,
    A brighter sunshine of their own.

JOEL BARLOW (1754–1812)

Poet and diplomat Joel Barlow's magnum opus, The Columbiad, *is an eight-volume epic that begins with Christopher Columbus as an old man able to survey America's past, present, and future. Published in 1807 with engravings executed in London, it was by far the costliest work published in its era.*

from The Columbiad

Now grateful truce suspends the burning war,
And groans and shouts promiscuous load the air;
When the tired Britons, where the smokes decay,
Quit their strong station and resign the day.
Slow files along the immeasurable train,
Thousands on thousands redden all the plain,
Furl their torn bandrols, all their plunder yield
And pile their muskets on the battle field.
Their wide auxiliar nations swell the crowd,
And the coopt navies from the neighboring flood
Repeat surrendering signals and obey
The landmen's fate on this concluding day.
 Cornwallis first, their late all conquering lord,
Bears to the victor chief his conquer'd sword,
Presents the burnisht hilt and yields with pain
The gift of kings, here brandisht long in vain.
Then bow their hundred banners, trailing far
Their wearied wings from all the skirts of war.
Battalion'd infantry and squadron'd horse
Dash the silk tassel and the golden torse;
Flags from the forts and ensigns from the fleet
Roll in the dust and at Columbia's feet
Prostrate the pride of thrones; they firm the base
Of freedom's temple, while her arms they grace.
Here Albion's crimson Cross the soil o'erspreads,
Her Lion crouches and her Thistle fades;
Indignant Erin rues her trampled Lyre,
Brunswick's pale Steed forgets his foamy fire,
Proud Hessia's Castle lies in dust o'erthrown,
And venal Anspach quits her broken Crown.
 Long trains of wheel'd artillery shade the shore,

Quench their blue matches and forget to roar;
Along the incumber'd plain, thick planted rise
High stacks of muskets glittering to the skies,
Numerous and vast. As when the toiling swains
Heap their whole harvest on the stubbly plains,
Gerb after gerb the bearded shock expands,
Shocks, ranged in rows, hill high the burden'd lands;
The joyous master numbers all the piles
And o'er his well earn'd crop complacent smiles:
Such growing heaps this iron harvest yield,
So tread the victors this their final field.
    Triumphant Washington with brow serene,
Regards unmoved the exhilarating scene,
Weighs in his balanced thought the silent grief
That sinks the bosom of the fallen chief,
With all the joy that laurel crowns bestow,
A world reconquer'd and a vanquisht foe.
Thus thro extremes of life, in every state,
Shines the clear soul, beyond all fortune great,
While smaller minds, the dupes of fickle chance,
Slight woes o'erwhelm and sudden joys entrance.
So the full sun, thro all the changing sky,
Nor blasts nor overpowers the naked eye;
Tho transient splendors, borrow'd from his light,
Glance on the mirror and destroy the sight.

ISAAC MCLELLAN (1806–1899)

Born in Portland, Maine, Isaac McLellan was a lawyer and sportsman who gained a wide readership with the publication of The Fall of the Indian *and* Poems of the Rod and Gun. *"New England's Dead" was long considered a school-reader classic.*

New England's Dead

New England's dead! New England's dead!
   On every hill they lie;
On every field of strife, made red
   By bloody victory.
Each valley, where the battle poured
   Its red and awful tide,
Beheld the brave New England sword
   With slaughter deeply dyed.
Their bones are on the northern hill,
   And on the southern plain,
By brook and river, lake and rill,
   And by the roaring main.

The land is holy where they fought,
   And holy where they fell;
For by their blood that land was bought,
   The land they loved so well.
Then glory to that valiant band,
The honored saviours of the land!
O, few and weak their numbers were,—
   A handful of brave men;
But to their God they gave their prayer,
   And rushed to battle then.
The God of battles heard their cry,
And sent to them the victory.

They left the ploughshare in the mould,
Their flocks and herds without a fold,
The sickle in the unshorn grain,
The corn, half-garnered, on the plain,
And mustered, in their simple dress,

For wrongs to seek a stern redress,
To right those wrongs, come weal, come woe,
To perish, or o'ercome their foe.
And where are ye, O fearless men?
    And where are ye to-day?
I call:—the hills replay again
    That ye have passed away:

That on old Bunker's lonely height,
    In Trenton, and in Monmouth ground,
The grass grows green, the harvest bright
    Above each soldier's mound.
The bugle's wild and warlike blast
    Shall muster them no more;
An army now might thunder past,
    And they heed not its roar.
The starry flag, 'neath which they fought
    In many a bloody day,
From their old graves shall rouse them not,
    For they have passed away.

RALPH WALDO EMERSON (1803–1882)

Ralph Waldo Emerson's poems, essays, and lectures made him a leading spokesman of the Transcendentalism movement. To this day, he is a preeminent figure of American letters. His best-known poems include "Threnody," "Brahma," and "The Rhodora."

Concord Hymn

Sung at the Completion of the Battle Monument, July 4, 1837

By the rude bridge that arched the flood,
    Their flag to April's breeze unfurled,
Here once the embattled farmers stood
    And fired the shot heard round the world.

The foe long since in silence slept;
    Alike the conqueror silent sleeps;
And Time the ruined bridge has swept
    Down the dark stream which seaward creeps.

On this green bank, by this soft stream,
    We set to-day a votive stone;
That memory may their deed redeem,
    While, like our sires, our sons are gone.

Spirit, that made those heroes dare
    To die, and leave their children free,
Bid Time and Nature gently spare
    The shaft we raise to them and thee.

WAR OF 1812
(1812–1815)

When we were within about two or three miles of the [Boston] lighthouse, we hove-to, hoisted our ensign, and fired a gun. The challenge was immediately accepted by the *Chesapeake;* who let fall their foretopsail and also fired a gun, hoisting at the same time a large white flag at the fore; which, upon close acquaintance, we found inscribed, "Free trade and sailor's rights," the idea for which they declared war against us . . . We continued hove-to until she was nearly within gun-shot . . . At ten minutes to six, being then within pistol-shot, she gallantly rounded-to, and ranged up close on our starboard quarter, and the battle began. The cannonading continued for eleven minutes.

SECOND LIEUTENANT PROVO WALLIS, H.M.S. *SHANNON,*
ON THE DEFEAT OF THE *CHESAPEAKE,* JUNE 1, 1813

JOHN NEAL (1793–1876)

Novelist and poet John Neal was born in Portland, Maine, of a Quaker family. He began his literary career while studying law in Baltimore. His long narrative poem, "The Battle of Niagara," was published in 1818 and concerns the American forces along the Niagara River in July, 1814, who fought with valor at Chippewa and Lundy's Lane.

from The Battle of Niagara

A Night-attack by Cavalry

Observed ye the cloud on that mountain's dim green
So heavily hanging, as if it had been
The tent of the Thunderer, the chariot of one
Who dare not appear in the blaze of the sun?
'T is descending to earth, and some horsemen are now
In a line of dark mist coming down from its brow.
'T is a helmeted band; from the hills they descend
Like the monarchs of storm when the forest trees bend.
No scimitars swing as they gallop along,
No clattering hoof falls sudden and strong,
No trumpet is filled and no bugle is blown,
No banners abroad on the wind are thrown,
No shoutings are heard and no cheerings are given,
No waving of red-flowing plumage to heaven,
No flashing of blades and no loosening of reins,
No neighing of steeds and no tossing of manes,
No furniture trailing, or warrior helms bowing,
Or crimson and gold-spotted drapery flowing;
But they speed like coursers whose hoofs are shod
With a silent shoe from the loosened sod. . . .
　　Dark and chill is the sky, and the clouds gather round;
There's nought to be seen, yet there comes a low sound
As if something were near that would pass unobserved.
O, if 't is that band, may their right-arms be nerved!
Hark, a challenge is given! a rash charger neighs—
And a trumpet is blown—and lo, there's a blaze—
And a clashing of sabres is heard, and a shout
Like a hurried order goes passing about;

And unfurling banners are tossed to the sky
As struggling to float on the wind passing by;
And unharness'd war-steeds are crowding together,
The horseman's thick plume and the foot-soldier's feather.
The battle is up! and the thunder is pealing,
And squadrons of cavalry coursing and wheeling
And line after line in their light are revealing.
One troop of high helms thro' the fight urge their way,
Unbroken and stern, like a ship thro' the spray:
Their pistols speak quick, and their blades are all bare,
And the sparkles of steely encounter are there.
    Away they still speed! with one impulse they bound,
With one impulse alike, as their foes gather round,
Undismayed, undisturbed; and above all the rest
One rides o'er the strife like a mane o'er its crest,
And holds on his way thro' the scimitars there
All plunging in light, while the slumbering air
Shakes wide with the rolling artillery-peal.
The tall one is first; and his followers deal
Around and around their desperate blows,
Like the army of shadows above when it goes
With the smiting of shields and the clapping of wings,
When the red-crests shake and the storm-pipe sings,
When the cloud-flag unfurls and the death-bugles sound,
When the monarchs of space on their dark chargers bound,
And the shock of their cavalry comes in the night
With furniture flashing and weapons of light.
So travelled this band in its pomp and its might.
    Away they have gone! and their path is all red,
Hedged in by two lines of the dying and dead—
By bosoms that burst unrevenged in the strife,
By swords that yet shake in the passing of life;
For so swift had that pageant of darkness sped,
So like a trooping of cloud-mounted dead,
That the flashing reply of the foe that was cleft
But fell on the shadows those troopers had left.
Far and away they are coursing again
O'er the clouded hill and the darkened plain;
Now choosing the turf for their noiseless route,
Now where the wet sand is strown thickest about,
Streams their long line: like a mist troop they ride

In a winding cloud o'er the near mountain's side,
While a struggling moon throws a luster as dim
As a sepulchre's lamp, and the vapours that swim
O'er the hills and the heavens divide as they fly—
The videttes of winds that are stationed on high.

PHILIP FRENEAU (1752–1832)

The War of 1812 was an unpopular war. The country was plagued by dissension, defeatism, and the fear that New England was on the verge of secession. Except for a few victories at sea, the military picture was dire at best. In August 1814, a British expedition to Chesapeake Bay scored an easy victory at Bladensburg and captured Washington, burning the Capitol and the White House.

ON THE CONFLAGRATIONS AT WASHINGTON

—Jam deiphobi dedit ampla ruinam,
Vulcano superante, domus; jam proximus ardet
Ucalegon.

VIRGIL

Now, George the third rules not alone,
For George the vandal shares the throne,
True flesh of flesh and bone of bone.

God save us from the fangs of both;
Or, one a vandal, one a goth,
May roast or boil us into froth.

Like danes, of old, their fleet they man
And rove from *Beersheba* to *Dan*,
To burn, and beard us—where they can.

They say, at George the fourth's command
This vagrant host were sent, to land
And leave in every house—a brand.

An idiot only would require
Such war—the worst they could desire—
The felon's war—the war of fire.

The warfare, now th' invaders make
Must surely keep us all awake,
Or life is lost for freedom's sake.

They said to Cockburn, "honest Cock!
To make a noise and give a shock
Push off, and burn their navy dock:

"Their capitol shall be emblazed!
How will the *buckskins* stand amazed,
And curse the day its walls were raised!"

Six thousand heroes disembark—
Each left at night his floating ark
And *Washington* was made their mark.

That few would fight them—few or none—
Was by their leaders clearly shown—
And *"down,"* they said, *"with Madison!"*

How close they crept along the shore!
As closely as if *Rodgers* saw her—
A frigate to a seventy-four.

A veteran host, by veterans led,
With *Ross* and *Cockburn* at their head—
They came—they saw—they burnt—and fled.

But not unpunish'd they retired;
They something paid, for all they fired,
In soldiers kill'd, and chiefs expired.

Five hundred veterans bit the dust,
Who came, inflamed with lucre's lust—
And so they waste—and so they must.

They left our congress naked walls—
Farewell to towers and capitols!
To lofty roofs and splendid halls!

To courtly domes and glittering things,
To folly, that too near us clings,
To courtiers who—tis well—had wings.

Farewell to all but glorious war,
Which yet shall guard *Potomac's* shore,
And honor lost, and fame restore.

To conquer armies in the field
Was, once, the surest method held
To make a hostile country yield.

The mode is this, now acted on;
In conflagrating *Washington,*
They held our independence gone!

Supposing *George's* house at Kew
Were burnt, (as we intend to do,)
Would that be burning England too?

Supposing, near the silver *Thames*
We laid in ashes their *saint James,*
Or *Blenheim* palace wrapt in flames;

Made Hampton Court to fire a prey,
And meanly, then, to sneak away,
And never ask them, what's to pay?

Would that be conquering London town?
Would that subvert the english throne,
Or bring the royal system down?

With all their glare of guards or guns,
How would they look like simpletons,
And not at all the *lion's sons!*

Supposing, then, we take our turn
And make it public law, to burn,
Would not old english honor spurn

At such a mean insidious plan
Which only suits some savage clan—
And surely not—the english man!

A doctrine has prevail'd too long;
A king, they hold, *can do no wrong*—
Merely a pitch-fork, without prong:

But de'il may trust such doctrines, more,—
One king, that wrong'd us, long before,
Has wrongs, by hundreds, yet in store.

He wrong'd us forty years ago;
He wrongs us yet, we surely know;
He'll wrong us till he gets a blow

That, with a vengeance, will repay
The mischiefs we lament this day,
This burning, damn'd, infernal play;

Will send *one city* to the sky,
Its buildings low and buildings high,
And buildings—built the lord knows why;

Will give him an eternal check
That breaks his heart or breaks his neck,
And plants our standard on QUEBEC.

FRANCIS SCOTT KEY (1779–1843)

While on a legal mission on the night of September 13, 1814, Maryland lawyer Francis Scott Key was detained by the British and forced to watch the massive bombardment of Fort McHenry in Baltimore. Throughout the bombardment, he was able to see only an enormous American flag, measuring thirty-six by twenty-nine feet, flying above the fort. The sight of it inspired his poem, the tune to which is derived from a British drinking song. An act of Congress made it America's official national anthem in 1931.

The Star-Spangled Banner

O say! can you see by the dawn's early light,
    What so proudly we hail'd at the twilight's last gleaming?
Whose broad stripes and bright stars, thro' the perilous fight,
O'er the ramparts we watched were so gallantly streaming?
And the rocket's red glare, the bombs bursting in air,
Gave proof thro' the night that our flag was still there.

    O say, does that star-spangled banner yet wave
    O'er the land of the free and the home of the brave?

On the shore, dimly seen thro' the mists of the deep,
There the foe's haughty host in dread silence reposes.
What is that which the breeze, o'er the towering steep,
    As it fitfully blows, half conceals, half discloses?
Now it catches the gleam of the morning's first beam,
In full glory reflected now shines on the stream;

    'Tis the star-spangled banner, O long may it wave
    O'er the land of the free and the home of the brave!

And where is that band who so vauntingly swore
    That the havoc of war and the battle's confusion,
A home and a country, shall leave us no more?
    Their blood has washed out their foul footsteps' pollution.
No refuge could save the hireling and slave,
From the terror of flight or the gloom of the grave,

And the star-spangled banner in triumph doth wave
O'er the land of the free and the home of the brave.

O! thus be it ever when free men shall stand
    Between their lov'd homes and the war's desolation!
Blest with vict'ry and peace, may the heav'n rescued land
    Praise the Pow'r that hath made and preserved us a nation!
Then conquer we must, when our cause it is just,
And this be our motto, "In God is our trust!"

And the star-spangled banner in triumph shall wave,
O'er the land of the free and the home of the brave!

OLIVER WENDELL HOLMES (1809–1894)

From 1847 until his retirement in 1882, Oliver Wendell Holmes was Parkman Professor of Anatomy and Physiology at Harvard University, where he also served as dean of the medical school. He wrote the following poem in tribute to the Constitution, perhaps the most famous vessel in U.S. naval history. On August 19, 1812, off the coast of Halifax, the 44-gun frigate destroyed the formidable British ship Guerriere, *while sustaining little damage to its own hull. Known thereafter as* Old Ironsides, *it was deemed unseaworthy in 1830, but public sentiment, aroused in part by the publication of Holmes' poem, helped save it from demolition. Today, the ship resides at the Boston Navy Yard, a national treasure.*

Old Ironsides

Ay, tear her tattered ensign down!
   Long has it waved on high,
And many an eye has danced to see
   That banner in the sky;
Beneath it rung the battle shout,
   And burst the cannon's roar;—
The meteor of the ocean air
   Shall sweep the clouds no more!

Her deck, once red with heroes' blood
   Where knelt the vanquished foe,
When winds were hurrying o'er the flood
   And waves were white below,
No more shall feel the victor's tread,
   Or know the conquered knee;—
The harpies of the shore shall pluck
   The eagle of the sea!

O better that her shattered hulk
   Should sink beneath the wave;
Her thunders shook the mighty deep,
   And there should be her grave;
Nail to the mast her holy flag,
   Set every thread-bare sail,
And give her to the god of storms,—
   The lightning and the gale!

MEXICAN-AMERICAN WAR
(1846–1848)

Dear friends: I presume you received a letter stating that I had enlisted in the Army . . . When we shall go away is uncertain, probably by the first of March, or at any rate as soon as Spring opens . . .

When I first came here, I with the other recruits was drilled one and a half hours in the A.M. . . . and the same in the P.M. when we had as much as you please of Right dress, Front, Right flank, Right face, Left flank, Left face, 'Bout face, Countermarch by file right and left, Left and right oblique march, Right and left wheel, Right and left turn, Right into lines, Common time, Quick time, Double quick time, Treble quick time, Mark time, etc., etc., etc., etc.

PRIVATE BARNA UPTON, THIRD UNITED STATES INFANTRY, GOVERNOR'S ISLAND, NEW YORK, FEBRUARY 8, 1845

Here's another letter from the rambling soldier. . . Today is muster day, and I have just come off parade. The Third Regiment is acknowledged to be the best disciplined regiment in the United States and [I] have nothing to say to the contrary. Every finger and toe and joint must be placed exactly according to custom, and I rather conclude that I can come it equal to the old buck. Sometimes a recollection of old times and early scenes makes me a little homesick, but the next roll of the drum drives it all away.

PRIVATE BARNA UPTON, THIRD UNITED STATES INFANTRY, CORPUS CHRISTI, TEXAS, AUGUST 31, 1845

RALPH WALDO EMERSON (1803–1882)

Emerson's ode to William Henry Channing was published in 1846. Channing was a vigorous political activist and a well-known Transcendentalist. With Emerson and Unitarian clergyman J. F. Clarke, he edited the memoirs of writer, lecturer, and ardent feminist Margaret Fuller in 1851.

Ode, Inscribed to W. H. Channing

Though loath to grieve
The evil time's patriot,
I cannot leave
My honied thought
For the priest's cant,
Or statesman's rant.

If I refuse
My study for their politique,
Which at the best is trick,
The angry Muse
Puts confusion in my brain.

But who is he that prates
Of the culture of mankind,
Of better arts and life?
Go, blindworm, go,
Behold the famous States
Harrying Mexico
With rifle and with knife!

Or who, with accent bolder,
Dare praise the freedom-loving mountaineer?
I found by thee, O rushing Contoocook!
And in thy valleys, Agiochook!
The jackals of the negro-holder.

The God who made New Hampshire
Taunted the lofty land
With little men;—
Small bat and wren

House in the oak:—
If earth-fire cleave
The upheaved land, and bury the folk,
The southern crocodile would grieve.

Virtue palters; Right is hence;
Freedom praised, but hid;
Funeral eloquence
Rattles the coffin-lid.

What boots thy zeal,
O glowing friend,
That would indignant rend
The northland from the south?
Wherefore? to what good end?
Boston Bay and Bunker Hill
Would serve things still;—
Things are of the snake.

The horseman serves the horse,
The neatherd serves the neat;
The merchant serves the purse,
The eater serves his meat;
'Tis the day of the chattel,
Web to weave, and corn to grind;
Things are in the saddle,
And ride mankind.

There are two laws discrete,
Not reconciled,—
Law for man, and law for thing;
The last builds town and fleet,
But it runs wild,
And doth the man unking.

'Tis fit the forest fall,
The steep be graded,
The mountain tunnelled,
The sand shaded,
The orchard planted,
The glebe tilled,

The prairie granted,
The steamer built.

Let man serve law for man;
Live for friendship, live for love,
For truth's and harmony's behoof;
The state may follow how it can,
As Olympus follows Jove.

    Yet do not I invite
The wrinkled shopman to my sounding woods,
Nor bid the unwilling senator
Ask votes of thrushes in the solitudes.
Every one to his chosen work;—
Foolish hands may mix and mar;
Wise and sure the issues are.
Round they roll till dark is light,
Sex to sex, and even to odd;—
The over-god
Who marries Right to Might,
Who peoples, unpeoples,—
He who exterminates
Races by stronger races,
Black by white faces,—
Knows to bring honey
Out of the lion;
Grafts gentlest scion
On pirate and Turk.

The Cossack eats Poland,
Like stolen fruit;
Her last noble is ruined,
Her last poet mute:
Straight, into double band
The victors divide;
Half for freedom strike and stand;—
The astonished Muse finds thousands at her side.

JOHN GREENLEAF WHITTIER (1807–1892)

John Greenleaf Whittier was a Quaker poet, a reformer, and a pioneer in regional literature, as well as a crusader for humanitarian causes. He was a member of the Massachusetts state legislature and helped found the Republican Party. Among contemporaneous poets, only Henry Wadsworth Longfellow surpassed his popularity. Fought on February 22–23, 1847, the battle of Buena Vista, described below in Whittier's poem, was a particularly hard and furious conflict between American forces commanded by General Zachary Taylor and the Mexican army under the leadership of General Santa Anna. On the night of February 23, Santa Anna withdrew his forces, leaving the control of northern Mexico in the hands of Taylor.

The Angels of Buena Vista

> *A letter-writer from Mexico during the Mexican war, when detailing some of the incidents at the terrible fight of Buena Vista, mentioned that Mexican women were seen hovering near the field of death, for the purpose of giving aid and succor to the wounded. One poor woman was found surrounded by the maimed and suffering of both armies, ministering to the wants of Americans as well as Mexicans with impartial tenderness.*

Speak and tell us, our Ximena, looking northward far away,
O'er the camp of the invaders, o'er the Mexican array,
Who is losing? who is winning? are they far or come they near?
Look aboard, and tell us, sister, whither rolls the storm we hear.

"Down the hills of Angostura still the storm of battle rolls;
Blood is flowing, men are dying; God have mercy on their souls!"
Who is losing? who is winning? "Over hill and over plain,
I see but smoke of cannon clouding through the mountain rain."

Holy Mother! keep our brothers! Look, Ximena, look once more.
"Still I see the fearful whirlwind rolling darkly as before,
Bearing on, in strange confusion, friend and foeman, foot and horse,
Like some wild and troubled torrent sweeping down its mountain course."

Look forth once more, Ximena! "Ah! the smoke has rolled away;
And I see the Northern rifles gleaming down the ranks of gray.
Hark! that sudden blast of bugles! there the troop of Minon wheels;
There the Northern horses thunder, with the cannon at their heels.

"Jesu, pity! how it thickens! now retreat and now advance!
Right against the blazing cannon shivers Puebla's charging lance!
Down they go, the brave young riders; horse and foot together fall;
Like a ploughshare in the fallow, through them ploughs the Northern ball."

Nearer came the storm and nearer, rolling fast and frightful on!
Speak, Ximena, speak and tell us, who has lost, and who has won?
"Alas! alas! I know not; friend and foe together fall,
O'er the dying rush the living: pray, my sisters, for them all!

"Lo! the wind the smoke is lifting. Blessed Mother, save my brain!
I can see the wounded crawling slowly out from heaps of slain.
Now they stagger, blind and bleeding; now they fall, and strive to rise;
Hasten, sisters, haste and save them, lest they die before our eyes!

"O my heart's love! O my dear one! lay thy poor head on my knee;
Dost thou know the lips that kiss thee? Canst thou hear me? canst thou see?
O my husband, brave and gentle! O my Bernal, look once more
On the blessed cross before thee! Mercy! mercy! all is o'er!"

Dry thy tears, my poor Ximena; lay thy dear one down to rest;
Let his hands be meekly folded, lay the cross upon his breast;
Let his dirge be sung hereafter, and his funeral masses said;
To-day, thou poor bereaved one, the living ask thy aid.

Close beside her, faintly moaning, fair and young, a soldier lay,
Torn with shot and pierced with lances, bleeding slow his life away;
But, as tenderly before him the lorn Ximena knelt,
She saw the Northern eagle shining on his pistol-belt.

With the stifled cry of horror straight she turned away her head;
With a sad and bitter feeling looked she back upon her dead;
But she heard the youth's low moaning, and his struggling breath of pain,
And she raised the cooling water to his parching lips again.

Whispered low the dying soldier, pressed her hand and faintly smiled;
Was that pitying face his mother's? did she watch beside her child?
All his stranger words with meaning her woman's heart supplied;
With her kiss upon his forehead, "Mother!" murmured he, and died!

"A bitter curse upon them, poor boy, who led thee forth,
From some gentle, sad-eyed mother, weeping, lonely, in the North!"
Spake the mournful Mexic woman, as she laid him with her dead,
And turned to soothe the living, and bind the wounds which bled.

Look forth once more, Ximena! "Like a cloud before the wind
Rolls the battle down the mountains, leaving blood and death behind;
Ah! they plead in vain for mercy; in the dust the wounded strive;
Hide your faces, holy angles! O thou Christ of God, forgive!"

Sink, O Night, among thy mountains! let the cool, gray shadows fall;
Dying brothers, fighting demons, drop thy curtain over all!
Through the thickening winter twilight, wide apart the battle rolled,
In its sheath the saber rested, and the cannon's lips grew cold.

But the noble Mexic women still their holy task pursued,
Through that long, dark night of sorrow, worn and faint and lacking food.
Over weak and suffering brothers, with a tender care they hung,
And the dying foeman blessed them in a strange and Northern tongue.

Not wholly lost, O Father! is this evil world of ours;
Upward, through its blood and ashes, spring afresh the Eden flowers;
From its smoking hell of battle, Love and Pity send their prayer,
And still thy white-winged angels hover dimly in our air!

JAMES RUSSELL LOWELL (1819–1891)

Poet, critic, editor, teacher, and diplomat, James Russell Lowell was among the most distinguished and popular American writers of the nineteenth century. He was the author of A Fable of Critics, Fireside Travels, *and* Democracy and Other Addresses. *Written in New England dialect and published in 1848,* The Biglow Papers *is a long poem that combines satire with piercing social criticism, its style in many ways anticipating Mark Twain's use of the vernacular. The following is told from the point of view of Birdofredum Sawin, a volunteer in the Mexican War.*

from The Biglow Papers

This 'ere 's about the meanest place a skunk could wal diskiver
(Saltillo's Mexican, I b'lieve, fer wut we call Salt-river);
The sort o' trash a feller gits to eat doos beat all nater,
I'd give a year's pay fer a smell o' one good blue-nose tater;
The country here thet Mister Bolles declared to be so charmin'
Throughout is swarmin' with the most alarmin' kind o' varmin.
He talked about delishis froots, but then it wuz a wopper all,
The holl on 't 's mud an' prickly pears, with here an' there a chapparal;
You see a feller peekin' out, an', fust you know, a lariat
Is round your throat an' you a copse, 'fore you can say, "Wut air ye at?"
You never see sech darned gret bugs (it may not be irrelevant
To say I've seen a *scarabœus pilularius* big ez a year old elephant),
The rigiment come up one day in time to stop a red bug
From runnin' off with Cunnle Wright,—'t wuz jest a common *cimex lectularius.*

One night I started up an eend an' thought I wuz to hum agin,
I heern a horn, thinks I it's Sol the fisherman hez come agin,
His bellowses is sound enough,—ez I'm a livin' creeter,
I felt a thing go thru my leg,—'t wuz nothin' more 'n a skeeter!
Then there's the yaller fever, tu, they can it here el vomito,—
(Come, thet wun't du, you landcrab there, I tell ye to le' *go* my toe!
My gracious! it's a scorpion thet's took a shine to play with 't,
I darsn't skeer the tarnal thing fer fear he'd run away with 't.)
Afore I come away from hum I hed a strong persuasion
Thet Mexicans worn't human beans,—an ourang outang nation,
A sort o' folks a chap could kill an' never dream on 't arter,
No more 'n a feller 'd dream o' pigs that he hed hed to slarter . . .

But wen I jined I worn't so wise ez thet air queen o' Sheby,
Fer, come to look at 'em, they aint much diff'rent from wut we be,
An' here we air ascrougin' 'em out o' thir own dominions,
Ashelterin' 'em, ez Caleb sez, under our eagle's pinions,
Wich means to take a feller up jest by the slack o' 's trowsis
An' walk him Spanish clean right out o' all his homes an' houses;
Wal, it doos seem a curus way, but then hooraw fer Jackson!
It must be right, fer Caleb sez it's reg'lar Anglo-saxon.
The Mex'cans don't fight fair, they say, they piz'n all the water,
An' du amazin' lots o' things thet is n't wut they ough' to;
Bein' they haint no lead, they make their bullets out o' copper
An' shoot the darned things at us, tu, wich Caleb sez aint proper;
He sez they'd ough' to stan' right up an' let us pop 'em fairly
(Guess wen he ketches 'em at thet he'll hev to git up airly),
Thet our nation's bigger 'n theirn an' so its rights air bigger,
An' thet it's all to make 'em free thet we air pullin' trigger,
Thet Anglo Saxondom's idee's abreakin' 'em to pieces,
An' thet idee's thet every man doos jet wut he damn pleases . . .

*   *   *

I spose you wonder ware I be; I can't tell, fer the soul o' me,
Exacly ware I be myself,—meanin' by thet the holl o' me.
Wen I left hum, I hed two legs, an' they worn't bad ones neither,
(The scaliest trick they ever played wuz bringin' on me hither,)
Now one on 'em's I dunno ware;—they thought I wuz adyin',
An' sawed it off because they said 't wuz kin' o' mortifyin':
I'm willin' to believe it wuz, an' yit I don't see, nuther,
Wy one shoud take to feelin' cheap a minnit sooner 'n t' other,
Sence both wuz equilly to blame; but things is ez they be;
It took on so they took it off, an' thet's enough fer me:
There's one good thing, though, to be said about my wooden new one,—
The liquor can't git into it ez 't used to in the true one;
So it saves drink; an' then, besides, a feller could n't beg
A gretter blessin' then to hev one ollers sober peg;
It's true a chap's in want o' two fer follerin' a drum,
But all the march I'm up to now is jest to Kingdom Come.

HENRY DAVID THOREAU (1817–1862)

Born in Concord, Massachusetts, Henry David Thoreau is among America's most important writers, known for such American classics as A Week on the Concord and Merrimack Rivers, Walden, *and* The Maine Woods. *In 1849, he was briefly imprisoned for refusing to pay a federal poll tax to support the Mexican-American War, a conflict he considered a land-grabbing scheme engineered by American imperialists and Southern slaveholders who were using, as he wrote in his essay, "Civil Disobedience," "the standing government as their tool."*

When with Pale Cheek and Sunken Eye I Sang

When with pale cheek and sunken eye I sang
Unto the slumbering world at midnight's hour,
How it no more resounded with war's clang,
And virtue was decayed in Peace's bower;

How in these days no hero was abroad,
But puny men, afraid of war's alarms,
Stood forth to fight the battles of their Lord,
Who scarce could stand beneath a hero's arms;

A faint, reproachful, reassuring strain,
From some harp's strings touched by unskillful hands
Brought back the days of chivalry again,
And the surrounding fields made holy lands.

A bustling camp and an embattled host
Extending far on either hand I saw,
For I alone had slumbered at my post,
Dreaming of peace when all around was war.

CIVIL WAR
(1861–1865)

Dear Madam,—I have been shown in the files of the War Department a statement of the Adjutant General of Massachusetts, that you are the mother of five sons who have died gloriously on the field of battle.

I feel how weak and fruitless must be any words of mine which should attempt to beguile you from the grief of a loss so overwhelming. But I cannot refrain from tendering to you the consolation that may be found in the thanks of the Republic they died to save.

I pray that our Heavenly father may assuage the anguish of your bereavement, and leave you only the cherished memory of the loved and lost, and the solemn pride that must be yours, to have laid so costly a sacrifice upon the altar of Freedom. Yours, very sincerely and respectfully.

LETTER TO MRS. LYDIA BIXBY,
PRESIDENT ABRAHAM LINCOLN, NOVEMBER 21, 1864

ELIZABETH AKERS ALLEN (1832–1911)

Elizabeth Akers Allen was born in Strong, Maine, and was the author of Forest Buds, from the Woods of Maine, Silver Bridge *and* Sunset and Sunset Song. *During the Civil War, she worked as a government clerk in Washington and tended wounded soldiers.*

In the Defences

Along the ramparts which surround the town
    I walk with evening, marking all the while
How night and autumn, closing softly down,
    Leave on the land a blessing and a smile.

In the broad streets the sounds of tumult cease,
    The gorgeous sunset reddens roof and spire,
The city sinks to quietude and peace,
    Sleeping, like Saturn, in a ring of fire;

Circled with forts, whose grim and threatening walls
    Frown black with cannon, whose abated breath
Waits the command to send the fatal balls
    Upon their errands of dismay and death.

And see, directing, guiding, silently
    Flash from afar the mystic signal lights,
As gleamed the fiery pillar in the sky
    Leading by night the wandering Israelites.

The earthworks, draped with summer weeds and vines,
    The rifle-pits, half hid with tangled briers,
But wait their time; for see, along the lines
    Rise the faint smokes of lonesome picket-fires,

Where sturdy sentinels on silent beat
    Cheat the long hours of wakeful loneliness
With thoughts of home, and faces dear and sweet,
    And, on the edge of danger, dream of bliss.

Yet at a word, how wild and fierce a change
    Would rend and startle all the earth and skies
With blinding glare, and noises dread and strange,
    And shrieks, and shouts, and deathly agonies.

The wide-mouthed guns would roar, and hissing shells
    Would pierce the shuddering sky with fiery thrills,
The battle rage and roll in thunderous swells,
    And war's fierce anguish shake the solid hills.

But now how tranquilly the golden gloom
    Creeps up the gorgeous forest-slopes, and flows
Down valleys blue with fringy aster-bloom,—
    An atmosphere of safety and repose.

Against the sunset lie the darkening hills,
    Mushroomed with tents, the sudden growth of war;
The frosty autumn air, that blights and chills,
    Yet brings its own full recompense therefor;

Rich colors light the leafy solitudes,
    And far and near the gazer's eyes behold
The oak's deep scarlet, warming all the woods,
    And spendthrift maples scattering their gold.

The pale beech shivers with prophetic woe,
    The towering chestnut ranks stand blanched and thinned,
Yet still the fearless sumac dares the foe,
    And waves its bloody guidons in the wind.

Where mellow haze the hill's sharp outline dims,
    Bare elms, like sentinels, watch silently,
The delicate tracery of their slender limbs
    Pencilled in purple on the saffron sky.

Content and quietude and plenty seem
    Blessing the place, and sanctifying all;
And hark! how pleasantly a hidden stream
    Sweetens the silence with its silver fall!

The failing grasshopper chirps faint and shrill,
    The cricket calls, in mossy covert hid,
Cheery and loud, as stoutly answering still
    The soft persistence of the katydid.

With dead moths tangled in its blighted bloom,
    The golden-rod swings lonesome on its throne,
Forgot of bees; and in the thicket's gloom,
    The last belated peewee cries alone.

The hum of voices, and the careless laugh
    Of cheerful talkers, fall upon the ear;
The flag flaps listlessly adown its staff;
    And still the katydid pipes loud and near.

And now from far the bugle's mellow throat
    Pours out, in rippling flow, its silver tide,
And up the listening hills the echoes float
    Faint and more faint, and sweetly multiplied.

Peace reigns; not now a soft-eyed nymph that sleeps
    Unvexed by dreams of strife or conqueror,
But Power, that, open-eyed and watchful, keeps
    Unwearied vigil on the brink of war.

Night falls; in silence sleep the patriot bands;
    The tireless cricket yet repeats its tune,
And the still figure of the sentry stands
    In black relief against the low full moon.

ANONYMOUS

"John Brown's Body" was a popular marching song among Union soldiers. Strongly abolitionist in tone, it commemorates Brown's raid on the government arsenal at Harper's Ferry in 1859 to establish a stronghold for escaped slaves. Brown was eventually hanged for treason.

John Brown's Body

Attributed to Thomas Brigham Bishop and Charles Sprague Hall

John Brown's body lies a-mould'ring in the grave,
John Brown's body lies a-mould'ring in the grave,
John Brown's body lies a-mould'ring in the grave,
   His soul goes marching on!

Chorus:
Glory, glory! Hallelujah!
Glory, glory! Hallelujah!
Glory, glory! Hallelujah!
His soul is marching on!

He captured Harper's Ferry with his nineteen men so true,
And he frightened old Virginia till she trembled through and through.
They hung him for a traitor, themselves the traitor crew,
   But his soul is marching on!

John Brown died that the slave might be free,
John Brown died that the slave might be free,
John Brown died that the slave might be free,
   And his soul is marching on!

The stars of Heaven are looking kindly down,
The stars of Heaven are looking kindly down,
The stars of Heaven are looking kindly down,
   On the grave of old John Brown.

Now has come the glorious jubilee,
Now has come the glorious jubilee,
Now has come the glorious jubilee,
   When all mankind are free.

HERMAN MELVILLE (1819–1891)

Author of Moby-Dick, Billy Budd, *and other American classics, Herman Melville led a life of almost total literary obscurity and died in poverty. One of the greatest of all Civil War poets, he never served in the war, though he was a staunch Unionist and made frequent visits to Fort Hamilton and the Brooklyn Navy Yard, once venturing to the Virginia front prior to the battle of the Wilderness in 1864. "The March into Virginia," "A Utilitarian View of the* Monitor's *Fight," and "The College Colonel" are some of his finest war poems. They first appeared in* Battle-Pieces and Aspects of the War, *his first volume of poetry, published in 1866.*

The March into Virginia

Ending in the First Manassas (July, 1861)

Did all the lets and bars appear
    To every just or larger end,
Whence should come the trust and cheer?
    Youth must its ignorant impulse lend—
Age finds place in the rear.
    All wars are boyish, and are fought by boys,
The champions and enthusiasts of the state:
    Turbid ardors and vain joys
        Not barrenly abate—
Stimulants to the power mature,
        Preparatives of fate.

Who here forecasteth the event?
What heart but spurns at precedent
And warnings of the wise,
Contemned foreclosures of surprise?
The banners play, the bugles call,
The air is blue and prodigal.
    No berrying party, pleasure-wooed,
No picnic party in the May,
Ever went less loth than they
    Into that leafy neighborhood.
In Bacchic glee they file toward Fate,
Moloch's uninitiate;
Expectancy, and glad surmise

Of battle's unknown mysteries.
All they feel is this: 'tis glory,
A rapture sharp, though transitory,
Yet lasting in belaureled story.
So they gaily go to fight,
Chatting left and laughing right.

But some who this blithe mood present,
    As on in lightsome files they fare,
Shall die experienced ere three days are spent—
    Perish, enlightened by the vollied glare;
Or shame survive, and, like to adamant,
    The throe of Second Manassas share.

A Utilitarian View of the *Monitor*'s Fight

Plain be the phrase, yet apt the verse,
    More ponderous than nimble;
For since grimed War here laid aside
His Orient pomp, 'twould ill befit
      Overmuch to ply
    The rhyme's barbaric cymbal.

Hail to victory without the gaud
    Of glory; zeal that needs no fans
Of banners; plain mechanic power
Plied cogently in War now placed—
      Where War belongs—
    Among the trades and artisans.

Yet this was battle, and intense—
    Beyond the strife of fleets heroic;
Deadlier, closer, calm 'mid storm;
No passion; all went on by crank,
      Pivot, and screw,
    And calculations of caloric.

Needless to dwell; the story's known.
    The ringing of those plates on plates
Still ringeth round the world—
The clangor of that blacksmiths' fray.
        The anvil-din
    Resounds this message from the Fates:

War shall yet be, and to the end;
    But war-paint shows the streaks of weather;
War yet shall be, but warriors
Are now but operatives; War's made
        Less grand than Peace,
    And a singe runs through lace and feather.

The College Colonel

He rides at their head;
    A crutch by his saddle just slants in view,
One slung arm is in splints, you see,
    Yet he guides his strong steed—how coldly too.

He brings his regiment home—
    Not as they filed two years before,
But a remnant half-tattered, and battered, and worn,
Like castaway sailors, who—stunned
        By the surf's loud roar,
    Their mates dragged back and seen no more—
Again and again breast the surge,
    And at last crawl, spent, to shore.

A still rigidity and pale—
    An Indian aloofness lones his brow;
He has lived a thousand years
Compressed in battle's pains and prayers,
    Marches and watches slow.

There are welcoming shouts, and flags;
    Old men off hat to the Boy,
Wreaths from gay balconies fall at his feet,
    But to *him*—there comes alloy.

It is not that a leg is lost,
    It is not that an arm is maimed,
It is not that the fever has racked—
    Self he has long disclaimed.

But all through the Seven Days' Fight,
    And deep in the Wilderness grim,
And in the field-hospital tent,
    And Petersburg crater, and dim
Lean brooding in Libby, there came—
    Ah heaven!—what *truth* to him.

JULIA WARD HOWE (1819–1910)

"Battle Hymn of the Republic" was first published in February 1862. Its well-known "Glory Hallelujah" chorus was not added until April of that year. During the war, it became the unofficial anthem of the Union Army. Julia Ward Howe was a poet and lecturer on social reform and was particularly interested in abolitionism and women's suffrage.

Battle Hymn of the Republic

Mine eyes have seen the glory of the coming of the Lord:
He is trampling out the vintage where the grapes of wrath are stored
He hath loosed the fateful lightning of his terrible swift sword:
    His truth is marching on.

    Glory, glory hallelujah,
    Glory, glory hallelujah,
    Glory, glory hallelujah,
    His truth is marching on.

I have seen Him in the watch-fires of a hundred circling camps;
They have builded Him an altar in the evening dews and damps;
I can read His righteous sentence by the dim and flaring lamps.
    His day is marching on.

I have read a fiery gospel, writ in burnished rows of steel:
"As ye deal with my condemners, so with you my grace shall deal;
Let the Hero, born of woman, crush the serpent with his heel,
    Since God is marching on."

He has sounded forth the trumpet that shall never call retreat;
He is sifting out the hearts of men before His judgment-seat:
Oh! be swift, my soul, to answer Him! be jubilant, my feet!
    Our God is marching on.

In the beauty of the lilies Christ was born across the sea,
With a glory in his bosom that transfigures you and me:
As he died to make men holy, let us die to make men free,
    While God is marching on.

JOHN GREENLEAF WHITTIER (1807–1892)

One of the most famous poems of the Civil War, "Barbara Frietchie" first appeared in 1864 in In War Time and Other Poems; *since then it has been a favorite among American readers. In September 1862, on his way to Antietam, Robert E. Lee divided his army, sending Stonewall Jackson to take the Union garrison at Harpers Ferry. En route, Jackson passed through the town of Frederick, Maryland, portrayed in Whittier's poem.*

Barbara Frietchie

Up from the meadows rich with corn,
Clear in the cool September morn,

The clustered spires of Frederick stand
Green-walled by the hills of Maryland.

Round about them orchards sweep,
Apple and peach tree fruited deep,

Fair as the garden of the Lord
To the eyes of the famished rebel horde,

On that pleasant morn of the early fall
When Lee marched over the mountain wall;

Over the mountains winding down,
Horse and foot, into Frederick town.

Forty flags with their silver stars,
Forty flags with their crimson bars,

Flapped in the morning wind: the sun
Of noon looked down, and saw not one.

Up rose old Barbara Frietchie then,
Bowed with her fourscore years and ten;

Bravest of all in Frederick town,
She took up the flag the men hauled down.

In her attic window the staff she set,
To show that one heart was loyal yet.

Up the street came the rebel tread,
Stonewall Jackson riding ahead.

Under his slouched hat left and right
He glanced; the old flag met his sight.

"Halt!"—dust-brown ranks stood fast.
"Fire!"—out blazed the rifle-blast.

It shivered the window, pane and sash;
It rent the banner with seam and gash.

Quick, as it fell, from the broken staff
Dame Barbara snatched the silken scarf.

She leaned far out on the window-sill,
And shook it forth with a royal will.

"Shoot, if you must, this old gray head,
But spare your country's flag," she said.

A shade of sadness, a blush of shame,
Over the face of the leader came;

The nobler nature within him stirred
To life at that woman's deed and word;

"Who touches a hair of yon gray head
Dies like a dog! March on!" he said.

All day long through Frederick street
Sounded the tread of marching feet:

All day long that free flag tost
Over the heads of the rebel host.

Ever its torn folds rose and fell
On the loyal winds that loved it well;

And through the hill-gaps sunset light
Shone over it with a warm good-night.

Barbara Frietchie's work is o'er,
And the Rebel rides on his raids no more.

Honor to her! and let a tear
Fall, for her sake, on Stonewall's bier.

Over Barbara Frietchie's grave,
Flag of Freedom and Union, wave!

Peace and order and beauty draw
Round thy symbol of light and law;

And ever the stars above look down
On thy stars below in Frederick town!

THOMAS BAILEY ALDRICH (1836–1907)

At the outbreak of the Civil War, novelist and poet Thomas Bailey Aldrich worked as a war correspondent for the New York Tribune *and later as an editor of the* Atlantic Monthly. *One of Aldrich's most famous sonnets, "Fredericksburg," describes one of the bloodiest battles of the Civil War. On December 13, 1862, at Fredericksburg, Virginia, Union soldiers, under the command of General Ambrose Burnside, attacked Confederate troops under Robert E. Lee. In the ensuing battle, Union casualties, more than twice the Confederate, totaled over twelve thousand.*

Fredericksburg

The increasing moonlight drifts across my bed,
And on the churchyard by the road, I know
It falls as white and noiselessly as snow. . . .
'T was such a night two weary summers fled;
The stars, as now, were waning overhead.
Listen! Again the shrill-lipped bugles blow
Where the swift currents of the river flow
Past Fredericksburg; far off the heavens are red
With sudden conflagration; on yon height,
Linstock in hand, the gunners hold their breath;
A signal rocket pierces the dense night,
Flings its spent stars upon the town beneath:
Hark!—the artillery massing on the right,
Hark!—the black squadrons wheeling down to Death!

SIDNEY LANIER (1842–1881)

Born in Macon, Georgia, Sidney Lanier served in the Confederate Army and saw action in several major engagements. He then became a flutist in the Peabody Orchestra in Baltimore and also taught at The Johns Hopkins University. His "The Dying Words of Stonewall Jackson" depicts Thomas Jonathan Jackson, a brilliant military tactician, who earned his nickname in the first battle of Manassas, when he and his brigade withstood Union troops "like a stone wall." Jackson died in 1863 when he was accidentally shot by his own men at the battle of Chancellorsville.

The Dying Words of Stonewall Jackson

"Order A. P. Hill to prepare for battle."
"Tell Major Hawks to advance the Commissary train."
"Let us cross the river and rest in the shade."

The stars of Night contain the glittering Day,
And rain his glory down with sweeter grace
Upon the dark World's grand, enchanted face
    All loth to turn away.

And so the Day, about to yield his breath,
Utters the Stars unto the listening Night
To stand for burning fare-thee-wells of light
    Said on the verge of death.

O hero-life that lit us like the Sun!
O hero-words that glittered like the Stars
And stood and shone above the gloomy wars
    When the hero-life was done!

The Phantoms of a battle came to dwell
I' the fitful vision of his dying eyes—
Yet even in battle-dreams, he sends supplies
    To those he loved so well.

His army stands in battle-line arrayed:
His couriers fly: all's done—now God decide!
And not till then saw he the Other Side
    Or would accept the Shade.

Thou Land whose Sun is gone, thy Stars remain!
Still shine the words that miniature his deeds—
O Thrice-Beloved, where'er thy great heart bleeds,
    Solace hast thou for pain!

WILL HENRY THOMPSON (1848–1918)

In this famous Civil War poem, Will Henry Thompson commemorates Pickett's charge on the Union center on Cemetery Hill on July 3, 1863, an assault that led to the near annihilation of his division.

The High Tide at Gettysburg

A cloud possessed the hollow field,
The gathering battle's smoky shield:
   Athwart the gloom the lightning flashed,
   And through the cloud some horsemen dashed,
And from the heights the thunder pealed.

Then, at the brief command of Lee,
Moved out that matchless infantry,
   With Pickett leading grandly down,
   To rush against the roaring crown
Of those dread heights of destiny.

Far heard above the angry guns,
A cry of tumult runs:
   The voice that rang through Shiloh's woods,
   And Chickamauga's solitudes:
The fierce South cheering on her sons!

Ah, how the withering tempest blew
Against the front of Pettigrew!
   A Khamsin wind that scorched and singed,
   Like that infernal flame that fringed
The British squares at Waterloo!

A thousand fell where Kemper led;
A thousand died where Garnett bled;
   In blinding flame and strangling smoke,
   The remnant through the batteries broke,
And crossed the works with Armistead.

"Once more in Glory's van with me!"
Virginia cried to Tennessee:
    "We two together, come what may,
    Shall stand upon those works today!"
The reddest day in history.

Brave Tennessee! In reckless way
Virginia heard her comrade say:
    "Close round this rent and riddled rag!"
    What time she set her battle flag
Amid the guns of Doubleday.

But who shall break the guards that wait
Before the awful face of Fate?
    The tattered standards of the South
    Were shrivelled at the cannon's mouth,
And all her hopes were desolate.

In vain the Tennesseean set
His breast against the bayonet;
    In vain Virginia charged and raged,
    A tigress in her wrath uncaged,
Till all the hill was red and wet!

Above the bayonets, mixed and crossed,
Men saw a gray, gigantic ghost
    Receding through the battle-cloud,
    And heard across the tempest loud
The death-cry of a nation lost!

The brave went down! Without disgrace
They leaped to Ruin's red embrace;
    They only heard Fame's thunders wake,
    And saw the dazzling sunburst break
In smiles on Glory's bloody face!

They fell, who lifted up a hand
And bade the sun in heaven to stand;
    They smote and fell, who set the bars
    Against the progress of the stars,
And stayed the march of Motherland.

They stood, who saw the future come
On through the fight's delirium;
    They smote and stood, who held the hope
    Of nations on that slippery slope,
Amid the cheers of Christendom!

God lives! He forged the iron will,
That clutched and held that trembling hill!
    God lives and reigns! He built and lent
    The heights for Freedom's battlement,
Where floats her flag in triumph still!

Fold up the banners! Smelt the guns!
Love rules. Her gentler purpose runs.
    A mighty mother turns in tears,
    The pages of her battle years,
Lamenting all her fallen sons!

LLOYD MIFFLIN (1846–1921)

Lloyd Mifflin, from Columbia, Pennsylvania, is known chiefly for his sonnets, of which "The Battlefield," a poem about Gettysburg, is one of the most recognized.

The Battlefield

Those were the conquered, still too proud to yield—
These were the victors, yet too poor for shrouds!
Here scarlet Slaughter slew her countless crowds
Heaped high in ranks where'er the hot guns pealed.
The brooks that wandered through the battlefield
Flowed slowly on in ever-reddening streams;
Here where the rank wheat waves and golden gleams,
The dreadful squadrons, thundering, charged and reeled.
Within the blossoming clover many a bone
Lying unsepulchred, has bleached to white;
While gentlest hearts that only love had known,
Have ached with anguish at the awful sight;
And War's gaunt Vultures that were lean, have grown
Gorged in the darkness in a single night!

AMBROSE BIERCE (1842–1914?)

Ambrose Bierce was an essayist, short-story writer, and journalist who fought in the battles of Shiloh, Murfreesboro, Chattanooga, Franklin, and Kenesaw Mountain, where he was wounded. He later worked as a journalist for the San Francisco Examiner. In 1913, he ventured to Mexico to join Pancho Villa's forces as an observer and died there under mysterious circumstances.

Corporal

Fiercely the battle raged and, sad to tell,
Our corporal heroically fell!
Fame from her height looked down upon the brawl
And said: "He had n't very far to fall."

THOMAS BUCHANAN READ (1822–1872)

Poet and portraitist Thomas Buchanan Read was a native of Chester County, Pennsylvania. "Sheridan's Ride," published in 1865, describes a battle at Cedar Creek, a small tributary of the Shenandoah River, on October 19, 1864. Union General Philip Sheridan was returning from Washington on his horse, Rienzi, when he heard a volley of fire. He rallied his confused men and led a successful but costly counterattack against General J. A. Early's Confederate troops. Read's popular poem was a staple in elementary school textbooks until after World War II.

Sheridan's Ride

Up from the South, at break of day,
Bringing to Winchester fresh dismay,
The affrighted air with a shudder bore,
Like a herald in haste, to the chieftain's door,
The terrible grumble, and rumble, and roar,
Telling the battle was on once more,
    And Sheridan twenty miles away.

And wider still those billows of war
Thundered along the horizon's bar;
And louder yet into Winchester rolled
The roar of that red sea uncontrolled,
Making the blood of the listener cold,
As he thought of the stake in that fiery fray,
    With Sheridan twenty miles away.

But there is a road from Winchester town,
A good, broad highway leading down;
And there, through the flush of the morning light,
A steed as black as the steeds of night
Was seen to pass, as with eagle flight;
As if he knew the terrible need,
He stretched away with the utmost speed;
Hills rose and fell, but his heart was gay,
    With Sheridan fifteen miles away.

Still sprang from those swift hoofs, thundering South,
The dust, like smoke from the cannon's mouth;

Or the trail of a comet, sweeping faster and faster,
Foreboding to traitors the doom of disaster,
The heart of the steed and the heart of the master
Were beating like prisoners assaulting their walls,
Impatient to be where the battlefield calls;
Every nerve of the charger was strained to full play,
    With Sheridan only ten miles away.

Under his spurning feet, the road
Like an arrowy Alpine river flowed,
And the landscape sped away behind
Like an ocean flying before the wind;
And the steed, like a barque fed with furnace ire,
Swept on, with his wild eye full of fire.
But, lo! he is nearing his heart's desire;
He is snuffing the smoke of the roaring fray,
    With Sheridan only five miles away.

The first that the general saw were the groups
Of stragglers, and then the retreating troops;
What was done? what to do? A glance told him both.
Then striking his spurs, with a terrible oath,
He dashed down the line 'mid a storm of huzzas,
And the wave of retreat checked its course there, because
The sight of the master compelled it to pause.
With foam and with dust the black charger was gray;
By the flash of his eye and the red nostril's play,
He seemed to the whole great army to say,
"I have brought you Sheridan all the way
    From Winchester down to save the day!"

Hurrah! hurrah for Sheridan!
Hurrah! hurrah for horse and man!
And when their statues are placed on high,
Under the dome of the Union sky,
The American soldier's Temple of Fame,
There, with the glorious general's name,
Be it said, in letters both bold and bright,
"Here is the steed that saved the day,
By carrying Sheridan into the fight,
    From Winchester, twenty miles away!"

WALT WHITMAN (1819–1892)

*One of America's essential poets, Walt Whitman never served in the Civil War, yet
he was nevertheless fascinated by the conflict, recording in his notebooks thousands
of observations that he later developed into poems. "I took the first scrap of paper,"
he recalled, "the first doorstep, the first desk, and wrote, wrote, wrote." The result
was some of the greatest poems produced about the Civil War, among them "Cavalry
Crossing a Ford," a kind of poetic photograph capturing a moment in the life of a
military unit; "Vigil Strange I Kept on the Field One Night," a poignant monologue
memorializing a young, unknown soldier dead on a battlefield; and "The Wound-
Dresser," one of Whitman's finest and most intensely autobiographical pieces, about
his work with the wounded in the hospitals of Washington, D.C.*

Cavalry Crossing a Ford

A line in long array, where they wind betwixt green islands;
They take a serpentine course—their arms flash in the sun—hark to the
    musical clank;
Behold the silvery river—in it the splashing horses, loitering, stop to drink;
Behold the brown-faced men—each group, each person, a picture—the
    negligent rest on the saddles;
Some emerge on the opposite bank—others are just entering the ford—while,
Scarlet, and blue, and snowy white,
The guidon flags flutter gaily in the wind.

Vigil Strange I Kept on the Field One Night

Vigil strange I kept on the field one night;
When you my son and my comrade dropt at my side that day,
One look I but gave which your dear eyes return'd with a look I shall never
    forget,
One touch of your hand to mine O boy, reach'd up as you lay on the ground,
Then onward I sped in the battle, the even-contested battle,
Till late in the night reliev'd to the place at last again I made my way,
Found you in death so cold dear comrade, found your body son of responding
    kisses, (never again on earth responding,)
Bared your face in the starlight, curious the scene, cool blew the moderate
    night-wind,
Long there and then in vigil I stood, dimly around me the battlefield spreading,

Vigil wondrous and vigil sweet there in the fragrant silent night,
But not a tear fell, not even a long-drawn sigh, long, long I gazed,
Then on the earth partially reclining sat by your side leaning my chin in my
    hands,
Passing sweet hours, immortal and mystic hours with you dearest comrade—
    not a tear, not a word,
Vigil of silence, love and death, vigil for you my son and my soldier,
As onward silently stars aloft, eastward new ones upward stole,
Vigil final for you brave boy, (I could not save you, swift was your death,
I faithfully loved you and cared for you living, I think we shall surely meet
    again,)
Till at latest lingering of the night, indeed just as the dawn appear'd,
My comrade I wrapt in his blanket, envelop'd well his form,
Folded the blanket well, tucking it carefully over head and carefully under feet,
And there and then and bathed by the rising sun, my son in his grave, in his
    rude-dug grave I deposited,
Ending my vigil strange with that, vigil of night and battle-field dim,
Vigil for boy of responding kisses, (never again on earth responding,)
Vigil for comrade swiftly slain, vigil I never forget, how as day brighten'd,
I rose from the chill ground and folded my soldier well in his blanket,
And buried him where he fell.

The Wound-Dresser

  I. An old man bending I come among new faces,
     Years looking backward resuming in answer to children,
     Come tell us old man, as from young men and maidens that love me,
     (Arous'd and angry, I'd thought to beat the alarum, and urge relentless war,
     But soon my fingers fail'd me, my face dropp'd and I resign'd myself,
     To sit by the wounded and soothe them, or silently watch the dead;)
     Years hence of these scenes, of these furious passions, these chances,
     Of unsurpass'd heroes, (was one side so brave? the other was equally brave;)
     Now be witness again, paint the mightiest armies of earth,
     Of those armies so rapid so wondrous what saw you to tell us?
     What stays with you latest and deepest? of curious panics,
     Of hard-fought engagements or sieges tremendous what deepest remains?

  II. O maidens and young men I love and that love me,
     What you ask of my days those the strangest and sudden your talking recalls,
     Soldier alert I arrive after a long march cover'd with sweat and dust,

In the nick of time I come, plunge in the fight, loudly shout in the rush of
    successful charge,
Enter the captur'd works—yet lo, like a swift-running river they fade,
Pass and are gone they fade—I dwell not on soldiers' perils or soldiers' joys,
(Both I remember well—many the hardships, few the joys, yet I was content.)

But in silence, in dreams' projections,
While the world of gain and appearance and mirth goes on,
So soon what is over forgotten, and waves wash the imprints off the sand,
With hinged knees returning I enter the doors, (while for you up there,
Whoever you are, follow without noise and be of strong heart.)
Bearing the bandages, water and sponge,
Straight and swift to my wounded I go,
Where they lie on the ground after the battle brought in,
Where their priceless blood reddens the grass the ground,
Or to the rows of the hospital tent, or under the roof'd hospital,
To the long rows of cots up and down each side I return,
To each and all one after another I draw near, not one do I miss,
An attendant follows holding a tray, he carries a refuse pail,
Soon to be fill'd with clotted rags and blood, emptied, and fill'd again.

I onward go, I stop,
With hinged knees and steady hand to dress wounds,
I am firm with each, the pangs are sharp yet unavoidable,
One turns to me his appealing eyes—poor boy! I never knew you,
Yet I think I could not refuse this moment to die for you, if that would
    save you.

III. On, on I go, (open doors of time! open hospital doors!)
    The crush'd head I dress, (poor crazed hand tear not the bandage away,)
    The neck of the cavalry-man with the bullet through and through I examine,
    Hard the breathing rattles, quite glazed already the eye, yet life struggles hard,
    (Come sweet death! be persuaded O beautiful death!
    In mercy come quickly.)

From the stump of the arm, the amputated hand,
I undo the clotted lint, remove the slough, wash off the matter and blood,
Back on his pillow the soldier bends with curv'd neck and side-falling head,
His eyes are closed, his face is pale, he dares not look on the bloody stump,
And has not yet look'd on it.

I dress a wound in the side, deep, deep,
But a day or two more, for see the frame all wasted and sinking,
And the yellow-blue countenance see.

I dress the perforated shoulder, the foot with the bullet-wound,
Cleanse the one with a gnawing and putrid gangrene, so sickening, so
    offensive,
While the attendant stands behind aside me holding the tray and pail.

I am faithful, I do not give out,
The fractur'd thigh, the knee, the wound in the abdomen,
These and more I dress with impassive hand, (yet deep in my breast a fire,
    a burning flame.)

IV. Thus in silence in dreams' projections,
    Returning, resuming, I thread my way through the hospitals,
    The hurt and wounded I pacify with soothing hand,
    I sit by the restless all the dark night, some are so young,
    Some suffer so much, I recall the experience sweet and sad,
    (Many a soldier's loving arms about this neck have cross'd and rested,
    Many a soldier's kiss dwells on these bearded lips.)

EMILY DICKINSON (1830–1886)

A native of Amherst, Massachusetts, Emily Dickinson led a life of near inviolable solitude. One of the greatest lyric poets of any era, she composed over 1,700 poems and fragments, only six of which were published during her lifetime.

My Triumph Lasted Till the Drums

My Triumph lasted till the Drums
Had left the Dead alone
And then I dropped my Victory
And chastened stole along
To where the finished Faces
Conclusion turned on me
And then I hated Glory
And wished myself were They.

What is to be is best descried
When it has also been—
Could Prospect taste of Retrospect
The tyrannies of Men
Were Tenderer—diviner
The Transitive toward.
A Bayonet's contrition
Is nothing to the Dead.

My Portion Is Defeat Today

My Portion is Defeat—today—
A paler luck than Victory—
Less Paeans—fewer Bells—
The Drums don't follow Me—with tunes—
Defeat—a somewhat slower—means—
More Arduous than Balls—
'Tis populous with Bone and stain—
And Men too straight to stoop again,
And Piles of solid Moan—
And Chips of Blank—in Boyish Eyes—

And scraps of Prayer—
And Death's surprise,
Stamped visible—in Stone—

There's somewhat prouder, over there—
The Trumpets tell it to the Air—
How different Victory
To Him who has it—and the One
Who to have had it, would have been
Contenteder—to die—

ALLEN TATE (1899–1979)

A poet, biographer, and editor, Allen Tate was born in Winchester, Kentucky. He was one of the founders of The Fugitive, *a journal that represented the writings of a Southern agrarian group of literary, social, and political conservatives. First published in 1927, "Ode to the Confederate Dead" is one of the most famous poems about the Civil War.*

Ode to the Confederate Dead

Row after row with strict impunity
The headstones yield their names to the element,
The wind whirrs without recollection;
In the riven troughs the splayed leaves
Pile up, of nature the casual sacrament
To the seasonal eternity of death;
Then driven by the fierce scrutiny
Of heaven to their election in the vast breath,
They sough the rumour of mortality.

Autumn is desolation in the plot
Of a thousand acres where these memories grow
From the inexhaustible bodies that are not
Dead, but feed the grass row after rich row.
Think of the autumns that have come and gone!—
Ambitious November with the humors of the year,
With a particular zeal for every slab,
Staining the uncomfortable angels that rot
On the slabs, a wing chipped here, an arm there:
The brute curiosity of an angel's stare
Turns you, like them, to stone,
Transforms the heaving air
Till plunged to a heavier world below
You shift your sea-space blindly
Heaving, turning like the blind crab.

    Dazed by the wind, only the wind
    The leaves flying, plunge

You know who have waited by the wall
The twilight certainty of an animal,
Those midnight restitutions of the blood
You know—the immitigable pines, the smoky frieze
Of the sky, the sudden call: you know the rage,
The cold pool left by the mounting flood,
Of muted Zeno and Parmenides.
You who have waited for the angry resolution
Of those desires that should be yours tomorrow,
You know the unimportant shrift of death
And praise the vision
And praise the arrogant circumstance
Of those who fall
Rank upon rank, hurried beyond decision—
Here by the sagging gate, stopped by the wall.

    Seeing, seeing only the leaves
    Flying, plunge and expire

Turn your eyes to the immoderate past,
Turn to the inscrutable infantry rising
Demons out of the earth—they will not last.
Stonewall, Stonewall, and the sunken fields of hemp,
Shiloh, Antietam, Malvern Hill, Bull Run.
Lost in that orient of the thick-and-fast
You will curse the setting sun.

    Cursing only the leaves crying
    Like an old man in a storm

You hear the shout, the crazy hemlocks point
With troubled fingers to the silence which
Smothers you, a mummy, in time.

                  The hound bitch
Toothless and dying, in a musty cellar
Hears the wind only.

Now that the salt of their blood
Stiffens the saltier oblivion of the sea,
Seals the malignant purity of the flood,
What shall we who count our days and bow
Our heads with a commemorial woe
In the ribboned coats of grim felicity,
What shall we say of the bones, unclean,
Whose verdurous anonymity will grow?
The ragged arms, the ragged heads and eyes
Lost in these acres of the insane green?
The gray lean spiders come, they come and go;
In a tangle of willows without light
The singular screech-owl's tight
Invisible lyric seeds the mind
With the furious murmur of their chivalry.

   We shall say only the leaves
   Flying, plunge and expire

We shall say only the leaves whispering
In the improbable mist of nightfall
That flies on multiple wing;
Night is the beginning and the end
And in between the ends of distraction
Waits mute speculation, the patient curse
That stones the eyes, or like the jaguar leaps
For his own image in a jungle pool, his victim.
What shall we say who have knowledge
Carried to the heart? Shall we take the act
To the grave? Shall we, more hopeful, set up the grave
In the house? The ravenous grave?

              Leave now
The shut gate and the decomposing wall:
The gentle serpent, green in the mulberry bush,
Riots with his tongue through the hush—
Sentinel of the grave who counts us all!

DUDLEY RANDALL (1914–2000)

In 1862, the first black troops entered the Civil War; when the war ended in 1865, roughly ten percent of the Union Army was black. In "Memorial Wreath," Dudley Randall memorializes these soldiers. A poet and translator, he was publisher of the influential Broadside Press, which introduced the work of many prominent contemporary African American poets.

Memorial Wreath

(For the more than 200,000 Negroes who served in the Union Army during the Civil War)

In this green month when resurrected flowers,
Like laughing children ignorant of death,
Brighten the couch of those who wake no more,
Love and remembrance blossom in our hearts
For you who bore the extreme sharp pang for us,
And bought our freedom with your lives.

       And now,
Honoring your memory, with love we bring
These fiery roses, white-hot cotton flowers
And violets bluer than cool northern skies
You dreamed of in the burning prison fields
When liberty was only a faint north star,
Not a bright flower planted by your hands
Reaching up hardy nourished with your blood.
Fit gravefellows you are for Lincoln, Brown
And Douglass and Toussaint . . . all whose rapt eyes
Fashioned a new world in this wilderness.

American earth is richer for your bones;
Our hearts beat prouder for the blood we inherit.

ROBERT LOWELL (1917–1977)

Poet Robert Lowell was a member of the prominent Bostonian family that also included poets James Russell Lowell and Amy Lowell. He remains one of America's most important twentieth-century poets. Lowell was long fascinated by Union Colonel Robert Gould Shaw, an ancestor. On July 18, 1863, Shaw and his black regiment, the 54th Massachusetts Infantry, suffered a terrible defeat while trying to overtake Fort Wagner on Morris Island near Charleston. Two hundred and seventy-two of the regiment's 650 men were lost.

For the Union Dead

"Relinquunt Omnia Servare Rem Publicam."

The old South Boston Aquarium stands
in a Sahara of snow now. Its broken windows are boarded.
The bronze weathervane cod has lost half its scales.
The airy tanks are dry.

Once my nose crawled like a snail on the glass;
my hand tingled
to burst the bubbles
drifting from the noses of the cowed, compliant fish.

My hand draws back. I often sigh still
for the dark downward and vegetating kingdom
of the fish and reptile. One morning last March,
I pressed against the new barbed and galvanized

fence on the Boston Common. Behind their cage,
yellow dinosaur steamshovels were grunting
as they cropped up tons of mush and grass
to gouge their underworld garage.

Parking spaces luxuriate like civic
sandpiles in the heart of Boston.
A girdle of orange, Puritan-pumpkin colored girders
braces the tingling Statehouse,

shaking over the excavations, as it faces Colonel Shaw
and his bell-cheeked Negro infantry
on St. Gaudens' shaking Civil War relief,
propped by a plank splint against the garage's earthquake.

Two months after marching through Boston,
half the regiment was dead;
at the dedication,
William James could almost hear the bronze Negroes breathe.

Their monument sticks like a fishbone
in the city's throat.
Its Colonel is as lean
as a compass-needle.

He has an angry wrenlike vigilance,
a greyhound's gentle tautness;
he seems to wince at pleasure,
and suffocate for privacy.

He is out of bounds now. He rejoices in man's lovely,
peculiar power to choose life and die—
when he leads his black soldiers to death,
he cannot bend his back.

On a thousand small town New England greens,
the old white churches hold their air
of sparse, sincere rebellion; frayed flags
quilt the graveyards of the Grand Army of the Republic.

The stone statues of the abstract Union Soldier
grow slimmer and younger each year—
wasp-waisted, they doze over muskets
and muse through their sideburns . . .

Shaw's father wanted no monument
except the ditch,
where his son's body was thrown
and lost with his "niggers."

The ditch is nearer.
There are no statues for the last war here;
on Boylston Street, a commercial photograph
shows Hiroshima boiling

over a Mosler Safe, the "Rock of Ages"
that survived the blast. Space is nearer.
When I crouch to my television set,
the drained faces of Negro school-children rise like balloons.

Colonel Shaw
is riding on his bubble,
he waits
for the blessèd break.

The Aquarium is gone. Everywhere,
giant finned cars nose forward like fish;
a savage servility
slides by on grease.

JAMES DICKEY (1923–1997)

Poet and novelist James Dickey was born in Atlanta, Georgia. He served as a fighter pilot in World War II and the Korean War and later worked as an advertising executive. The recipient of numerous honors for his poetry, including the National Book Award, he served two appointments as Poetry Consultant to the Library of Congress and was Poet-in-Residence and Carolina Professor at the University of South Carolina. His books include Into the Stone and Other Poems, Buckdancer's Choice, *and* Flying, May Day, Sermon, and Other Poems.

Hunting Civil War Relics at Nimblewill Creek

As he moves the mine detector
A few inches over the ground,
Making it vitally float
Among the ferns and weeds,
I come into this war
Slowly, with my one brother,
Watching his face grow deep
Between the earphones,
For I can tell
If we enter the buried battle
Of Nimblewill
Only by his expression.

Softly he wanders, parting
The grass with a dreaming hand,
No dead cry yet takes root
In his clapped ears
Or can be seen in his smile.
But underfoot I feel
The dead regroup,
The burst metals all in place,
The battle lines be drawn
Anew to include us
In Nimblewill,
And I carry the shovel and pick

More as if they were
Bright weapons that I bore.
A bird's cry breaks
In two, and into three parts.
We cross the creek; the cry
Shifts into another,
Nearer, bird, and is
Like the shout of a shadow—
Lived-with, appallingly close—
Or the soul, pronouncing
"Nimblewill":
Three tones; your being changes.

We climb the bank;
A faint light glows
On my brother's mouth.
I listen, as two birds fight
For a single voice, but he
Must be hearing the grave,
In pieces, all singing
To his clamped head,
For he smiles as if
He rose from the dead within
Green Nimblewill
And stood in his grandson's shape.

No shot from the buried war
Shall kill me now,
For the dead have waited here
A hundred years to create
Only the look on the face
Of my one brother,
Who stands among them, offering
A metal dish
Afloat in the trembling weeds,
With a long-buried light on his lips
At Nimblewill
And the dead outsinging two birds.

I choke the handle
Of the pick, and fall to my knees
To dig wherever he points,
To bring up mess tin or bullet,
To go underground
Still singing, myself,
Without a sound,
Like a man who renounces war,
Or one who shall lift up the past,
Not breathing "Father,"
At Nimblewill,
But saying, "Fathers! Fathers!"

INDIAN WARS
(1860–1890)

The only good Indians I ever saw were dead.

GENERAL PHILIP SHERIDAN, 1868

Our chiefs are killed . . . The old men are all dead . . . The little children are freezing to death. My people, some of them, have run away to the hills and have no blankets, no food. No one knows where they are, perhaps freezing to death. I want to have time to look for my children and see how many of them I can find. Maybe I shall find them among the dead. Hear me my chiefs, I am tired. My heart is sick and sad. From where the sun now stands I will fight no more forever.

CHIEF JOSEPH OF THE NEZ PERCÉ, 1877

WILLIAM HEYEN (1940–)

William Heyen is the author of The Swastika Poems, The Host: Selected Poems 1965–1990, *and* Crazy Horse in Stillness. *For many years, he was Professor of English and Poet-in-Residence at the State University of New York, Brockport. "Unknown" considers the Washita River Massacre in Oklahoma on November 27, 1868, at which Colonel George Armstrong Custer and his 7th Cavalry slaughtered over 103 Cheyenne villagers, including Chief Black Kettle, and captured 53 women and children. During the battle, Arapahos from a neighboring village killed a platoon of 19 soldiers, commanded by Major Joe Elliott.*

Unknown

Custer desired the Indians "be completely humbled."
We suppose, in the end, some were & some were not.
Some of the living were humbled, & some were not.
Some of the dead were humbled, & some were not.

In 1868, Major Elliott & his men were wiped out.
General Custer asked Dr. Lippincott to report
on the character & number of wounds received by each,
as well as to mutilations to which they had been subjected.

"Sergeant-Major Walter Kennedy, bullet hole in right temple,
head partly cut off, seventeen bullet holes in back and two in legs."
By the time of his death, quick or drawn-out,
the Sergeant-Major may or may not have been completely humbled.

"Corporal Henry Mercer, bullet hole in right axilla,
one in region of heart, three in back, eight arrow wounds in back,
right ear cut off, head scalped, skull fractured, throat cut"—
the Corporal may or may not have been completely humbled.

It's a long list. It ends with those unidentifiable:
"Unknown, head cut off, body partially destroyed by wolves."
"Unknown, scalped, skull fractured, three bullet holes
and thirteen arrow holes in back." Maybe, at the exact

instant of his death, each forever-to-be-Unknown
was completely humbled, . . . but maybe not. Those of us
now scanning the report for intuitions & familiar names
must be completely humbled. Some are & some are not.

ARCHIBALD MACLEISH (1892–1982)

Archibald MacLeish served as Undersecretary of State as well as Director of the Office of Facts and Figures during World War II, and he led an amazingly prolific literary life. His books include Conquistador, J. B., *and* Collected Poems: 1917–1952—*all recipients of the Pulitzer Prize. "Wildwest," based on Black Elk's memories of Crazy Horse recorded by John Neihardt, imagines Custer's Last Stand, the famous battle of June 25, 1876, in which hundreds of Cheyenne and Sioux warriors, under the leadership of Crazy Horse and Sitting Bull, slaughtered Custer's battalion of 210 men in the Little Big Horn valley of southeastern Montana.*

Wildwest

There were none of my blood in this battle:
There were Minneconjous, Sans Arcs, Brules,
Many nations of Sioux: they were few men galloping.

This would have been in the long days in June:
They were galloping well deployed under the plum-trees:
They were driving riderless horses: themselves they were few.

Crazy Horse had done it with few numbers.
Crazy Horse was small for a Lakota.
He was riding always alone thinking of something:

He was standing alone by the picket lines by the ropes:
He was young then, he was thirty when he died:
Unless there were children to talk he took no notice.

When the soldiers came for him there on the other side
On the Greasy Grass in the villages we were shouting
"Hoka Hey! Crazy Horse will be riding!"

They fought in the water: horses and men were drowning:
They rode on the butte: dust settled in sunlight:
Hoka Hey! they lay on the bloody ground.

No one could tell of the dead which man was Custer . . .
That was the end of his luck: by that river.
The soldiers beat him at Slim Buttes once:

They beat him at Willow Creek when the snow lifted:
That last time they beat him was the Tongue.
He had only the meat he had made and of that little.

Do you ask why he should fight? It was his country:
My God should he not fight? It was his.
But after the Tongue there were no herds to be hunting:

He cut the knots of the tails and he led them in:
He cried out "I am Crazy Horse! Do not touch me!"
There were many soldiers between and the gun glinting . . .

And a Mister Josiah Perham of Maine had much of the
land Mister Perham was building the Northern Pacific
railroad that is Mister Perham was saying at lunch that

forty say fifty millions of acres in gift and
government grant outright ought to be worth a
wide price on the Board at two-fifty and

later a Mister Cooke had relieved Mister Perham and
later a Mister Morgan relieved Mister Cooke:
Mister Morgan converted at prices current:

It was all prices to them: they never looked at it:
why should they look at the land? they were Empire Builders:
it was all in the bid and the asked and the ink on their books . . .

When Crazy Horse was there by the Black Hills
His heart would be big with the love he had for that country
And all the game he had seen and the mares he had ridden

And how it went out from you wide and clean in the sunlight

DUANE NIATUM (1938–   )

Duane Niatum is a member of the Klallam tribe. He is the author of a number of books of poetry, fiction, and nonfiction, and the editor of Harper's Anthology of 20th Century Native American Poetry. *His "A Tribute to Chief Joseph" honors the leader of the Nez Percé, who surrendered to the U.S. Army in 1877. Chief Joseph and his tribe were then shipped to Leavenworth, Kansas, where they were held as prisoners of war. From there, they were sent to the Indian Territory, where many perished of malaria and other diseases. On September 21, 1904, Chief Joseph died in exile on the Colville Reservation in Washington.*

A Tribute to Chief Joseph (1840?–1904)

Never reaching the promised land in Canada,
HIN-MAH-TOO-YAH-LAT-KET:
"Thunder-rolling-in-the-mountains,"
the fugitive chief sits in a corner
of the prison car headed for Oklahoma,
chained to his warriors,
a featherless hawk in exile.

He sees out the window
geese rise from the storm's center
and knows more men died
by snow blizzard
than by cavalry shot.

Still his father's shield
of Wallowa Valley deer and elk
flashes in his eyes
and coyote runs the circles
and a cricket swallows the dark.

How many songs this elder
sang to break the cycle
of cold weather and disease
his people coughed and breathed
in this land of drifting ice.

Now sleepless as the door-guard,
the train rattles like dirt in his teeth,
straw in his eyes.

Holding rage in the palm of his fist,
his people's future spirals to red-forest dust,
leaves his bones on the track,
his soul in the whistle.

SITTING BULL (1831–1890)

A prominent leader in the Sioux warfare against the whites, Chief Sitting Bull fought hard against any and all forced settlement on reservations. A medicine man and seasoned warrior, he constantly composed war songs about his bold courage and his love of the land. "Two War Songs" were among his favorites. After the battle of Little Big Horn, Sitting Bull and three thousand of his followers fled to Canada, where they lived in exile for four years, often under extreme conditions. On July 19, 1881, with the understanding that they would receive a governmental pardon, he and 186 others returned to the United States, only to have the government break its promise. Sitting Bull chanted "Last Song" from his cell at Fort Randall, where he was jailed as a military prisoner.

Two War Songs

Translated from the Teton Sioux by W. S. Campbell

1.
Young men, help me, do help me!
I love my country so;
That is why I am fighting.

2.
No chance for me to live;
Mother, you might as well mourn.

Last Song

Translated from the Teton Sioux by Frances Densmore

A warrior
I have been.
Now
It is all over.
A hard time
I have.

WALT WHITMAN (1819–1892)

Whitman's subject in "Interpolation Sounds," General Philip Sheridan (also the focus of Thomas Buchanan Read's "Sheridan's Ride"), was transferred after the Civil War to the western plains. There he conducted military campaigns against the Cheyenne, Comanche, Arapaho, Sioux and other Native American nations. Though not considered a brilliant general, he was a fierce, brutal fighter who masterminded such massacres as Washita River and authorized initial strikes against the bands of Sitting Bull and Crazy Horse that culminated in the battle of Little Big Horn.

Interpolation Sounds

> *(General Philip Sheridan was buried at the Cathedral, Washington, D. C., August 1888, with all the pomp, music, and ceremonies of the Roman Catholic service.)*

Over and through the burial chant,
Organ and solemn service, sermon, bending priests,
To me come interpolation sounds not in the show—plainly to me, crowding
    up the aisle and from the window.
Of sudden battle's hurry and harsh noises—war's grim game to sight and ear
    in earnest;
The scout call'd up and forward—the general mounted and his aids around
    him—the new-brought word—the instantaneous order issued;
The rifle crack—the cannon thud—the rushing forth of men from their tents;
The clank of cavalry—the strange celerity of forming ranks—the slender
    bugle note;
The sound of horses' hoofs departing—saddles, arms, accoutrements.

TRADITIONAL

In 1890, Wovoka, a religious leader among the Paiute, prophesized the end of white westward expansion and the return of the land to the Native Americans. His message resonated particularly among the Sioux, Cheyenne, and Arapaho, all of whom had recently been confined to reservations. The rituals accompanying his messianic message were known as Ghost Dances, of which "The Whole World Is Coming" is one of the best examples. The dance played a significant role among the Sioux prior to the battle of Wounded Knee on December 29, 1890, when over two hundred defenseless men, women, and children were slaughtered by U. S. troops. The Sioux, wearing shirts called ghost shirts, believed they would be impervious to soldiers' bullets. Wounded Knee is considered to be the last battle of the Indian Wars.

The Whole World Is Coming

Translated from the Sioux by James Mooney

A whole world is coming.
A nation is coming, a nation is coming,
The Eagle has brought the message to the tribe.
The father says so, the father says so.
Over the whole earth they are coming.
The buffalo are coming, the buffalo are coming,
The Crow has brought the message to the tribe,
The father says so, the father says so.

SPANISH-AMERICAN WAR
(1898)

Over all of us in 1898 was the shadow of the Civil War and the men who fought it to the end that had come only thirty-five years before our enlistment. Our motives were as mixed as theirs. I think many of company C went along with my old chum Bohunk Calkins saying, "I want to find out whether I'll run when the shootin' begins."

FROM *ALWAYS THE YOUNG STRANGERS*, CARL SANDBURG

EDGAR LEE MASTERS (1869–1950)

Born in Garnett, Kansas, of pioneer stock, Edgar Lee Masters was catapulted into fame with the 1915 publication of Spoon River Anthology, *poetic epitaphs revealing the secret lives of people buried in a Midwestern cemetery. The speaker in "Harry Wilmans," among those buried, served under George Dewey, who, on May 1, 1898, sailed into the harbor of Manila, Philippine Islands, and in a matter of hours defeated the Spanish fleet there. On August 13, after the armistice had taken place, Dewey commanded a land and sea assault that led to the occupation of Manila.*

Harry Wilmans

I was just turned twenty-one,
And Henry Phipps, the Sunday-school superintendent,
Made a speech in Bindle's Opera House.
"The honor of the flag must be upheld," he said,
"Whether it be assailed by a barbarous tribe of Tagalogs
Or the greatest power in Europe."
And we cheered and cheered the speech and the flag he waved
As he spoke.
And I went to the war in spite of my father,
And followed the flag till I saw it raised
By our camp in a rice field near Manila,
And all of us cheered and cheered it.
But there were flies and poisonous things;
And there was the deadly water,
And the cruel heat,
And the sickening, putrid food;
And the smell of the trench just back of the tents
Where the soldiers went to empty themselves;
And there were the whores who followed us, full of syphilis;
And beastly acts between ourselves or alone,
With bullying, hatred, degradation among us,
And days of loathing and nights of fear
To the hour of the charge through the steaming swamp,
Following the flag,
Till I fell with a scream, shot through the guts.
Now there's a flag over me in Spoon River!
A flag! A flag!

WILLIAM VAUGHN MOODY (1869–1910)

Poet and dramatist William Vaughn Moody taught at Harvard University and the University of Chicago. His many works include A History of English Literature, *written with Robert Morss Lovett, and the popular verse play,* The Great Divide.

On a Soldier Fallen in the Philippines

Streets of the roaring town,
Hush for him, hush, be still!
He comes, who was stricken down
Doing the word of our will.
Hush! Let him have his state,
Give him his soldier's crown.
The grists of trade can wait
Their grinding at the mill,
But he cannot wait for his honor, now the trumpet has been blown.
Wreathe pride now for his granite brow, lay love on his breast of stone.

Toll! Let the great bells toll
Till the clashing air is dim.
Did we wrong this parted soul?
We will make it up to him.
Toll! Let him never guess
What work we set him to.
Laurel, laurel, yes;
He did what we bade him do.
Praise, and never a whispered hint but the fight he fought was good;
Never a word that the blood on his sword was his country's own heart's-blood.

A flag for the soldier's bier
Who dies that his land may live;
O, banners, banners here,
That he doubt not nor misgive!
That he heed not from the tomb
The evil days draw near
When the nation, robed in gloom,
With its faithless past shall strive.
Let him never dream that his bullet's scream went wide of its island mark,
Home to the heart of his darling land where she stumbled and sinned in the dark.

STEPHEN CRANE (1871–1900)

A novelist, poet, and short-story writer, Stephen Crane was the author of Maggie: A Girl of the Streets, The Open Boat and Other Tales, *and the classic Civil War novel,* The Red Badge of Courage. *While Crane never served in war, he worked as a newspaper correspondent in both the Greco-Turkish War of 1897 and the Spanish-American War. "Do Not Weep, Maiden, for War Is Kind" appeared in 1899.*

Do Not Weep, Maiden, for War Is Kind

Do not weep, maiden, for war is kind.
Because your lover threw wild hands toward the sky
And the affrighted steed ran on alone,
Do not weep.
War is kind.

    Hoarse, booming drums of the regiment,
    Little souls who thirst for fight,
    These men were born to drill and die.
    The unexplained glory flies above them,
    Great is the battle-god, great, and his kingdom—
    A field where a thousand corpses lie.

Do not weep, babe, for war is kind.
Because your father tumbled in the yellow trenches,
Raged at his breast, gulped and died,
Do not weep.
War is kind.

    Swift blazing flag of the regiment,
    Eagle with crest of red and gold,
    These men were born to drill and die.
    Point for them the virtue of slaughter,
    Make plain to them the excellence of killing
    And a field where a thousand corpses lie.

Mother whose heart hung humble as a button
On the bright splendid shroud of your son,
Do not weep.
War is kind.

FIRST WORLD WAR
(1914–1918)

Well Mother, this is the proudest day of my life. We leave for "over there" tonight, and I am thankful that I can take a place among men who will bring freedom to the world. I do not want you to worry about me at all, for I am coming back and will be 100 percent better for having gone, for in the army one gains knowledge of life, that is impossible to gain elsewhere . . .

PRIVATE LESTER HENSLER, BATTALION "E"
312 FIELD ARTILLERY, CAMP MEADE, MARYLAND, 1917

VACHEL LINDSAY (1879–1931)

Vachel Lindsay studied art in Chicago and New York but, unable to find suitable employment, became a troubadour, conducting tramping-tours of the country, reciting his poems and prose, and lecturing on art and temperance. Written in 1914, "Abraham Lincoln Walks at Midnight" depicts the ghost of Lincoln pacing the streets of Springfield, Illinois, tormented by the dreadful slaughter of war.

Abraham Lincoln Walks at Midnight

It is portentous, and a thing of state
That here at midnight, in our little town
A mourning figure walks, and will not rest,
Near the old court-house pacing up and down,

Or by his homestead, or in shadowed yards
He lingers where his children used to play,
Or through the market, on the well-worn stones
He stalks until the dawn-stars burn away.

A bronzed, lank man! His suit of ancient black,
A famous high top-hat and plain worn shawl
Make him the quaint great figure that men love,
The prairie-lawyer, master of us all.

He cannot sleep upon his hillside now.
He is among us:—as in times before!
And we who toss and lie awake for long
Breathe deep, and start, to see him pass the door.

His head is bowed. He thinks on men and kings.
Yea, when the sick world cries, how can he sleep?
Too many peasants fight, they know not why,
Too many homesteads in black terror weep.

The sins of all the war-lords burn his heart.
He sees the dreadnaughts scouring every main.
He carries on his shawl-wrapped shoulders now
The bitterness, the folly and the pain.

He cannot rest until a spirit-dawn
Shall come;—the shining hope of Europe free:
The league of sober folk, the Workers' Earth,
Bringing long peace to Cornland, Alp and Sea.

It breaks his heart that kings must murder still,
That all his hours of travail here for men
Seem yet in vain. And who will bring white peace
That he may sleep upon his hill again?

ALAN SEEGER (1888–1916)

Alan Seeger graduated from Harvard University in 1910, traveled to Paris, and at the start of World War I enlisted in the French Foreign Legion. Fiercely idealistic about war, he wrote in a letter home on May 22, 1915, about dying during battle: "If it must be, let it come in the heat of action. Why flinch? It is by far the noblest form in which death can come. It is in a sense almost a privilege." Seeger was killed at Belloy-en-Santere, in the battle of the Somme, on July 4, 1916, a battle that cost the British and French forces 620,000 casualties. "The Aisne (1914–15)" and "Rendezvous" are two of his most famous war poems.

The Aisne (1914–15)

We first saw fire on the tragic slopes
Where the flood-tide of France's early gain,
Big with wrecked promise and abandoned hopes,
Broke in a surf of blood along the Aisne.

The charge her heroes left us, we assumed,
What, dying, they reconquered, we preserved,
In the chill trenches, harried, shelled, entombed,
Winter came down on us, but no man swerved.

Winter came down on us. The low clouds, torn
In the stark branches of the riven pines,
Blurred the white rockets that from dusk till morn
Traced the wide curve of the close-grappling lines.

In rain, and fog that on the withered hill
Froze before dawn, the lurking foe drew down;
Or light snows fell that made forlorner still
The ravaged country and the ruined town;

Or the long clouds would end. Intensely fair,
The winter constellations blazing forth—
Perseus, the Twins, Orion, the Great Bear—
Gleamed on our bayonets pointing to the north.

And the lone sentinel would start and soar
On wings of strong emotion as he knew
That kinship with the stars that only War
Is great enough to lift man's spirit to.

And ever down the curving front, aglow
With the pale rockets' intermittent light,
He heard, like distant thunder, growl and grow
The rumble of far battles in the night,—

Rumours, reverberant, indistinct, remote,
Borne from red fields whose martial names have won
The power to thrill like a far trumpet-note,—
Vic, Vailly, Soupir, Hurtelise, Craonne . . .

Craonne, before thy cannon-swept plateau,
Where like sere leaves lay strewn September's dead,
I found for all things I forfeited
A recompense I would not now forgo.

For that high fellowship was ours then
With those who, championing another's good,
More than dull Peace or its poor votaries could,
Taught us the dignity of being men.

There we drained deeper the deep cup of life,
And on sublimer summits came to learn,
After soft things, the terrible and stern,
After sweet Love, the majesty of Strife;

There where we faced under those frowning heights
The blast that maims, the hurricane that kills;
There where the watch-lights on the winter hills
Flickered like balefire through inclement nights;

There where, firm links in the unyielding chain,
Where fell the long-planned blow and fell in vain—
Hearts worthy of the honour and the trail,
We helped to hold the lines along the Aisne.

Rendezvous

I have a rendezvous with Death
At some disputed barricade,
When Spring comes back with rustling shade
And apple-blossoms fill the air—
I have a rendezvous with Death
When Spring brings back blue days and fair.

It may be he shall take my hand
And lead me into his dark land
And close my eyes and quench my breath—
It may be I shall pass him still.
I have a rendezvous with Death
On some scarred slope of battered hill,
When Spring comes round again this year
And the first meadow-flowers appear.

God knows 'twere better to be deep
Pillowed in silk and scented down,
Where love throbs out in blissful sleep,
Pulse nigh to pulse, and breath to breath,
Where hushed awakenings are dear . . .
But I've a rendezvous with Death
At midnight in some flaming town,
When Spring trips north again this year,
And I to my pledged word am true,
I shall not fail that rendezvous.

ROBERT LOWELL (1917–1977)

Lowell first published "Verdun" in History. *It describes the longest and one of the bloodiest battles of World War I, fought in 1916 at Verdun, a village in northeastern France. Two million were engaged, and in the end over 650,000 lives were lost.*

Verdun

I bow down to the great goiter of Verdun,
I know what's buried there, ivory telephone,
ribs, hips bleached to parchment, a pale machinegun—
they lie fatigued from too much punishment,
cling by a string to friends they knew firsthand,
to the God of our fathers still twenty like themselves.
Their medals and rosettes have kept in bloom,
they stay young, only living makes us age.
I know the sort of town they came from, straight brownstone,
each house cooled by a rectilinear private garden,
a formal greeting and a slice of life.
The city says, "I am the finest city"—
landmass held by half a million bodies
for Berlin and Paris, twin cities saved at Verdun.

JANET LEWIS (1899–1998)

Novelist and poet Janet Lewis lived most of her life in Los Altos, California, with her husband, the poet and critic Yvor Winters. She was the author of The Indians in the Woods, The Dear Past and Other Poems 1919–1994, *and* the Invention of the Flute. *The Seventh Zouaves, described in Lewis's poem below, were French infantrymen recruited in Algeria from the Zouaves, a group of Berbers.*

Trophy, W. W. I

A cross.
I had it from a friend, a Russian woman,
Who found it in a shop in London.
The double cross of Lorraine,
Made of tin, cleverly worked, lusterless,
Set with six bits of glass
Faceted to shine like emeralds,
Inscribed on the back in block letters, lightly scratched,
Verdun.

Verdun, a word to echo
With the sound of guns,
Continual, near, remote, ominous,
The guns of August.
Inscribed also, lightly, the years.
On the lower foot of the cross,
Nineteen-fourteen, nineteen-fifteen, and above,
Above the top crossbar,
Nineteen-sixteen, nineteen-seventeen,
The years of my girlhood.
There is no nineteen-eighteen.

The name, hard to decipher,
Begins with an A. Perhaps Audujart,
Of the Seventh Zouaves.
Did he carry it with him
Through all those years of cold,
Of stifled fear, and mud,
And endless boredom? Did he make
This cross?

Into whose hands
Was it finally surrendered?
Those of a sweetheart, of a sister,
Of a mother surviving the loss
Of other sons? To be held
Close to the heart, to receive
Warm breath, murmuring a name,
The touch of lips?

No one can speak for it.
In itself it says:
Verdun
And the death of a man.

AMY LOWELL (1874–1925)

Amy Lowell was a leading figure in the Imagist movement. One of the most colorful personalities in early twentieth-century American letters, she was virtually a legend in her lifetime, attracting overflowing crowds to her lectures and poetry readings. In London at the outbreak of World War I, Lowell helped organize war relief at the American Consulate and donated thousands of dollars of her own money to the war effort. "Patterns," first published in 1916, remains her best-known poem.

Patterns

I walk down the garden paths,
And all the daffodils
Are blowing, and the bright blue squills.
I walk down the patterned garden paths
In my stiff, brocaded gown.
With my powdered hair and jewelled fan,
I too am a rare
Pattern, as I wander down
The garden paths.

My dress is richly figured,
And the train
Makes a pink and silver stain
On the gravel, and the thrift
Of the borders.
Just a plate of current fashion
Tripping by in high-heeled, ribboned shoes.
Not a softness anywhere about me,
Only whalebone and brocade.
And I sink on a seat in the shade
Of a lime tree. For my passion
Wars against the stiff brocade.
The daffodils and squills
Flutter in the breeze
As they please.
And I weep;
For the lime tree is in blossom
And one small flower has dropped upon my bosom.

And the plashing of waterdrops
In the marble fountain
Comes down the garden paths.
The dripping never stops.
Underneath my stiffened gown
Is the softness of a woman bathing in a marble basin,
A basin in the midst of hedges grown
So thick, she cannot see her lover hiding,
But she guesses he is near,
And the sliding of the water
Seems the stroking of a dear
Hand upon her.
What is Summer in a fine brocaded gown!
I should like to see it lying in a heap upon the ground.
All the pink and silver crumpled up on the ground.

I would be the pink and silver as I ran along the paths,
And he would stumble after,
Bewildered by my laughter.
I should see the sun flashing from his sword-hilt and the buckles on his shoes.
I would choose
To lead him in a maze along the patterned paths,
A bright and laughing maze for my heavy-booted lover.
Till he caught me in the shade,
And the buttons of his waistcoat bruised my body as he clasped me,
Aching, melting, unafraid.
With the shadows of the leaves and the sundrops,
And the plopping of the waterdrops,
All about us in the open afternoon—
I am very like to swoon
With the weight of this brocade,
For the sun sifts through the shade.

Underneath the fallen blossom
In my bosom,
Is a letter I have hid.
It was brought to me this morning by a rider from the duke.
"Madam, we regret to inform you that Lord Hartwell
Died in action Thursday se'nnight."
As I read it in the white, morning sunlight,
The letters squirmed like snakes.
"Any answer, Madam," said my footman.

"No," I told him.
"See that the messenger takes some refreshment.
No, no answer."
And I walked into the garden,
Up and down the patterned paths,
In my stiff, correct brocade.
The blue and yellow flowers stood up proudly in the sun,
Each one.
I stood upright too,
Held rigid to the pattern
By the stiffness of my gown.
Up and down I walked.
Up and down.

In a month he would have been my husband.
In a month, here, underneath this lime,
We would have broken the pattern;
He for me, and I for him,
He as Colonel, I as Lady,
On this shady seat.
He had a whim
That sunlight carried blessing.
And I answered, "It shall be as you have said."
Now he is dead.

In Summer and in Winter I shall walk
Up and down
The patterned garden paths
In my stiff, brocaded gown.
The squills and daffodils
Will give place to pillared roses, and to asters and to snow.
I shall go
Up and down,
In my gown.
Gorgeously arrayed,
Boned and stayed.
And the softness of my body will be guarded from embrace
By each button, hook, and lace.
For the man who should loose me is dead,
Fighting with the Duke in Flanders,
In a pattern called a war.
Christ! What are patterns for?

ROBERT FROST (1874–1963)

One of America's most enduring and important poets, Robert Frost was born in San Francisco and was taken at the age of ten to the New England farm country with which his poetry is so strongly identified. After spending three years in England, he returned to the United States in 1915 to settle on a New Hampshire farm, having already achieved a reputation as a significant American poet. He went on to win four Pulitzer Prizes for his poetry. "Not to Keep" is one of Frost's few war poems and was first published in 1917.

Not to Keep

They sent him back to her. The letter came
Saying . . . and she could have him. And before
She could be sure there was no hidden ill
Under the formal writing, he was in her sight—
Living.—They gave him back to her alive—
How else? They are not known to send the dead—
And not disfigured visibly. His face?—
His hands? She had to look—to ask
"What was it, dear?" And she had given all
And still she had all—*they* had—they the lucky!
Wasn't she glad now? Everything seemed won,
And all the rest for them permissible ease.
She had to ask "What was it, dear?"
                                        "Enough,
Yet not enough. A bullet through and through,
High in the breast. Nothing but what good care
And medicine and rest—and you a week,
Can cure me of to go again." The same
Grim giving to do over for them both.
She dared no more than ask him with her eyes
How was it with him for a second trial.
And with his eyes he asked her not to ask.
They had given him back to her, but not to keep.

E. E. CUMMINGS (1894–1962)

Edward Estlin Cummings joined the service of the American volunteer Norton Harjes Ambulance Corps in France before the U.S. entered World War I. In 1917, he was confined for months in a French concentration camp on an unfounded charge of treasonable correspondence. One of the most influential poets of his generation, he was the author of fifteen volumes of poetry, *including* Tulips and Chimneys, Is 5, *and* 95 Poems. The Enormous Room, *a prose account of his internment in France, is considered a classic of World War I literature.*

i sing of Olaf glad and big

i sing of Olaf glad and big
whose warmest heart recoiled at war:
a conscientious object-or
his wellbelovéd colonel (trig
westpointer most succinctly bred)
took erring Olaf soon in hand;
but—though an host of overjoyed
noncoms (first knocking on the head
him) do through icy waters roll
that helplessness which others stroke
with brushes recently employed
anent this muddy toiletbowl,
while kindred intellects evoke
allegiance per blunt instruments—
Olaf (being to all intents
a corpse and wanting any rag
upon what God unto him gave)
responds, without getting annoyed
"I will not kiss your fucking flag"

straightway the silver bird looked grave
(departing hurriedly to shave)

but—through all kinds of officers
(a yearning nation's blueeyed pride)
their passive prey did kick and curse
until for wear their clarion
voices and boots were much the worse,

and egged the firstclassprivates on
his rectum wickedly to tease
by means of skilfully applied
bayonets roasted hot with heat—
Olaf (upon what were once knees)
does almost ceaselessly repeat
"there is some shit I will not eat"

our president, being of which
assertions duly notified
threw the yellowsonofabitch
into a dungeon, where he died

Christ (of His mercy infinite)
i pray to see; and Olaf, too

preponderatingly because
unless statistics lie he was
more brave than me: more blond than you.

my sweet old etcetera

my sweet old etcetera
aunt lucy during the recent

war could and what
is more did tell you just
what everybody was fighting

for,
my sister

isabel created hundreds
(and
hundreds) of socks not to
mention shirts fleaproof earwarmers

etcetera wristers etcetera, my
mother hoped that

i would die etcetera
bravely of course my father used
to become hoarse talking about how it was
a privilege and if only he
could meanwhile my

self etcetera lay quietly
in the deep mud et

cetera
(dreaming,
et
    cetera, of
Your smile
eyes knees and of your Etcetera)

MALCOLM COWLEY (1898–1989)

Malcolm Cowley served in World War I and became an expatriate in France. He led a distinguished literary career that included volumes of poetry, criticism, and literary history, most notably Exile's Return, Many Windowed Houses: Collected Essays on Writers and Writing, *and* Second Flowering.

Château de Soupir, 1917

Jean tells me that the Senator
came here to see his mistresses.
With a commotion at the door
the servants ushered him, Jean says,
through velvets and mahoganies
to where the odalisque was set,
the queen pro tempore, Yvette.

An eighteenth-century chateau
remodeled to his Lydian taste,
painted and gilt fortissimo:
the Germans, grown sardonical,
had used a bust of Cicero
as shield for a machine-gun nest
at one end of the banquet hall.

The trenches run diagonally
across the gardens and the lawns,
and jagged wire from tree to tree.
The lake is desolate of swans.
In tortured immobility
the deities of stone or bronze
abide each new catastrophe.

Phantasmagorical at nights,
yellow and white and amethyst,
the star-shells flare, the Verey lights
hiss upward, brighten, and persist
until a tidal wave of mist
rolls over us and makes us seem
the drowned creatures of a dream,

ghosts among earlier ghosts. Yvette,
the tight skirt raised above her knees,
beckons her lover *en fillette,*
then nymphlike flits among the trees,
while he, beard streaming in the breeze,
pants after her, a portly satyr,
his goat feet shod in patent leather.

The mist creeps riverward. A fox
barks underneath a blasted tree.
An enemy machine gun mocks
this ante-bellum coquetry
and then falls silent, while a bronze
Silenus, patron of these lawns,
lies riddled like a pepper box.

JOHN PEALE BISHOP (1892-1944)

Born in Jefferson County, West Virginia, John Peale Bishop entered Princeton in 1913. Among his fellow students were Edmund Wilson and novelist F. Scott Fitzgerald, who used Bishop as his model for Tom D'Invilliers in This Side of Paradise. *After graduation, he was first lieutenant in the 33rd Infantry in France. Although he saw no action during the war, he served in Europe until 1919. His books include* Green Fruit, Minute Particulars, *and* The Collected Poems of John Peale Bishop.

In the Dordogne

We stood up before day
And shaved by metal mirrors
In the faint flame of a faulty candle.
And we hurried down the wide stone stairs
With a clirr of spur chains
On stone. And we thought
When the cocks crew
That the ghosts of a dead dawn
Would rise and be off. But they stayed
Under the window, crouched on the staircase,
The windows now the color of morning.

The colonel slept in the bed of Sully,
Slept on: but we descended
And saw in a niche in the white wall
A Virgin and Child, serene
Who were stone: we saw sycamores:
Three aged mages
Scattering gifts of gold.
But when the wind blew, there were autumn odors
And the shadowed trees
Had the dapplings of young fawns.

And each day one died or another
Died: each week we sent out thousands
That returned by hundreds
Wounded or gassed. And those that died

We buried close to the old wall
Within a stone's throw of Périgord
Under the tower of the troubadours.

And because we had courage;
Because there was courage and youth
Ready to be wasted; because we endured
And were prepared for all endurance;
We thought something must come of it:
That the Virgin would raise her Child and smile;
The trees gather up their gold and go;
That courage would avail something
And something we had never lost
Be regained through wastage, by dying,
By burying the others under the English tower.

The colonel slept on in the bed of Sully
Under the ravelling curtains; the leaves fell
And were blown away; the young men rotted
Under the shadow of the tower
In a land of small clear silent streams
Where the coming on of evening is
The letting down of blue and azure veils
Over the clear and silent streams
Delicately bordered by poplars.

ERNEST HEMINGWAY (1899–1961)

Ernest Hemingway is known primarily for such novels as The Sun Also Rises, A Farewell to Arms, For Whom the Bell Tolls, *and* The Old Man and the Sea. *In World War I, he joined a volunteer ambulance unit in France and later transferred to the Italian infantry. On July 8, 1918, at the battle of Piave, he was wounded by a trench mortar explosion, the first American wounded in Italy, and was later awarded the Italian Cross for Valor for saving the lives of three Italian soldiers. "Champs d'Honneur" and "Killed Piave—July 8—1918," a poem about a dead soldier remembered by his wife or lover, were published in 1923.*

Champs d'Honneur

Soldiers never do die well;
   Crosses mark the places,
Wooden crosses where they fell;
   Stuck above their faces.
Soldiers pitch and cough and twitch;
   All the world roars red and black,
Soldiers smother in a ditch;
   Choking through the whole attack.

Killed Piave—July 8—1918

Desire and
All the sweet pulsing aches
And gentle hurtings
That were you,
Are gone into the sullen dark,
Now in the night you come unsmiling
To lie with me
A dull, cold, rigid bayonet
On my hot-swollen, throbbing soul.

WALLACE STEVENS (1879–1955)

One of the most important American poets of the twentieth century, Wallace Stevens was born in Reading, Pennsylvania, but lived his entire adult life in Hartford, Connecticut, where he worked at the Hartford Accident and Indemnity Company. In 1950, he received the Bollingen Prize in Poetry, and, in 1955, he was awarded both the Pulitzer Prize and the National Book Award for his Collected Poems. *"The Death of a Soldier" was written in 1918.*

The Death of a Soldier

Life contracts and death is expected,
As in a season of autumn.
The soldier falls.

He does not become a three-days personage,
Imposing his separation,
Calling for pomp.

Death is absolute and without memorial,
As in a season of autumn,
When the wind stops,

When the wind stops and, over the heavens,
The clouds go, nevertheless,
In their direction.

ARCHIBALD MACLEISH (1892–1982)

Archibald MacLeish served as a volunteer ambulance driver in World War I and then at the front as a captain of field artillery. Written in 1926, "Memorial Rain" pays tribute to MacLeish's brother, who died while flying a mission over Belgium.

Memorial Rain

For Kenneth MacLeish, 1894–1918

Ambassador Puser the ambassador
Reminds himself in French, felicitous tongue,
What these (young men no longer) lie here for
In rows that once, and somewhere else, were young . . .

    All night in Brussels the wind had tugged at my door:
    I had heard the wind at my door and the trees strung
    Taut, and to me who had never been before
    In that country it was a strange wind, blowing
    Steadily, stiffening the walls, the floor,
    The roof of my room. I had not slept for knowing
He too, dead, was a stranger in that land
    And felt beneath the earth in the wind's flowing
    A tightening of roots and would not understand,
Remembering lake winds in Illinois,
That strange wind. I had felt his bones in the sand
    Listening.

        . . . Reflects that these enjoy
Their country's gratitude, that deep repose,
That peace no pain can break, no hurt destroy,
That rest, that sleep . . .

        At Ghent the wind rose.
    There was a smell of rain and a heavy drag
    Of wind in the hedges but not as the wind blows
    Over fresh water when the waves lag
    Foaming and the willows huddle and it will rain:
    I felt him waiting.

. . . Indicates the flag
Which (may he say) enisles in Flanders plain
This little field these happy, happy dead
Have made America . . .

                               In the ripe grain
The wind coiled glistening, darted, fled,
Dragging its heavy body: at Waereghem
The wind coiled in the grass above his head:
Waiting—listening . . .

                . . . Dedicates to them
This earth their bones have hallowed, this last gift
A Grateful country . . .

                          Under the dry grass stem
The words are blurred, are thickened, the words sift
Confused by the rasp of the wind, by the thin grating
Of ants under the grass, the minute shift
And tumble of dusty sand separating
From dusty sand. The roots of the grass strain,
Tighten, the earth is rigid, waits—he is waiting—

And suddenly, and all at once, the rain!

The living scatter, they run into houses, the wind
Is trampled under the rain, shakes free, is again
Trampled. The rain gathers, running in thinned
Spurts of water that ravel in the dry sand,
Seeping in the sand under the grass roots, seeping
Between cracked boards to the bones of a clenched hand:
The earth relaxes, loosens; he is sleeping,
He rests, he is quiet, he sleeps in a strange land.

EDITH WHARTON (1862–1937)

Author of over forty volumes of fiction, nonfiction, and poetry, Edith Wharton was awarded the Pulitzer Prize for her novel, The Age of Innocence. *Living in Paris during World War I, she worked tirelessly in the relief effort, established the American Hostels for Refugees, made repeated visits to the front, organized the Children of Flanders Rescue Committee, and made the war the centerpiece of much of her writing. In 1915, she was awarded the Cross of the Legion of Honor by the French government.*

On Active Service

American Expeditionary Force

(R.S., August 12th, 1918)
He is dead that was alive.
How shall friendship understand?
Lavish heart and tireless hand
Bidden not to give or strive,
Eager brain and questing eye
Like a broken lens laid by.

He, with so much left to do,
Such a gallant race to run,
What concern had he with you,
Silent Keeper of things done?

Tell us not that, wise and young,
Elsewhere he lives out his plan.
Our speech was sweetest to his tongue,
And his great gift was to be man.

Long and long shall we remember,
In our breasts his grave be made.
It shall never be December
Where so warm a heart is laid,
But in our saddest selves a sweet voice sing,
Recalling him, and Spring.

MIKHAIL NAIMY (1889–1988)

Born in Baskinta, Lebanon, Mikhail Naimy remains one of the most acclaimed poets in the Arab world. After studying for the Orthodox priesthood in Poltava, Russia, he came to the United States in 1911 and received a law degree from the University of Washington, Seattle. During World War I, he served on the French front with the U.S. Army. "My Brother" is one of his most famous poems.

My Brother

Translated from the Arabic by Sharif S. Elmusa and Gregory Orfalea

Brother, if on the heels of war Western man celebrates his deeds,
Consecrates the memory of the fallen and builds monuments for heroes,
Do not yourself sing for the victors nor rejoice over those trampled by
    victorious wheels;
Rather kneel as I do, wounded, for the end of our dead.

Brother, if after the war a soldier comes home
And throws his tired body into the arms of friends,
Do not hope on your return for friends.
Hunger struck down all to whom we might whisper our pain.

Brother, if the farmer returns to till his land,
And after long exile rebuilds a shack which cannon had wrecked,
Our waterwheels have dried up
And the foes have left no seedling except the scattered corpses.

Brother, misery nestled everywhere—through our will.
Do not lament. Others do not hear our woe.
Instead follow me with a pick and spade that we may dig a trench in which
    to hide our dead.

Dear brother, who are we without a neighbor, kin or country?
We sleep and we wake clad in shame.

The world breathes our stench, as it did that of the dead.
Bring the spade and follow me—dig another trench for those still alive.

LOUISE BOGAN (1897–1970)

Louise Bogan was born in Livermore Falls, Maine, and led a stormy, often hidden life. Her early success as a poet earned her a place in the prestigious New York literary circles of the 1920s. Her many books include Body of This Death *and* The Blue Estuaries: Poems 1923–1968. *In October 1918, a few weeks before the armistice, Bogan's thirty-two year-old brother, Charles, was killed in the battle of Haumont Wood in France. German artillery was so relentless during the battle that whole companies were reduced to two or three survivors each.*

To My Brother Killed: Haumont Wood: October, 1918

O you so long dead,
You masked and obscure,
I can tell you, all things endure:
The wine and the bread;

The marble quarried for the arch;
The iron become steel;
The spoke broken from the wheel;
The sweat of the long march;

The hay-stacks cut through like loaves
And the hundred flowers from the seed;
All things indeed
Though struck by the hooves

Of disaster, of time due,
Of fell loss and gain,
All things remain,
I can tell you, this is true.

Though burned down to stone
Though lost from the eye,
I can tell you, and not lie,—
Save of peace alone.

KAY BOYLE (1902–1993)

A native of St. Paul, Minnesota, Kay Boyle began her literary life in Paris during the 1920s, becoming friends with such writers as Samuel Beckett and James Joyce. A recipient of numerous awards and honors for her writing, including two Guggenheim Fellowships, two O. Henry Awards, and the Before Columbus Foundation Award for a lifetime of work, she was the author of more than twenty books ranging from novels to children's stories. "Mothers" and "The People's Cry" were some of her first poems and come from notebooks written during World War I.

Mothers

In the still of night
Have we wept.
And our hearts, shattered and aching
Have prayed.
In the cold, cold moonlight
Have we sobbed
And dreamed of what might have been.
And our hearts have bled from stabs
Given unheeding.
We are the women who have suffered alone—
Alone and in silence.

The People's Cry

Great King, there is no hatred in this heart for you,
There is no anger in my soul.
Only a man's deep pity for a brother,
Do I feel, only a wish that you could understand.
We fought, Great King, for what you thought was right—
We were the puppets and you pulled the strings.
We did not know for what we fought—
'Twas to protect our honor, so you said, and we our souls aflame,
Answered the trumpets' call.
Honor—what does it mean?
Does it mean a bloody war?
Is not *our* honor greater, higher than this, O King?
Higher than death and destruction, highest above all?

Is not to protect our honor to stand, wondrous and fine,
Helping those countries about to grow as we have done?
Is not honor a marvelous love and a heart that holds all men?
King, that's what we call honor, and you we feel are wrong.
But if you *are* right and honor *is* death and hate and kill,
If the honor we fight for is stained by a brother's blood—
King, we would rather die in the fight,
Die rather than see our children rejoice in the fact
That we murdered our brothers so.
But King, because you have said it,
Our children will think it right
That we fought "to protect our honor,"
So King, we die in the fight.

EZRA POUND (1885–1972)

In 1908, Ezra Pound traveled to Europe and was soon at the center of literary Modernism. One of the most influential poets of the twentieth century, he was in London during World War I. Following the war, he moved to Paris, where he lived until 1924, a force in the expatriate circle that included Hemingway and Joyce. In 1924, he moved again, this time to Rapallo, Italy, where he remained for the next two decades. His chief works include The Cantos, Hugh Selwyn Mauberley, *and* The Pisan Cantos, *recipient of the Bollingen Prize.*

from Hugh Selwyn Mauberley

These fought in any case,
And some believing,
             pro domo, in any case . . .

Some quick to arm,
some for adventure,
some from fear of weakness,
some from fear of censure,
some for love of slaughter, in imagination,
learning later . . .
some in fear, learning love of slaughter;
Died some, pro patria,
             non 'dulce' non 'et decor' . . .
walked eye-deep in hell
believing in old men's lies, then unbelieving
came home, home to a lie,
home to many deceits,
home to old lies and new infamy;
usury age-old and age-thick
and liars in public places.

Daring as never before, wastage as never before.
Young blood and high blood,
fair cheeks, and fine bodies;

fortitude as never before
frankness as never before,
disillusions as never told in the old days,
hysterias, trench confessions,
laughter out of dead bellies.

*   *   *

There died a myriad,
And of the best, among them,
For an old bitch gone in the teeth,
For a botched civilization,

Charm, smiling at the good mouth,
Quick eyes gone under earth's lid,

For two gross of broken statues,
For a few thousand battered books.

T. S. ELIOT (1888–1965)

In 1914, T. S. Eliot traveled to Europe and did not return again to the United States until 1932, when he accepted a lectureship at Harvard University. A Nobel Laureate in literature, he was the author of Prufrock and Other Observations, The Waste Land, Four Quartets, *and other works that helped set the stage for the Modernist period. Eliot's "Triumphal March" from "Coriolan," a poem inspired by Beethoven's "Coriolan Overture," was written between World Wars I and II and is considered a post-war poem.*

Triumphal March

Stone, bronze, stone, steel, stone, oakleaves, horses' heels
Over the paving.
And the flags. And the trumpets. And so many eagles.
How many? Count them. And such a press of people.
We hardly knew ourselves that day, or knew the City.
This is the way to the temple, and we so many crowding the way.
So many waiting, how many waiting? what did it matter, on such a day?
Are they coming? No, not yet. You can see some eagles. And hear the trumpets.
Here they come. Is he coming?
The natural wakeful life of our Ego is a perceiving.
We can wait with our stools and our sausages.
What comes first? Can you see? Tell us. It is

  5,800,000 rifles and carbines,
    102,000 machine guns,
     28,000 trench mortars,
     53,000 field and heavy guns,
I cannot tell how many projectiles, mines and fuses,
     13,000 aeroplanes,
     24,000 aeroplane engines,
     50,000 ammunition waggons,
now 55,000 army waggons,
     11,000 field kitchens,
      1,150 field bakeries.

What a time that took. Will it be he now? No,
Those are the golf club Captains, these the Scouts,
And now the *société gymnastique de Poissy*

And now come the Mayor and the Liverymen. Look
There he is now, look:
There is no interrogation in his eyes
Or in the hands, quiet over the horse's neck,
And the eyes watchful, waiting, perceiving, indifferent.
O hidden under the dove's wing, hidden in the turtle's breast,
Under the palmtree at noon, under the running water
At the still point of the turning world. O hidden.

Now they go up to the temple. Then the sacrifice.
Now come the virgins bearing urns, urns containing
Dust
Dust
Dust of dust, and now
Stone, bronze, stone, steel, stone, oakleaves, horses' heels
Over the paving.

That is all we could see. But how many eagles! and how many trumpets!
(And Easter Day, we didn't get to the country,
So we took young Cyril to church. And they rang a bell
And he said right out loud, *crumpets.*)
                              Don't throw away that sausage,
It'll come in handy. He's artful. Please, will you
Give us a light?
Light
Light
Et les soldats faisaient la haie? ILS LA FAISAIENT.

CARL SANDBURG (1878–1967)

Carl Sandburg was born in Galesburg, Illinois, of a Swedish immigrant family. After a series of itinerant jobs from milkman to farmhand, he enlisted in the army and went through the Puerto Rico campaign in the Spanish-American War. His best known books include Chicago Poems; Cornhuskers; The People, Yes; *and his monumental biography of Abraham Lincoln.*

Grass

Pile the bodies high at Austerlitz and Waterloo.
Shovel them under and let me work—
        I am the grass; I cover all.

And pile them high at Gettysburg
And pile them high at Ypres and Verdun.
Shovel them under and let me work.
Two years, ten years, and passengers ask the conductor:
        What place is this?
        Where are we now?

        I am the grass.
        Let me work.

SARA TEASDALE (1884–1933)

Sara Teasdale's first poems were published when she was still in her teens, and her first book appeared when she was twenty-one. Her adult life, however, was a severely troubled one, and she died in 1933 from an overdose of sleeping pills that caused her to drown in her bath. "There Will Come Soft Rains" was first published in 1920.

There Will Come Soft Rains

There will come soft rains and the smell of the ground,
And swallows circling with their shimmering sound;

And frogs in the pools singing at night,
And wild plum-trees in tremulous white;

Robins will wear their feathery fire
Whistling their whims on a low fence-wire;

And not one will know of the war, not one
Will care at last when it is done.

Not one would mind, neither bird nor tree
If mankind perished utterly;

And Spring herself, when she woke at dawn,
Would scarcely know that we were gone.

CONRAD AIKEN (1889–1973)

Poet and novelist Conrad Aiken was the author of more than twenty volumes of poetry, including Earth Triumphant; Selected Poems, *recipient of the 1929 Pulitzer Prize;* The Soldier; *and* Collected Poems, *winner of the National Book Award. "The Wars and the Unknown Soldier" honors three major memorials to the unknown dead of the First World War—the Tomb of the Unknowns in Washington, D. C., Westminster Abbey in London, and the Arc de Triomphe in Paris.*

The Wars and the Unknown Soldier

I

Dry leaves, soldier, dry leaves, dead leaves:
voices of leaves on the wind that bears them to destruction,
impassioned prayer, impassioned hymn of delight
of the gladly doomed to die. Stridor of beasts,
stridor of men, praisers of lust and battle,
numberless as waves, the waves singing
to the wind that beats them down.

                  Under Osiris,
him of the Egyptian priests, Osymandyas the King,
eastward into Asia we passed, swarmed over Bactria,
three thousand years before Christ.

                  The history of war
is the history of mankind.
            So many dead:
look at them there in the dark, look at them going,
the longest parade of all, the parade of the dead:
between then and now, seven thousand million dead:
dead on the field of battle.

                  The people which is not ready
to guard its gods, and its household gods, with the sword,
who knows but it will find itself with nothing
save honor to defend—?
            Consider, soldier,
whatever name you go by, doughboy, dogface,

(*solidus,* a piece of silver, the soldier's pay,)
marine or tommy, God's mercenary—consider our lot
in the days of the single combat. You have seen on the seashore,
in the offshore wind blown backward, a wavecrest
windwhipped and quivering, borne helpless and briefly
to fall underfoot of an oncoming seawall, foam-smothered,
sea-trapped, lost; and the roar, and the foamslide regathered,
once more to recede, wind-thwarted again: thus deathward
the battle lines whelmed and divided. The darkling battalions
locked arms in chaos, the bravest, the heroes,
kept in the forefront; and this line once broken,
our army was done for.

II

In the new city of marble and bright stone,
the city named for a captain: in the capital:
under the solemn echoing dome, in the still tomb,
lies an unknown soldier.

    (Concord: Valley Forge: the Wilderness: Antietam: Gettysburg: Shiloh)

                In the brown city,
old and shabby, by the muddy Thames, in the gaunt avenue
where Romans blessed with Latin the oyster and the primrose,
the stone shaft speaks of another. Those who pass
bare their heads in the rain, pausing to listen.

    (Hastings: Blenheim: Waterloo: Trafalgar: Balaklava: Gallipoli)

Across grey water, red poppies on cliffs and chalk,
hidden under the arch, in the city of light,
the city beloved of Abelard, rests a third,
nameless as those, but the fluttering flame
substituting for a name.
                Three unknown soldiers:
three, let us say, out of many. On the proud arch
names shine like stars, the names of battles and victories;
but never the name of man, you, the unknown.
Down there runs the river, under dark walls of rock,
parapets of rock, stone steps that green to the water.

There they fished up in the twilight another unknown,
the one they call *L'Inconnue de la Seine:* drowned hands,
drowned hair, drowned eyes: masked like marble she listens
to the drip-drop secret of silence; and the pale eyelids
enclose and disclose what they know, the illusion
found like fire under Lethe. Devotion here sainted,
the love here deathless. The strong purpose turns
from the daggered lamplight, from the little light to the lesser,
from stone to stone stepping, from the next-to-the-last
heartbeat and footstep even to the sacred, to the last.
Love: devotion: sacrifice: death: can we call her unknown
who was not unknown to herself? whose love lives still
as if death itself were alive and divine?

                              And you, the soldier:
you who are dead: is it not so with you?
Love: devotion: sacrifice: death: can we call you unknown,
you who knew what you did? The soldier is crystal:
crystal of man: clear heart, clear duty, clear purpose.
No soldier can be unknown. Only he is unknown
who is unknown to himself.

SECOND WORLD WAR
(1939–1945)

Twenty years after, on the other side of the globe, again the filth of murky fox-holes, the stench of ghostly trenches, the slime of dripping dugouts, those boiling suns of relentless heat, those torrential rains of devastating storms, the loneliness and utter desolation of jungle trails, the bitterness of long separation from those they loved and cherished, the deadly pestilence of tropical disease, the horror of stricken areas of war.

FROM "DUTY, HONOR, COUNTRY," AN ADDRESS AT
WEST POINT, GENERAL DOUGLAS MACARTHUR, MAY 12, 1962

ELIZABETH BISHOP (1911-1979)

Born in Worcester, Massachusetts, and raised in Nova Scotia, Elizabeth Bishop spent much of her life traveling and living in Brazil. While she wrote and published sparingly, she won almost every significant American poetry prize during her lifetime, including the Pulitzer Prize (for Poems-North & South*), the National Book Award (for* Questions of Travel*), and the National Book Critics Circle Award (for* Geography III*). Employing subtle, complex military imagery, "Roosters" was written at the advent of World War II while Bishop was in Key West, Florida.*

Roosters

At four o'clock
in the gun-metal blue dark
we hear the first crow of the first cock

just below
the gun-metal blue window
and immediately there is an echo

off in the distance,
then one from the backyard fence,
then one, with horrible insistence,

grates like a wet match
from the broccoli patch,
flares, and all over town begins to catch.

Cries galore
come from the water-closet door,
from the dropping-plastered henhouse floor,

where in the blue blur
their rustling wives admire,
the roosters brace their cruel feet and glare

with stupid eyes
while from their beaks there rise
the uncontrolled, traditional cries.

Deep from protruding chests
in green-gold medals dressed,
planned to command and terrorize the rest,

the many wives
who lead hens' lives
of being courted and despised;

deep from raw throats
a senseless order floats
all over town. A rooster gloats

over our beds
from rusty iron sheds
and fences made from old bedsteads,

over our churches
where the tin rooster perches,
over our little wooden northern houses,

making sallies
from all the muddy alleys,
marking out maps like Rand McNally's:

glass-headed pins,
oil-golds and copper greens,
anthracite blues, alizarins,

each one an active
displacement in perspective;
each screaming, "This is where I live!"

Each screaming
"Get up! Stop dreaming!"
Roosters, what are you projecting?

You, whom the Greeks elected
to shoot at on a post, who struggled
when sacrificed, you whom they labeled

"Very combative . . ."
what right have you to give
commands and tell us how to live,

cry "Here!" and "Here!"
and wake us here where are
unwanted love, conceit and war?

The crown of red
set on your little head
is charged with all your fighting blood.

Yes, that excrescence
makes a most virile presence,
plus all that vulgar beauty of iridescence.

Now in mid-air
by twos they fight each other.
Down comes a first flame-feather,

and one is flying,
with raging heroism defying
even the sensation of dying.

And one has fallen,
but still above the town
his torn-out, bloodied feathers drift down;

and what he sung
no matter. He is flung
on the gray ash-heap, lies in dung

with his dead wives
with open, bloody eyes,
while those metallic feathers oxidize.

St. Peter's sin
was worse than that of Magdalen
whose sin was of the flesh alone;

of spirit, Peter's,
falling, beneath the flares,
among the "servants and officers."

Old holy sculpture
could set it all together
in one small scene, past and future:

Christ stands amazed,
Peter, two fingers raised
to surprised lips, both as if dazed.

But in between
a little cock is seen
carved on a dim column in the travertine,

explained by *gallus canit;*
flet Petrus underneath it.
There is inescapable hope, the pivot;

yes, and there Peter's tears
run down our chanticleer's
sides and gem his spurs.

Tear-encrusted thick
as a medieval relic
he waits. Poor Peter, heart-sick,

still cannot guess
those cock-a-doodles yet might bless,
his dreadful rooster come to mean forgiveness,

a new weathervane
on basilica and barn,
and that outside the Lateran

there would always be
a bronze cock on a porphyry
pillar so the people and the Pope might see

that even the Prince
of the Apostles long since
had been forgiven, and to convince

all the assembly
that "Deny deny deny"
is not all the roosters cry.

In the morning
a low light is floating
in the backyard, and gilding

from underneath
the broccoli, leaf by leaf;
how could the night have come to grief?

gilding the tiny
floating swallow's belly
and lines of pink cloud in the sky,

the day's preamble
like wandering lines in marble.
The cocks are now almost inaudible.

The sun climbs in,
following "to see the end,"
faithful as enemy, or friend.

EDNA ST. VINCENT MILLAY (1892–1950)

Born in Maine, Edna St. Vincent Millay graduated from Vassar College, having already gained fame for the publication of "Renascence," the title poem of her first book of poetry. She was the author of numerous other collections, including The Ballad of the Harp-Weaver, *which received the Pulitzer Prize,* The Buck in the Snow, *and* Make Bright the Arrows. *The fate of Czechoslovakia in World War II, subject of Millay's poem below, was sealed as early as March 1939 with the signing of the Munich Agreement, which called for the cession of the Sudetenland to Germany. During the war, over 350,000 Czechoslovakians died as a result of Nazi oppression.*

Czecho-Slovakia

If there were balm in Gilead, I would go
To Gilead for your wounds, unhappy land,
Gather your balsam there, and with this hand,
Made deft by pity, cleanse and bind and sew
And drench with healing, that your strength might grow,
(Though love be outlawed, kindness contraband)
And you, O proud and felled, again might stand;
But where to look for balm, I do not know.
The oils and herbs of mercy are so few;
Honour's for sale; allegiance has its price;
The barking of a fox has bought us all;
We save our skins a craven hour or two.—
While Peter warms him in the servants' hall
The thorns are platted and the cock crows twice.

JOHN BERRYMAN (1914–1972)

John Berryman's books include the poetry collections Homage to Mistress Bradstreet, *77* Dream Songs *(winner of the Pulitzer Prize), and* Delusions, *as well as collections of fiction and essays. He was a renowned teacher of literature and, before his suicide in 1972, taught at several universities, including the University of Iowa and the University of Minnesota. One of his best-known poems, "The Moon and the Night and the Men" addresses King Leopold's surrender of Belgium to Germany on May 28, 1940, following an overwhelming Nazi invasion that involved 134,000 soldiers, 41,000 motor vehicles, and more than 1,600 tanks and reconnaissance vehicles.*

The Moon and the Night and the Men

On the night of the Belgian surrender the moon rose
Late, a delayed moon, and a violent moon
For the English or the American beholder;
The French beholder. It was a cold night,
People put on their wraps, the troops were cold
No doubt, despite the calendar, no doubt
Numbers of refugees coughed, and the sight
Or sound of some killed others. A cold night.

On Outer Drive there was an accident:
A stupid well-intentioned man turned sharp
Right and abruptly he became an angel
Fingering an unfamiliar harp,
Or screamed in hell, or was nothing at all.
Do not imagine this is unimportant.
He was a part of the night, part of the land,
Part of the bitter and exhausted ground
Out of which memory grows.

                Michael and I
Stared at each other over chess, and spoke
As little as possible, and drank and played.
The chessmen caught in the European eye,
Neither of us I think had a free look
Although the game was fair. The move one made
It was difficult at last to keep one's mind on.

'. . . hurt and unhappy' said the man in London.
We said to each other, The time is coming near
When none shall have books or music, none his dear,
And only a fool will speak aloud his mind.
History is approaching a speechless end,
As Henry Adams said. Adams was right.
Fulfilled the treachery four years before
Begun—or was he well-intentioned, more
Roadmaker to hell than king? At any rate,
The moon came up late and the night was cold,
Many men died—although we know the fate
Of none, nor of anyone, and the war
Goes on, and the moon in the breast of man is cold.

STANLEY KUNITZ (1905–   )

Stanley Kunitz is the recipient of every major poetry award and honor in American literature, including the Pulitzer and Bollingen prizes, a National Medal of Arts, and the National Book Award. He served as U.S. Poet Laureate and was founder of both the Fine Arts Work Center in Provincetown, Massachusetts, and Poets House in New York City. In 1943, he was drafted into the army as a nonaffiliated pacifist, with the understanding that he would be assigned to a service unit, such as the medical corps. Instead, his papers were lost and he spent three years being shuttled from camp to camp. "The Last Picnic" was written following the bombing of Pearl Harbor on December 7, 1941.

The Last Picnic

The guests in their summer colors have fled
Through field and hedgerow. Come, let's pick
The bones and feathers of our fun
And kill the fire with a savage stick.

The figures of our country play,
The mocking dancers, in a swirl
Of laughter waved from the evening's edge,
Wrote finis to a pastoral.

Now the tongue of the military man,
Summoning the violent,
Calls the wild dogs out of their holes
And the deep Indian from his tent,

Not to be tamed, not to be stamped
Under. Earth-faced, behind this grove,
Our failures creep with soldier hearts,
Pointing their guns at what we love.

When they shall paint our sockets gray
And light us like a stinking fuse,
Remember that we once could say,
Yesterday we had a world to lose.

LANGSTON HUGHES (1902–1967)

Poet, novelist, and essayist Langston Hughes led a long and distinguished literary career. His many books include The Weary Blues, Shakespeare in Harlem, One-Way Ticket, *and* Ask Your Momma. *Despite Hughes's hope for the abolishment of the discriminatory Jim Crow laws referenced in the poem below, most black troops in World War II were not utilized in battle; they were quartered in segregated units and often given menial jobs. As the casualty rate of white troops mounted, gradual integration occurred in the ranks. In 1948, three years after the conclusion of the war, President Harry Truman officially ended segregation in the military.*

Jim Crow's Last Stand

There was an old Crow by the name of Jim.
The Crackers were in love with him.
They liked him so well they couldn't stand
To see Jim Crow get out of hand.
But something happened, Jim's feathers fell.
Now that Crow's begun to look like hell.

DECEMBER 7, 1941:

Pearl Harbor put Jim Crow on the run.
That Crow can't fight for Democracy
And be the same old Crow he used to be—
Although right now, even yet today,
He still tries to act in the same old way.
But India and China and Harlem, too,
Have made up their minds Jim Crow is through.
Nehru said, before he went to jail,
Catch that Jim Crow bird, pull the feathers out his tail!
Marian Anderson said to the DAR,
I'll sing for you—but drop that color bar.
Paul Robeson said, out in Kansas City,
To Jim Crow my people is a pity.
Mrs. Bethune told Martin Dies,
You ain't telling nothing but your Jim Crow lies—
If you want to get old Hitler's goat,
Abolish poll tax so folks can vote.

Joe Louis said, We gonna win this war
Cause the good Lord knows what *we're* fighting for!

DECEMBER 7, 1941:

When Dorie Miller took gun in hand—
Jim Crow started his last stand.
Our battle yet is far from won
But when it is, Jim Crow'll be done.
We gonna bury that son-of-a-gun!

WILLIAM CARLOS WILLIAMS (1883–1963)

*William Carlos Williams was born in Rutherford, New Jersey, where he later prac-
ticed medicine. One of the most influential and original poets of the twentieth century, he was the author of such important works as* Spring & All, In the American
Grain, Paterson, *and* Pictures from Brueghel. *"War, the Destroyer!" was written
in 1942 and concerns a photograph by Barbara Morgan showing a bomb exploding
above the figure of dancer Martha Graham, who was dressed in a long black robe to
suggest the specter of death.*

War, the Destroyer!

   (for Martha Graham)

What is war,
the destroyer
but an appurtenance

to the dance?
The deadly serious
who would have us suppress

all exuberance
because of it
are mad. When terror blooms—

leap and twist
whirl and prance—
that's the show

of this the circumstance.
We cannot change it
not by writing, music

neither prayer.
Then fasten it
on the dress, in the hair

to incite and impel.
And if dance be
the answer, dance!

body and mind—
substance, balance, elegance!
with that, blood red

displayed flagrantly
in its place
beside the face.

W. D. SNODGRASS (1926–   )

W. D. Snodgrass served in the navy in the Pacific during World War II. His books of poetry include Heart's Needle, *which received the Pulitzer Prize,* After Experience, *and* The Führer Bunker: The Complete Cycle. *In* "After Experience Taught Me . . . ," *the stanzas aligned left are quotations from the Jewish philosopher, Baruch Spinoza; the indented stanzas are quotations from a hand-to-hand combat instructor with whom Snodgrass studied in the navy.*

After Experience Taught Me . . .

After experience taught me that all the ordinary
Surroundings of social life are futile and vain;

> I'm going to show you something very
> Ugly: someday, it might save your life.

Seeing that none of the things I feared contain
In themselves anything either good or bad

> What if you get caught without a knife;
> Nothing—even a loop of piano wire;

Excepting only in the effect they had
Upon my mind, I resolved to inquire

> Take the first two fingers of this hand;
> Fork them out—kind of a "V for Victory"—

Whether there might be something whose discovery
Would grant me supreme, unending happiness.

> And jam them into the eyes of your enemy.
> You have to do this hard. Very hard. Then press

No virtue can be thought to have priority
Over this endeavor to preserve one's being.

> Both fingers down around the cheekbone
> And setting your foot high into the chest

No man can desire to act rightly, to be blessed,
To live rightly, without simultaneously

    You must call up every strength you own
    And you can rip off the whole facial mask.

Wishing to be, to act, to live. He must ask
First, in other words, to actually exist.

    And you, whiner, who wastes your time
        Dawdling over the remorseless earth,
    What evil, what unspeakable crime
        Have you made your life worth?

WINFIELD TOWNLEY SCOTT (1910–1968)

Winfield Townley Scott served as literary editor of the Providence Journal *and also taught at Brown and New York universities. His books include* Wind the Clock, Dark Sister, *and* Collected Poems. *The battle of Guadacanal, described in "The U.S. Soldier with the Japanese Skull," began on August 7, 1942, and was the first major test of land strength between Japanese and American forces in the Pacific theater. The battle lasted five months and its toll was heavy—6,111 Army and Marine casualties, including 1,752 men killed. The American victory helped turn the tide of the war in the Pacific.*

The U.S. Soldier with the Japanese Skull

Bald-bare, bone-bare, and ivory yellow: skull
Carried by a thus two-headed U.S. sailor
Who got it from a Japanese soldier killed
At Guadalcanal in the ever-present war: our

Bluejacket, I mean, aged 20, in August strolled
Among the little bodies on the sand and hunted
Souvenirs; teeth, tags, diaries, boots; but bolder still
Hacked off this head and under a leopard tree skinned it:

Peeled with a lifting knife the jaw and cheeks, bared
The nose, ripped off the black-haired scalp and gutted
The dead eyes to these thoughtful hollows: a scarred
But bloodless job, unless it be said brains bleed.

Then, his ship underway, dragged this aft in a net
Many days and nights—the cold bone tumbling
Beneath the foaming wake, weed-worn and salt-cut
Rolling safe among fish and washed with Pacific;

Till on a warm and level-keeled day hauled in
Held to the sun and the sailor, back to a gun-rest,
Scrubbed the cured skull with lye, perfecting this;
Not foreign as he saw it first; death's familiar cast.

Bodiless, fleshless, nameless, it and the sun
Offend each other in strange fascination
As though one of the two were mocked; but nothing is in
This head, or it fills with what another imagines

As: here were love and hate and the will to deal
Death or to kneel before it, death emperor,
Recorded orders without reasons, bomb-blast, still
A child's morning, remembered moonlight on Fujiyama:

All scoured out now by the keeper of this skull
Made elemental, historic, parentless by our
Sailor boy who thinks of home, voyages laden, will
Not say, 'Alas! I did not know him at all.'

ISABELLA GARDNER (1915–1981)

A cousin of Robert Lowell, Isabella Gardner was a professional actress as well as the author of Birthdays from the Ocean, West of Childhood: Poems 1950–1965, *and* Isabella Gardner: The Collected Poems.

The Searchlight

from an anti-aircraft battery

In smug delight we swaggered through the park
and arrogant pressed arm and knee and thigh.
We could not see the others in the dark.
We stopped and peered up at the moonless sky
and at grey bushes and the bristling grass
You in your Sunday suit, I in my pleated gown,
deliberately we stooped (brim-full of grace,
each brandied each rare-steaked) and laid us down.

We lay together in that urban grove
an ocean from the men engaged to die.
As we embraced a distant armoured eye
aroused our dusk with purposed light, a grave
rehearsal for another night. The field
bloomed lovers, dined and blind and target-heeled.

RICHARD EBERHART (1904–)

Richard Eberhart worked as an advertising copywriter, a deck hand on a tramp steamer, and a tutor to the son of the King of Siam. During the war, he was an aerial gunnery officer in the navy. He is the author of A Bravery of *Earth,* Reading the Spirit, *and* Selected Poems, *which was awarded the Pulitzer Prize in 1965.*

The Fury of Aerial Bombardment

You would think the fury of aerial bombardment
Would rouse God to relent; the infinite spaces
Are still silent. He looks on shock-pried faces.
History, even, does not know what is meant.

You would feel that after so many centuries
God would give man to repent; yet he can kill
As Cain could, but with multitudinous will,
No farther advanced than in his ancient furies.

Was man made stupid to see his own stupidity?
Is God by definition indifferent, beyond us all?
Is the eternal truth man's fighting soul
Wherein the Beast ravens in its own avidity?

Of Van Wettering I speak, and Averill,
Names on a list, whose faces I do not recall
But they are gone to early death, who late in school
Distinguished the belt feed lever from the belt holding pawl.

HOWARD NEMEROV (1920–1991)

The author of numerous books, including The Image and the Law, War Stories, *and* Collected Poems, *for which he won the Pulitzer Prize, Howard Nemerov enlisted in the Royal Canadian Air Force in 1942 and became a pilot flying anti-submarine and anti-shipping patrols for the RAF Coastal Command over the North Atlantic and the North Sea.*

The War in the Air

For a saving grace, we didn't see our dead,
Who rarely bothered coming home to die
But simply stayed away out there
In the clean war, the war in the air.

Seldom the ghosts came back bearing their tales
Of hitting the earth, the incompressible sea,
But stayed up there in the relative wind,
Shades fading in the mind,

Who had no graves but only epitaphs
Where never so many spoke for never so few:
Per ardua, said the partisans of Mars,
Per aspera, to the stars.

That was the good war, the war we won
As if there were no death, for goodness' sake,
With the help of the losers we left out there
In the air, in the empty air.

RANDALL JARRELL (1914–1965)

In 1942, following the publication of his first book, Blood for a Stranger, *Randall Jarrell entered the U.S. Army Air Corps and was stationed from 1942 to 1946 on bases in Texas, Illinois, and Arizona. Unable to qualify as a pilot, he served as a control tower operator and worked with B-29 crews. Before and after the war, he taught at a number of colleges and universities, including Sarah Lawrence, Kenyon, Princeton, and the University of North Carolina. He led a distinguished literary career, publishing collections of poetry, essays, children's books, translations, and anthologies. "Losses" and "The Death of the Ball Turret Gunner" are two of Jarrell's finest poems about the war.*

Losses

It was not dying: everybody died.
It was not dying: we had died before
In the routine crashes—and our fields
Called up the papers, wrote home to our folks,
And the rates rose, all because of us.
We died on the wrong page of the almanac,
Scattered on mountains fifty miles away;
Diving on haystacks, fighting with a friend,
We blazed up on the lines we never saw.
We died like aunts or pets or foreigners.
(When we left high school nothing else had died
For us to figure we had died like.)

In our new planes, with our new crews, we bombed
The ranges by the desert or the shore,
Fired at towed targets, waited for our scores—
And turned into replacements and woke up
One morning, over England, operational.
It wasn't different: but if we died
It was not an accident but a mistake
(But an easy one for anyone to make).
We read our mail and counted up our missions—
In bombers named for girls, we burned
The cities we had learned about in school—
Till our lives wore out; our bodies lay among
The people we had killed and never seen.

When we lasted long enough they gave us medals;
When we died they said, "Our casualties were low."
They said, "Here are the maps"; we burned the cities.

It was not dying—no, not ever dying;
But the night I died I dreamed that I was dead,
And the cities said to me: "Why are you dying?
We are satisfied, if you are; but why did I die?"

The Death of the Ball Turret Gunner

From my mother's sleep I fell into the State,
And I hunched in its belly till my wet fur froze.
Six miles from earth, loosed from its dream of life,
I woke to black flak and the nightmare fighters.
When I died they washed me out of the turret with a hose.

ROBERT LOWELL (1917–1977)

On October 13, 1943, after refusing to be inducted into the armed forces, Robert Lowell was sentenced to one year and a day in the Federal Correctional Center at Danbury, Connecticut. While waiting to be sent there, he was incarcerated in New York's West Street Jail. Fellow inmate Louis (Lepke) Buchalter was head of a notorious crime syndicate known as Murder Incorporated that operated in New York in the thirties and forties. Lepke was eventually executed in the electric chair.

Memories of West Street and Lepke

Only teaching on Tuesdays, book-worming
In pajamas fresh from the washer each morning,
I hog a whole house on Boston's
"hardly passionate Marlborough Street,"
where even the man
scavenging filth in the back alley trash cans,
has two children, a beach wagon, a helpmate,
and is a "young Republican."
I have a nine months' daughter,
young enough to be my granddaughter.
Like the sun she rises in her flame-flamingo infants' wear.

These are the tranquillized *Fifties*,
and I am forty. Ought I to regret my seed time?
I was a fire-breathing Catholic C. O.,
and made my manic statement,
telling off the state and president, and then
sat waiting sentence in the bull pen
beside a Negro boy with curlicues
of marijuana in his hair.

Given a year,
I walked on the roof of the West Street Jail, a short
enclosure like my school soccer court,
and saw the Hudson River once a day
through sooty clothesline entanglements
and bleaching khaki tenements.
Strolling, I yammered metaphysics with Abramowitz,
a jaundice-yellow ("it's really tan")

and fly-weight pacifist,
so vegetarian,
he wore rope shoes and preferred fallen fruit.
He tried to convert Bioff and Brown,
the Hollywood pimps, to his diet.
Hairy, muscular, suburban,
wearing chocolate double-breasted suits,
they blew their tops and beat him black and blue.

I was so out of things, I'd never heard
of the Jehovah's Witnesses.
"Are you a C. O.?" I asked a fellow jailbird.
"No," he answered, "I'm a J. W."
He taught me the "hospital tuck,"
and pointed out the T shirted back
of *Murder Incorporated's* Czar Lepke,
there piling towels on a rack,
or dawdling off to his little segregated cell full
of things forbidden the common man:
a portable radio, a dresser, two toy American
flags tied together with a ribbon of Easter palm.
Flabby, bald, lobotomized,
he drifted in a sheepish calm,
where no agonizing reappraisal
jarred his concentration on the electric chair—
hanging like an oasis in his air
of lost connections . . . .

EDWIN ROLFE (1909–1954)

Poet and journalist Edwin Rolfe was often called the poet laureate of the Abraham Lincoln Battalion, a group of American volunteers who fought in the Spanish Civil War from 1936 to 1939. The author of To My Contemporaries *and* Permit Me Refuge, *he was drafted into the U.S. Army in 1943. While in training at Camp Wolters in Texas, however, he became ill and was discharged. "No Man Knows War" is one of his best-known poems.*

No Man Knows War

Needless to catalogue heroes. No man
weighted with rifle, digging with nails in earth,
quickens at the name. Hero's a word for
peacetime. Battle
knows only three realities: enemy, rifle, life.

No man knows war or its meaning who has not
stumbled from tree to tree, desperate for cover,
or dug his face deep in earth, felt the ground pulse with
the ear-breaking fall of death. No man knows war
who never has crouched in his foxhole, hearing
the bullets an inch from his head, nor the zoom of
planes like a Ferris wheel strafing the trenches . . .

War is your comrade struck dead beside you,
his shared cigarette still alive in your lips.

EDWARD FIELD (1924–)

Edward Field served as a bomber navigator with the U.S. Army Air Corps and flew numerous combat missions over Europe. His books include Stand Up, Friend, With Me *and* A New Geography of Poets.

World War II

It was over Target Berlin the flak shot up our plane
just as we were dumping bombs on the already smoking city
on signal from the lead bomber in the squadron.
The plane jumped again and again as the shells burst under us
sending jagged pieces of steel rattling through our fuselage.
I'll never understand
how none of us got ripped by those fragments.

Then, being hit, we had to drop out of formation right away
losing speed and altitude,
and when I figured out our course with trembling hands on the instruments
(I was navigator)
we set out on the long trip home to England
alone, with two of our four engines gone
and gas streaming out of holes in the wing tanks.
That morning at briefing
we had been warned not to go to nearby Poland
partly liberated then by the Russians,
although later we learned that another crew in trouble
had landed there anyway,
and patching up their plane somehow,
returned gradually to England
roundabout by way of Turkey and North Africa.
But we chose England, and luckily
the Germans had no fighters to send up after us then
for this was just before they developed their jet.
To lighten our load we threw out
guns and ammunition, my navigation books, all the junk
and made it over Holland
with a few goodbye fireworks from the shore guns.

Over the North Sea the third engine gave out
and we dropped low over the water.
The gas gauge read empty but by keeping the nose down
a little gas at the bottom of the tank sloshed forward
and kept our single engine going.
High overhead, the squadrons were flying home in formation
—the raids had gone on for hours after us.
Did they see us down there in our trouble?
We radioed our final position for help to come
but had no idea if anyone
happened to be tuned in and heard us,
and we crouched together on the floor
knees drawn up and head down
in regulation position for ditching;
listened as the engine stopped, a terrible silence,
and we went down into the sea with a crash,
just like hitting a brick wall,
jarring bones, teeth, eyeballs panicky.
Who would ever think water could be so hard?
You black out, and then come to
with water rushing in like a sinking-ship movie.

All ten of us started getting out of there fast:
There was a convenient door in the roof to climb out by,
one at a time. We stood in line,
water up to our thighs and rising.
The plane was supposed to float for twenty seconds
but with all those flak holes
who could say how long it really would?
The two life rafts popped out of the sides into the water
but one of them only half inflated
and the other couldn't hold everyone
although they all piled into it, except the pilot,
who got into the limp raft that just floated.
The radio operator and I, out last,
(Did that mean we were least aggressive, least likely to survive?)
we stood on the wing watching the two rafts
being swept off by waves in different directions.
We had to swim for it.
Later they said the cords holding rafts to plane
broke by themselves, but I wouldn't have blamed them

for cutting them loose, for fear
that by waiting the plane would go down
and drag them with it.

I headed for the overcrowded good raft
and after a clumsy swim in soaked heavy flying clothes
got there and hung onto the side.
The radio operator went for the half-inflated raft
where the pilot lay with water sloshing over him,
but he couldn't swim, even with his life vest on,
being from the Great Plains—
his strong farmer's body didn't know
how to wallow through the water properly
and a wild current seemed to sweep him farther off.
One minute we saw him on top of a swell
and perhaps we glanced away for a minute
but when we looked again he was gone—
just as the plane went down sometime around then
when nobody was looking.

It was midwinter and the waves were mountains
and the water ice water.
You could live in it twenty-five minutes
the Ditching Survival Manual said.
Since most of the crew were squeezed on my raft
I had to stay in the water hanging on.
My raft? It was their raft, they got there first so they would live.
Twenty-five minutes I had.
Live, live, I said to myself.
You've got to live.
There looked like plenty of room on the raft
from where I was and I said so
but they said no.
When I figured the twenty-five minutes were about up
and I was getting numb,
I said I couldn't hold on anymore,
and a little rat-faced boy from Alabama, one of the gunners,
got into the icy water in my place,
and I got on the raft in his.
He insisted on taking off his flying clothes
which was probably his downfall because even wet clothes are protection,

and then worked hard, kicking with his legs, and we all paddled,
to get to the other raft,
and we tied them together.
The gunner got in the raft with the pilot
and lay in the wet.
Shortly after, the pilot started gurgling green foam from his mouth—
maybe he was injured in the crash against the instruments—
and by the time we were rescued,
he and the little gunner were both dead.

That boy who took my place in the water
who died instead of me
I don't remember his name even.
It was like those who survived the death camps
by letting others go into the ovens in their place.
It was him or me, and I made up my mind to live.
I'm a good swimmer,
but I didn't swim off in that scary sea
looking for the radio operator when he was washed away.
I suppose, then, once and for all,
I chose to live rather than be a hero, as I still do today,
although at that time I believed in being heroic, in saving the world,
even if, when opportunity knocked,
I instinctively chose survival.

As evening fell the waves calmed down
and we spotted a boat, far off, and signaled with a flare gun,
hoping it was English not German.
The only two who cried on being found
were me and a boy from Boston, a gunner.
The rest of the crew kept straight faces.

It was a British air-sea rescue boat:
They hoisted us up on deck,
dried off the living and gave us whisky and put us to bed,
and rolled the dead up in blankets,
and delivered us all to a hospital on shore
for treatment or disposal.
None of us even caught cold, only the dead.

This was a minor accident of war:
Two weeks in a rest camp at Southport on the Irish Sea
and we were back at Grafton-Underwood, our base,
ready for combat again,
the dead crewmen replaced by living ones,
and went on hauling bombs over the continent of Europe,
destroying the Germans and their cities.

KENNETH REXROTH (1905–1982)

Kenneth Rexroth was born in Indiana and lived most of his life in California, first in San Francisco where, for a short time, he was associated with the Beat movement, and later in Santa Barbara. A distinguished poet, translator, and essayist, he was the author of fifty-four volumes of poetry, essays, and translations from a dozen languages.

Un Bel Di Vedremo

"Hello NBC, this is London speaking . . . "
I move the dial, I have heard it all,
Day after day—the terrible waiting,
The air raids, the military communiqués,
The between the lines whispering
Of quarreling politicians,
The mute courage of the people.
The dial moves over aggressive
Advertisements, comedians, bands hot and sweet,
To a record concert—La Scala—Madame Butterfly.
I pause, listening idly, and suddenly
I feel as though I had begun to fall
Slowly, buoyantly, through infinite, indefinite space.
Milano, fretting in my seat,
In my lace collar and velvet suit,
My beautiful mother weeping
Happily beside me. My God,
How long ago it was, further far
Than Rome or Egypt, that other
World before the other war.
Stealing downstairs to spy on the champagne suppers;
Watching the blue flame of the chafing dish
On Sunday nights: driving over middle Europe
Behind a café au lait team,
The evenings misty, smelling of cattle
And the fat Danubian earth.
It will never be again
The open work stockings,
The lace evening gowns,
The pink roses on the slippers;
Debs eating roast chicken and drinking whiskey,

On the front porch with grandpa;
The neighbors gaping behind their curtains;
The Japanese prints and the works of Huneker.
Never again will a small boy
Curled in the hammock in the murmurous summer air,
Gnaw his knuckles, reading *The Jungle;*
Never again will he gasp as Franz Josef
And the princesses sweep through
The lines of wolf caped hussars.
It is a terrible thing to sit here
In the uneasy light above this strange city
And listen to the poignant sentimentality
Of an age more dead than the Cro Magnon.
It is a terrible thing to see a world die twice,
"The first time as tragedy;
The second as evil farce."

THOMAS MCGRATH (1916–1990)

During World War II, Thomas McGrath served in the air force in the Aleutian Islands of Alaska. After the war, he worked as a scriptwriter in Hollywood until he was blacklisted for his left-wing political convictions. His books of poetry include Letter to an Imaginary Friend, The Movie at the End of the World: Collected Poems, *and* Passages Toward the Dark.

Remembering That Island

Remembering that island lying in the rain
(Lost in the North Pacific, lost in time and the war)
With a terrible fatigue as of repeated dreams
Of running, climbing, fighting in the dark,
I feel the wind rising and the pitiless cold surf
Shaking the headlands of the black north.

And the ships come in again out of the fog—
As real as nightmare I hear the rattle of blocks
When the first boat comes down, the ghostly whisper of feet
At the barge pier—and wild with strain I wait
For the flags of my first war, the remembered faces,
And mine not among them to make the nightmare safe.

Then without words, with a heavy shuffling of gear,
The figures plod in the rain, in the shoreside mud,
Speechless and tired; their faces, lined and hard,
I search for my comrades, and suddenly—there—there—
Harry, Charlie, and Bob, but their faces are worn, old,
And mine is among them. In a dream as real as war

I see the vast stinking Pacific suddenly awash
Once more with bodies, landings on all beaches,
The bodies of dead and living go back to appointed places,
A ten year old resurrection,
And myself once more in the scourging wind, waiting, waiting
While the rich oratory and the lying famous corrupt
Senators mine our lives for another war.

LUCIEN STRYK (1924–   )

Lucien Stryk served in the army during the war and later taught at Northern Illinois University. He is the author of Taproot, And Still the Birds Sang, *and several volumes of translations of Chinese and Japanese poetry.*

The Pit

Twenty years. I still remember
The sun-blown stench, and the pit
At least two hundred yards from
The cove we'd anchored guns in.
They were blasting at the mountains,
The beach was nearly ours.

The smell kept leaking back.
I thought of garbage cans
Behind chopsuey restaurants
Of home, strangely appealing on
A summer's night, meaning another
Kind of life. Which made the difference.

When the three of us, youngest in
The crew, were handed poles and told
To get the deadmen underground
Or join them, we saw it a sullen
Sort of lark. And lashed to trees,
The snipers had us dancing.

Ducks for those vultures in the boughs,
Poles poking through the powder-
Bitten grass, we zigzagged
Toward the pit as into
The arse of death, the wittiest
Of us said but did not laugh.

At last we reached it, half full
Of sand and crawling. We clamped
Nose, mouth, wrenched netted helmets

To the chin, yet poles probed forward
Surgically, touching for spots
The maggots had not jelled.

Somehow we got the deadmen under,
Along with empty lobster tins,
Bottles, gear and ammo. Somehow
We plugged the pit and slipped back
To the guns. Then for days
We had to helmet bathe downwind.

I stuck my pole, clean end high,
Behind the foxhole, a kind of
Towelpeg and a something more.
I'd stare it out through jungle haze,
And wonder. Ask anyone who
Saw it: nobody won that war.

ALAN DUGAN (1923–2003)

Alan Dugan served in the U.S. Army Air Corps during World War II as an aircraft engine repairman in the Marianas, a strategic group of islands midway between Japan and New Guinea. The author of numerous books, including Poems *and* Poems 7: New and Complete Poetry, *he was the recipient of the National Book Award and the Pulitzer Prize.*

Portrait from the Infantry

He smelled bad and was red-eyed with the miseries
of being scared while sleepless when he said
this: "I want a private woman, peace and quiet,
and some green stuff in my pocket. Fuck
the rest." Pity the underwear and socks,
long burnt, of an accomplished murderer,
oh God, of germans and replacements, who
refused three stripes to keep his B.A.R.,
who fought, fought not to fight some days
like any good small businessman of war,
and dug more holes than an outside dog
to modify some Freudian's thesis: "No
man can stand three hundred days
of fear and mutilation and death." What he
theorized was a joke: "To keep a tight
asshole, dry socks and a you-deep hole
with you at all times." Afterwards,
met in a sports shirt with a round wife, he was
the clean slave of a daughter, a power brake
and beer. To me, he seemed diminished
in his dream, or else enlarged, who knows?,
by its accomplishment: personal life
wrung from mass issues in a bloody time
and lived out hiddenly. Aside from sound
baseball talk, his only interesting remark
was, in pointing to his wife's belly, "If
in the approach to it, I turn my back
to it, then I walk backwards: I
approach it as a limit. Even if I fall
to hands and knees, I crawl to it.
Backwards or forwards I approach it.

There is the land on one hand, rising, and
the ocean on the other, falling away;
what the sky does, I can not look to see,
but it's around, as ever, all around.
The courteous vultures move away in groups
like functionaries. The dogs circle and stare
like working police. One wants a heel
and gets it. I approach it, concentrating so
on not approaching it, going so far away
that when I get there I am sideways like
the crab, too limited by carapace to say:

"Oh here I am arrived, all; yours today."
No: kneeling and facing away, I will
fall over backwards in intensity of life
and lie convulsed, downed struggling,
sideways even, and should as vulture ask
an eye as its aperitif, I grant it,
glad for the moment wrestling by a horse
whose belly has been hollowed from the rear,
who's eyeless. The wild dog trapped in its ribs
grins as it eats its way to freedom. Not
conquered outwardly, and after rising once,
I fall away inside, and see the sky around
rush out away in the vulture's craw
and barely can not hear them calling, "Here's one."
he comes out left foot first" (the way
you Forward March!), "I am going to stuff
him back up." "Isn't he awful?" she said.

KARL SHAPIRO (1913–2000)

Karl Shapiro served as a medical corps clerk in the South Pacific, mostly in New Guinea. After the war, he was Poetry Consultant at the Library of Congress and taught at The Johns Hopkins University, the University of Nebraska, the University of Chicago, and the University of California at Davis, and also served as editor of Poetry *and* Prairie Schooner. *He was the author of* Poems, V-Letter and Other Poems, *winner of the Pulitzer Prize, and* Selected Poems.

Troop Train

It stops the town we come through. Workers raise
Their oily arms in good salute and grin.
Kids scream as at a circus. Business men
Glance hopefully and go their measured way.
And women standing at their dumbstruck door
More slowly wave and seem to warn us back,
As if a tear blinding the course of war
Might once dissolve our iron in their sweet wish.

Fruit of the world, O clustered on ourselves
We hang as from a cornucopia
In total friendliness, with faces bunched
To spray the streets with catcalls and with leers.
A bottle smashes on the moving ties
And eyes fixed on a lady smiling pink
Stretch like a rubber-band and snap and sting
The mouth that wants the drink-of-water kiss.

And on through crummy continents and days,
Deliberate, grimy, slightly drunk we crawl,
The good-bad boys of circumstance and chance,
Whose bucket-helmets bang the empty wall
Where twist the murdered bodies of our packs
Next to the guns that only seem themselves.
And distance like a strap adjusted shrinks,
Tightens across the shoulder and holds firm.

Here is a deck of cards; out of this hand
Dealer, deal me my luck, a pair of bulls,
The right draw to a flush, the one-eyed jack.
Diamonds and hearts are red but spades are black,
And spades are spades and clubs are clovers—black.
But deal me winners, souvenirs of peace.
This stands to reason and arithmetic,
Luck also travels and not all come back.

Trains lead to ships and ships to death or trains,
And trains to death or trucks, and trucks to death,
Or trucks lead to the march, the march to death,
Or that survival which is all our hope;
And death leads back to trucks and trains and ships,
But life leads to the march, O flag! at last
The place of life found after trains and death—
Nightfall of nations brilliant after war.

LINCOLN KIRSTEIN (1907–1996)

Author of Rhymes of a PFC, *Lincoln Kirstein served in the U. S. Army from 1943
to 1945. He was sent overseas and attached to the Arts, Monuments, and Archives
section of General George Patton's Third Army, helping to search for plundered art
works after the Nazi defeat. Before World War II, he founded the School of
American Ballet and served as its director for many years. Following the war, he co-
founded and directed the New York Ballet Company, administered several other distinguished arts institutions, and wrote extensively on dance.*

Vaudeville

Pete Petersen, before this bit, a professional entertainer;
He and a partner tossed two girls on the Two-a-Day,
Swung them by their heels and snatched them in mid-air,
Billed as "Pete's Meteors: Acrobatic Adagio & Classical Ballet."

His vulnerable grin, efficiency, or bland physique
Lands him in Graves' Registration, a slot few strive to seek.
He follows death around picking up pieces,
Recovering men and portions of men so that by dawn
Only the landscape bares its wounds, the dead are gone.

Near Echternach, after the last stand they had the heart to make
With much personal slaughter by small arms at close range,
I drive for an officer sent down to look things over.
There is Pete slouched on a stump, catching his wind.

On your feet: salute. "Yes, sir?"
"Bad here, what?" "Yes, sir."

Good manners or knowing no word can ever condone
What happened, what he had to do, has done,
Spares further grief. Pete sits down.
A shimmering pulsation of exhaustion fixes him
In its throbbing aura like footlights when the curtain rises.

His act is over. Nothing now till the next show.

He takes his break while stagehands move the scenery,
And the performing dogs are led up from below.

LOUIS SIMPSON (1923–   )

Louis Simpson was born in Jamaica in the West Indies and immigrated to the United States in 1940. He served as an infantryman in the 101st Airborne Division in France, Holland, Belgium, and Germany, and was wounded twice. He later taught at Columbia University, the University of California at Berkeley, and the State University of New York at Stony Brook. His books include At the End of the Open Road, Searching for the Ox, *and* In the Room We Share. *The Carentan of his poem below is a small town in France that was liberated by American forces on June 11, 1944, five days after the Normandy invasion.*

Carentan O Carentan

Trees in the old days used to stand
And shape a shady lane
Where lovers wandered hand in hand
Who came from Carentan.

This was the shining green canal
Where we came two by two
Walking at combat-interval.
Such trees we never knew.

The day was early June, the ground
Was soft and bright with dew.
Far away the guns did sound,
But here the sky was blue.

The sky was blue, but there a smoke
Hung still above the sea
Where the ships together spoke
To towns we could not see.

Could you have seen us through a glass
You would have said a walk
Of farmers out to turn the grass,
Each with his own hay-fork.

The watchers in their leopard suits
Waited till it was time,

And aimed between the belt and boot
And let the barrel climb.

I must lie down at once, there is
A hammer at my knee.
And call it death or cowardice,
Don't count again on me.

Everything's all right, Mother,
Everyone gets the same
At one time or another.
It's all in the game.

I never strolled, nor ever shall,
Down such a leafy lane.
I never drank in a canal,
Nor ever shall again.

There is a whistling in the leaves
And it is not the wind,
The twigs are falling from the knives
That cut men to the ground.

Tell me, Master-Sergeant,
The way to turn and shoot.
But the Sergeant's silent
That taught me how to do it.

O Captain, show us quickly
Our place upon the map.
But the Captain's sickly
And taking a long nap.

Lieutenant, what's my duty,
My place in the platoon?
He too's a sleeping beauty,
Charmed by that strange tune.

Carentan O Carentan
Before we met with you
We never yet had lost a man
Or known what death could do.

GEORGE OPPEN (1908–1984)

George Oppen joined the Communist Party in 1935 and worked as a labor organizer for years. During World War II, he served in an anti-tank company of the 103rd Infantry Division in Europe until he was seriously wounded by shellfire. In 1950, he moved to Mexico to avoid an FBI investigation and lived there until 1960. His books include Of Being Numerous, *winner of the Pulitzer Prize.*

Survival: Infantry

And the world changed.
There had been trees and people,
Sidewalks and roads

There were fish in the sea.

Where did all the rocks come from?
And the smell of explosives
Iron standing in mud
We crawled everywhere on the ground without seeing the earth again

We were ashamed of our half life and our misery: we saw that everything
   had died.

And the letters came. People who addressed us thru our lives
They left us gasping. And in tears
In the same mud in the terrible ground

RICHARD WILBUR (1921–   )

In 1944–1945, Richard Wilbur served in the Alsace-Lorraine region of France as a staff sergeant and cryptographer with the U.S. Army. Poet Laureate of the United States from 1987 to 1988, he won the National Book Award and the Pulitzer Prize for Things of This World; *the Bollingen Prize for* Walking to Sleep; *and another Pulitzer Prize for* New and Collected Poems.

First Snow in Alsace

The snow came down last night like moths
Burned on the moon; it fell till dawn,
Covered the town with simple cloths.

Absolute snow lies rumpled on
What shellbursts scattered and deranged,
Entangled railings, crevassed lawn.

As if it did not know they'd changed,
Snow smoothly clasps the roofs of homes
Fear-gutted, trustless and estranged.

The ration stacks are milky domes;
Across the ammunition pile
The snow has climbed in sparkling combs.

You think: beyond the town a mile
Or two, this snowfall fills the eyes
Of soldiers dead a little while.

Persons and persons in disguise,
Walking the new air white and fine,
Trade glances quick with shared surprise.

At children's windows, heaped, benign,
As always, winter shines the most,
And frost makes marvelous designs.

The night guard coming from his post,
Ten first-snows back in thought, walks slow
And warms him with a boyish boast:

He was the first to see the snow.

H. D. (1886–1961)

H. D. (Hilda Doolittle) went to Europe in 1911, married the British author Richard Aldington in 1913, and lived in England thereafter. An early member of the Imagist school, she published works of poetry, prose, and translation including Sea Garden, Hymen, *and* Red Roses for Bronze. *Following a mental breakdown after World War II, she moved to Switzerland, where she lived and wrote until her death in Zurich.*

Christmas 1944

I

The stratosphere was once where angels were;
if we are dizzy and a little mad,
forgive us, we have had
experience of a world beyond our sphere,
there—where no angels are;

the angel host, and choir
is driven further, higher,
or (so it seems to me) descended to our level,
to share our destiny;

we do not see the fire,
we do not even hear
the whirr and distant roar,
we have gone hence before

the sound manifests;
are we here? or there?
we do not know,
waiting from hour to hour,

hoping for what? dispersal
of our poor bodies' frame?
what do we hope for?
name remembered? faults forgot?

or do we hope to rise upward?
no—no—not to those skies;
rather we question here,
what do I love?

what have I left un-loved?
what image would I choose
had I one thing, as gift,
redeemed from dust and ash?

I ask, what would I take?
which doll clutch to my breast?
should some small tender ghost,
descended from the host

of cherubim and choirs, speak:
'look, they are all here,
all, all your loveliest treasures,
look and then choose—but *one*—

we have our journey now,
poor child—come.'

II

A Dresden girl and boy
held up the painted dial,
but I had quite forgot
I had that little clock;

I'll take the clock—but how?
why, it was broken, lost,
dismantled long ago;

but there's another treasure,
that slice of amber-rock,
a traveller once brought
me from the Baltic coast,

and with it (these are small)
the little painted swallow—
where are they? one, I left,
I know at a friend's house;

and there's that little cat
that lapped milk from my tray
at breakfast-time—but where?

at some hotel perhaps?
or staying with a friend?
or was it in a dream?

a small cat with grey fur;
perhaps you may remember?

> it's true I lent or gave away the amber,
> the swallow's somewhere else in someone's house,
> the clock was long ago, dismantled, lost,
> the cat was dream or memory or both;
> but I'll take these—is it too much?

III

We are a little dizzy
and quite mad,
but we have had
strange visitations
from the stratosphere,
of angels drawn to earth
and nearer angels;

we think and feel and speak
like children lost,
for one Child too, was cast
at Christmas, from a house
of stone with wood for beam
and lintel and door-shaft;

go—go—there is no room
for you, in this our Inn:

to Him, the painted swallow,
to Him, the lump of amber,
to Him, the boy and girl
with roses and love-knots,
to Him, the little cat
to play beneath the Manger:

if we are dizzy
and a little mad,
forgive us, we have had
strange visitations
from the stratosphere.

DENISE LEVERTOV (1923–1997)

Denise Levertov was born in England and served as a nurse in a small hospital in Fitzroy Square in the heart of London during World War II. In 1948, she moved to the United States and taught at a number of schools over the ensuing decades, including Stanford University and City College of New York. In the early 1960s, she was poetry editor of The Nation. *Her books include* Freeing the Dust, *winner of the Lenore Marshall Poetry Prize,* With Eyes at the Back of Our Heads, *and* The Sorrow Dance.

Christmas 1944

Bright cards above the fire bring no friends near,
fire cannot keep the cold from seeping in.
Spindrift sparkle and candles on the tree
make brave pretence of light; but look out of doors:
Evening already surrounds the curtained house,
draws near, watches;
gardens are blue with frost, and every carol
bears a burden of exile, a song of slaves.
Come in, then, poverty, and come in, death:
this year too many lie cold, or die in cold
for any small room's warmth to keep you out.
You sit in empty chairs, gleam in unseeing eyes;
having no home now, you cast your shadow
over the atlas, and rest in the restlessness
of our long nights as we lie, dreaming of Europe.

A painted bird or boat above the fire,
a fire in the hearth, a candle in the dark,
a dark excited tree, fresh from the forest,
are all that stand between us and the wind.
The wind has tales to tell of sea and city,
a plague on many houses, fear knocking on the doors;
how venom trickles from the open mouth of death,
and trees are white with rage of alien battles.
Who can be happy while the wind recounts
its long sagas of sorrow? Though we are safe
in a flickering circle of winter festival
we dare not laugh; or if we laugh, we lie,
hearing hatred crackle in the coal,
the voice of treason, the voice of love.

MARIANNE MOORE (1887–1972)

Marianne Moore was born in St. Louis and lived most of her adult life in New York City. Among her many honors were the Bollingen Prize, the National Book Award, and, for her Collected Poems, *the Pulitzer Prize. Of "In Distrust of Merits," Moore wrote, "It's truthful. It is testimony—to the fact that war is intolerable, and unjust."*

In Distrust of Merits

Strengthened to live, strengthened to die for
    medals and positioned victories?
They're fighting, fighting, fighting the blind
    man who thinks he sees—
who cannot see that the enslaver is
enslaved; the hater, harmed. O shining O
       firm star, O tumultuous
          ocean lashed till small things go
      as they will, the mountainous
        wave makes us who look, know

depth. Lost at sea before they fought! O
    star of David, star of Bethlehem,
O black imperial lion
    of the Lord—emblem
of a risen world—be joined at last, be
joined. There is hate's crown beneath which all is
      death; there's love's without which none
         is king; the blessed deeds bless
      the halo. As contagion
        of sickness makes sickness,

contagion of trust can make trust. They're
    fighting in deserts and caves, one by
one, in battalions and squadrons;
    they're fighting that I
may yet recover from the disease, My
Self; some have it lightly; some will die. "Man
      wolf to man"; yes. We devour
        ourselves. The enemy could not
      have made a greater breach in our
        defenses. One pilot-

ing a blind man can escape him, but
    Job disheartened by false comfort knew
that nothing can be so defeating
    as a blind man who
can see. O alive who are dead, who are
proud not to see, O small dust of the earth
        that walks so arrogantly,
            trust begets power and faith is
        an affectionate thing. We
            vow, we make this promise

to the fighting—it's a promise—"We'll
            never hate black, white, red, yellow, Jew,
Gentile, Untouchable." We are
    not competent to
make our vows. With set jaw they are fighting,
fighting, fighting—some we love whom we know,
        some we love but know not—that
            hearts may feel and not be numb.
        It cures me; or am I what
            I can't believe in? Some

in snow, some on crags, some in quicksands,
    little by little, much by much, they
are fighting fighting fighting that where
    there was death there may
be life. "When a man is prey to anger,
he is moved by outside things; when he holds
        his ground in patience patience
            patience, that is action or
        beauty," the soldier's defense
            and hardest armor for

the fight. The world's an orphans' home. Shall
    we never have peace without sorrow?
without pleas of the dying for
    help that won't come? O
quiet form upon the dust, I cannot
look and yet I must. If these great patient
        dyings—all these agonies
            and woundbearings and bloodshed—
        can teach us how to live, these

dyings were not wasted.

Hate-hardened heart, O heart of iron,
    iron is iron till it is rust.
There never was a war that was
    not inward; I must
fight till I have conquered in myself what
causes war, but I would not believe it.
      I inwardly did nothing.
        O Iscariotlike crime!
      Beauty is everlasting
        and dust is for a time.

HARVEY SHAPIRO (1924–   )

Harvey Shapiro served in the U.S. Army Air Corps during World War II, flying thirty-five combat missions over central Europe as a B-17 radio gunner based in Italy. He served as editor of Commentary, The New Yorker, *and* The New York Times Book Review. *His books include* The Eye, How Charlie Shavers Died and Other Poems, *and* Poets of World War II.

Battle Report

1.
I praise an age that has no monuments,
That if millions die within a war—
A few I knew, a few I saw go down—
They die forever, and what's to be said?

2.
It is always a prayer to the remembering Muses:
Remember me. Remember through all time
That I sing this,
You who write the genealogies
And the spirits crowd round without number.

3.
The Adriatic was no sailor's sea.
We raced above that water for our lives
Hoping the green curve of Italy
Would take us in. Rank, meaningless fire

That had no other object but our life
Raged in the stunned engine. I acquired
From the scene that flickered like a silent film
New perspective on the days of man.

Now the aviators, primed for flight,
Gave to the blue expanse can after can
Of calibers, armored clothes, all
The rich paraphernalia of our war.

Death in a hungry instant took us in.
He touched me where my lifeblood danced
And said, the cold water is an ample grin
For all your twenty years.

Monotone and flawless, the blue sky
Shows to my watching face this afternoon
The chilled signal of our victory.
Again the lost plane drums home.

4.

No violence rode in the glistening chamber.
For the gunner the world was unhinged.
Abstract as a drinker and single
He hunched to his task, the dumb show
Of surgical fighters, while flak, impersonal,
Beat at the floor that he stood on.

The diamond in his eye was fear;
It barely flickered.
From target to target he rode.
The images froze, the flak hardly mattered.
Europe rolled to its murderous kneess
Under the sex of guns and of cannon.

In an absence of pain he continued,
The oxygen misting his veins like summer.
The bomber's long sleep and the cry of the gunner,
Who knows that the unseen mime in his blood
Will startle to terror,
Years later, when love matters.

5.

My pilot dreamed of death before he died.
That stumbling Texas boy
Grew cold before the end, and told
The bombardier, who told us all.
We worried while we slept.
And when he died, on that dark morning
Over Italy in clouds,
We clapped him into dirt.

We counted it for enmity
That he had fraternized with death.
From hand to hand
We passed in wonderment
The quicksilver of our lives.

6.

In the blue oxygen, what I saw,
My valve fluttering its song,
My ears tight to the static.
I perceived that I was rocked
In the body of the plane.
Rarefied air frosted my lashes.
Congealed breath sparkled my scarf.

So gloved and chuted, wired into my bones,
I rode the day. Austria,
An ant's plan underfoot.
In that perilous seat above cities
I mixed into my own breathings
And waited, exposed as a stone.
Sunlight through plexiglass above my head
Was light without sun, a blue wash of cold.

This I recall, seated in my room,
Having sloughed off the glory and the pose
That place where the oxygen faltered
And the mask of my face went closed,
And they pried me, sleeping, from the sea.

Walker under water, can you believe
That even now the sun touches
That phalanx of fins, the vectoring Forts?
It is mainly cold I remember, and the warmth
When my mask, clotted with breath, grew dark.

7.

I turn my rubber face to the blue square
Given me to trace the fighters
As they weave their frost, and see
Within this sky the traffic

Fierce and heavy for the day:
All those who stumbling home at dark
Found their names fixed
Beside a numbered Fort, and heard
At dawn the sirens rattling the night away,
And rose to that cold resurrection
And are now gathered over Italy.

In this slow dream's rehearsal,
Again I am the death-instructed kid,
Gun in its cradle, sun at my back,
Cities below me without sound.
That tensed, corrugated hose
Feeding to my face the air of substance,
I face the mirroring past.
We swarm the skies, determined armies,
To seek the war's end, the silence stealing,
The mind grown hesitant as breath.

CHARLES SIMIC (1938–   )

Born in Yugoslavia, Charles Simic teaches at the University of New Hampshire. His books include Dismantling the Silence, Austerities, *and* Hotel Insomnia. *Awards for his poetry and translations include the Pulitzer Prize, the Edgar Allan Poe Award, the PEN Translation Prize, and a MacArthur Foundation Fellowship.*

Prodigy

I grew up bent over
a chessboard.

I loved the word *endgame.*

All my cousins looked worried.

It was a small house
near a Roman graveyard.
Planes and tanks
shook its windowpanes.

A retired professor of astronomy
taught me how to play.

That must have been in 1944.

In the set we were using,
the paint had almost chipped off
the black pieces.

The white King was missing
and had to be substituted for.

I'm told but do not believe
that that summer I witnessed
men hung from telephone poles.

I remember my mother
blindfolding me a lot.

She had a way of tucking my head
suddenly under her overcoat.

In chess, too, the professor told me,
the masters play blindfolded,
the great ones on several boards
at the same time.

RICHARD HUGO (1923–1982)

During World War II, Richard Hugo was a B-24 bombardier in the U.S. Army Air Corps and was stationed in Italy, making bombing runs over Yugoslavia. He was awarded both the Distinguished Flying Cross and the Air Medal. He later worked for the Boeing Company and from 1964 until his death he taught at the University of Montana. His books include A Run of Jacks, Good Luck in Cracked Italian, *and* Making Certain It Goes On.

Letter to Simic from Boulder

Dear Charles: And so we meet once in San Francisco and I
learn I bombed you long ago in Belgrade when you were five.
I remember. We were after a bridge on the Danube
hoping to cut the German armies off as they fled north
from Greece. We missed. Not unusual, considering I
was one of the bombardiers. I couldn't hit my ass if
I sat on the Norden or ride a bomb down singing
The Star Spangled Banner. I remember Belgrade opened
like a rose when we came in. Not much flak. I didn't know
about the daily hangings, the 80,000 Slavs who dangled
from German ropes in the city, lessons to the rest.
I was interested mainly in staying alive, that moment
the plane jumped free from the weight of bombs and we went home.
What did you speak then? Serb, I suppose. And what did your mind
do with the terrible howl of bombs? What is Serb for "fear"?
It must be the same as in English, one long primitive wail
of dying children, one child fixed forever in dead stare.
I don't apologize for the war, or what I was. I was
willingly confused by the times. I think I even believed
in heroics (for others, not for me). I believed the necessity
of that suffering world, hoping it would learn not to do
it again. But I was young. The world never learns. History
has a way of making the past palatable, the dead
a dream. Dear Charles, I'm glad you avoided the bombs, that you
live with us now and write poems. I must tell you though,
I felt funny that day in San Francisco. I kept saying
to myself, he was one on the ground that day, the sky
eerie mustard and our engines roaring everything
out of the way. And the world comes clean in moments

like that for survivors. The world comes clean as clouds
in summer, the pure puffed white, soft birds careening
in and out, our lives with a chance to drift on slow
over the world, our bomb bays empty, the target forgotten,
the enemy ignored. Nice to meet you finally after
all that mindless hate. Next time, if you want to be sure
you survive, sit on the bridge I'm trying to hit and wave.
I'm coming in on course but nervous and my cross hairs flutter.
Wherever you are on earth, you are safe. I'm aiming but
my bombs are candy and I've lost the lead plane. Your friend, Dick.

JOSEPH LANGLAND (1917–)

Joseph Langland served in the infantry during World War II, receiving four European Theater Battle Stars. Following the war, he taught English at Dana College, the University of Wyoming, and the University of Massachusetts. His books include The Green Town, The Wheel of Summer, *and* Selected Poems. *In "Buchenwald, Near Weimar," he describes a concentration camp situated in central Germany, which supplied forced labor to local armament manufacturers. Of the 238,980 imprisoned at Buchenwald from 1937 to 1945, 56,545 perished.*

Buchenwald, Near Weimar

Through barbed-wire enclosures,
Their bodies bloodless under metallic thorns
Like an unauthorized crucifixion,
The animal faces of handsome Europe steered
And grinned and begged and leered.

They had piled some bodies up,
Naked to God, like cordwood for a fire.
If eyes and faces turned,
Or jaws hung out among the shriveled limbs,
They sang, thank God, no hymns.

Pallid with black dishonor,
Nailed to the numerals of striped uniforms,
Stripped of their native hair,
They snared me with their unashamed display
And mocked at my dismay.

A rapid frantic babbling
I took for a Slavic tongue, a complete stranger,
But a wrinkled skeleton
Wavered up the wire and whispered in English,
His mind is sick. In anguish

The proud white brow of man,
Where the eye nobly shines, had crashed down.
It groveled on the ground,
More than Greece failing, more than Rome

Razed in its charred home.
   The low gray barracks stood
Dumb, in a chained line, in the torn-up land.
   The bleak doggy eyes
Rolled to and fro, compounded with despair,
   Blind to the exit there.

   I could not touch them; I could
Not ask forgiveness, not even comfort them.
   I came from another land
And stood at the deathbed of my own father again
In that vast mad graveyard of falling men.

ANTHONY HECHT (1923–   )

Anthony Hecht is the author of such books as A Summoning of Stones, The Darkness and the Light, *and* The Hard Hours, *which won a Pulitzer Prize. He served as a rifleman in the 97th Infantry Division and helped liberate the Flossenberg concentration camp on May 4, 1945. In the last months of the war, over 14,000 people died or were executed at the camp, including the renowned German theologian and pastor Dietrich Bonhoeffer.*

"More Light! More Light!"

for Heinrich Blücher and Hannah Arendt

Composed in the Tower before his execution
These moving verses, and being brought at that time
Painfully to the stake, submitted, declaring thus:
'I implore my God to witness that I have made no crime.'

Nor was he forsaken of courage, but the death was horrible,
The sack of gunpowder failing to ignite.
His legs were blistered sticks on which the black sap
Bubbled and burst as he howled for the Kindly Light.

And that was but one, and by no means one of the worst;
Permitted at least his pitiful dignity;
And such as were by made prayers in the name of Christ,
That shall judge all men, for his soul's tranquillity.

We move now to outside a German wood.
Three men are there commanded to dig a hole
In which the two Jews are ordered to lie down
And be buried alive by the third, who is a Pole.

Not light from the shrine at Weimar beyond the hill
Nor light from heaven appeared. But he did refuse.
A Luger settled back deeply in its glove.
He was ordered to change places with the Jews.

Much casual death had drained away their souls.
The thick dirt mounted toward the quivering chin.
When only the head was exposed the order came
To dig him out again and to get back in.

No light, no light in the blue Polish eye.
When he finished a riding boot packed down the earth.
The Luger hovered lightly in its glove.
He was shot in the belly and in three hours bled to death.

No prayers or incense rose up in those hours
Which grew to be years, and every day came mute
Ghosts from the ovens, sifting through crisp air,
And settled upon his eyes in a black soot.

MURIEL RUKEYSER (1913–1980)

Muriel Rukeyser was the author of more than fifteen volumes of poetry, plus books of prose, plays, film scripts, children's books, and translations. In 1943, she worked in the Graphics Division of the Office of War Information. The recipient of numerous distinguished honors for her writing, she was a member of the American Academy and Institute of Arts and Letters and served as president of PEN America.

Easter Eve 1945

Wary of time O it seizes the soul tonight
I wait for the great morning of the west
confessing with every breath mortality.
Moon of this wild sky struggles to stay whole
and on the water silvers the ships of war.
I go alone in the black-yellow light
all night waiting for day, while everywhere the sure
death of light, the leaf's sure return to the root
is repeated in million, death of all man to share.
Whatever world I know shines ritual death,
wide under this moon they stand gathering fire,
fighting with flame, stand fighting in their graves.
All shining with life as the leaf, as the wing shines,
the stone deep in the mountain, the drop in the green wave.
Lit by their energies, secretly, all things shine.
Nothing can black that glow of life;   although
         each part go crumbling down
         itself shall rise up whole.

Now I say there are new meanings;   now I name
death our black honor and feast of possibility
to celebrate casting of life on life.   This earth-long day
between blood and resurrection where we wait
remembering sun, seed, fire;   remembering
that fierce Judaean Innocent who risked
every immortal meaning on one life.
Given to our year as sun and spirit are,
as seed we are blessed only in needing freedom.
Now I say that the peace the spirit needs is peace,
not lack of war, but fierce continual flame.

For all men : effort is freedom, effort's peace,
it fights.   And along these truths the soul goes home,
        flies in its blazing to a place
        more safe and round than Paradise.

Night of the soul, our dreams in the arms of dreams
dissolving into eyes that look upon us.
Dreams the sources of action, the meeting and the end,
a resting-place among the flight of things.
And love which contains all human spirit, all wish,
the eyes and hands, sex, mouth, hair, the whole woman—
fierce peace I say at last, and the sense of the world.
In the time of conviction of mortality
whatever survive, I remember what I am.—
The nets of this night are on fire with sun and moon
pouring both lights into the open tomb.
Whatever arise, it comes in the shape of peace,
fierce peace which is love, in which move all the stars,
and the breathing of universes, filling, falling away,
and death on earth cast into the human dream.
        What fire survive forever
        myself is for my time.

ROBERT CREELEY (1926–   )

Robert Creeley served in India and Burma with the American Field Service during World War II. Later, he lived in France, Spain, and Guatemala. He has taught at Black Mountain College, the University of New Mexico, and San Francisco State University. His books include For Love: Poems 1950-1960, Selected Poems, *and* The Collected Poems of Robert Creeley. *"Return" was written upon Creeley's return home from India in 1945.*

Return

Quiet as is proper for such places;
The street, subdued, half-snow, half-rain,
Endless, but ending in the darkened doors.
Inside, they who will be there always,
Quiet as is proper for such people—
Enough for now to be here, and
To know my door is one of these.

JOHN CIARDI (1916–1986)

John Ciardi's books of poetry include Homeward to America, Live Another Day, *and his widely acclaimed translation of Dante's* Divine Comedy. *During World War II, he was a B-29 gunner and flew sixteen combat missions over Japan. Once his superiors learned of his writing skills, he was given the job of writing letters of condolence to next of kin whose loved ones died while in service. Ciardi also addressed casualties of war in his own writing, both on an intimate level, as in "A Box Comes Home," and on a massive one, as in "V-J Day" (short for Victory over Japan), which resonates with the dropping of American atomic bombs on Hiroshima and Nagasaki.*

A Box Comes Home

I remember the United States of America
As a flag-draped box with Arthur in it
And six marines to bear it on their shoulders.

I wonder how someone once came to remember
The Empire of the East and the Empire of the West.
As an urn maybe delivered by chariot.

You could bring Germany back on a shield once
And France in a plume. England, I suppose,
Kept coming back a long time as a letter.

Once I saw Arthur dressed as the United States
Of America. Now I see the United States
Of America as Arthur in a flag-sealed domino.

And I would pray more good of Arthur
Than I can wholly believe. I would pray
An agreement with the United States of America

To equal Arthur's living as it equals his dying
At the red-taped grave in Woodmere
By the rain and oakleaves on the domino.

V-J Day

On the tallest day in time the dead came back.
Clouds met us in the pastures past a world.
By short wave the releases of a rack
Exploded on the interphone's new word.

Halfway past Iwo we jettisoned to sea
Our gift of bombs like tears and tears like bombs
To spring a frolic fountain daintily
Out of the blue metallic seas of doom.

No fire-shot cloud pursued us going home.
No cities cringed and wallowed in the flame.
Far out to sea a blank millennium
Changed us alive, and left us still the same.

Lightened, we banked like jays, antennae squawking.
The four wild metal halos of our props
Blurred into time. The interphone was talking
Abracadabra to the cumulus tops:

Dreamboat three-one to Yearsend—loud and clear,
Angels one-two, on course at one-six-nine.
Magellan to Balboa. Propwash to Century.
How do you read me? Bombay to Valentine.

Fading and out. And all the dead were homing.
(Wisecrack to Halfmast. Doom to Memory.)
On the tallest day in time we saw them coming,
Wheels jammed and flaming on a metal sea.

JAMES DICKEY (1923–1997)

"Victory" is set on Okinawa, the strategically important island 340 miles from mainland Japan that was captured by American forces in June 1945. To secure the island, the U.S. committed over 500,000 men and 1,200 warships, an invasion that in magnitude rivaled Normandy. Three months later, on September 2, 1945, the Japanese formally signed the document signifying their surrender.

Victory

By September 3rd I had made my bundle
Of boards and a bag of nails. America, I was high
On Okinawa, with the fleet lying on its back
Under me, whispering "I can't help it"
                               and all ships firing up fire
Fighting liquids   sucking seawater, hoses climbing and coloring
The air, for Victory. I was clear-seeing
The morning   far-seeing backward
And forward from the cliff. I turned on the ground
And dug in, my nails and bag of magic
Boards from the tent-floor trembling to be
A throne. I was ready to sail
The island toward life
After death, left hand following right into the snail
shelled ground, then knocking down and nailing down my chair like a box
seat in the worldwide window of peace   and sat and lay down my arms
On the stomped grains of ammo-crates heavy with the soles
Of buddies who had helped me wreck the tent
In peace-joy, and of others long buried
At sea. The island rocked with the spectrum
Bombardment of the fleet   and there I was
For sure   saved and plucked naked to my shirt
And lids. I raised my head to the sun.
What I saw was two birthdays

Back, in the jungle, before I sailed high on the rainbow
Waters of victory   before the sun
Of armistice morning burned into my chest
The great V of Allied Conquest. Now it was not here
With the ships sucking up fire

Water and spraying it wild
Through every color, or where, unthreatened, my navel burned
Burned like an entry-wound. Lord, I deepened
Memory, and lay in the light high and wide
Open, murmuring "I can't help it" as I went
South in my mind.

Yes Mother

there were two fine hands
Driving the jeep: mine, much better than before, for you had sent
Whiskey. What could I do but make the graveyards soar! O you coming
Allied Victory, I rambled in the night of two birthdays
Ago, the battle of Buna stoned
In moonlight   stone-dead left and right   going nowhere
Near friend or foe, but turned off into the thickest
Dark. O yes, Mother, let me tell you: the vines split and locked:
About where you'd never know me is
Where I stalled

and sat bolt up-
right in the moonlit bucket
Seat throne of war

cascading the bottle to drink
To victory, and to what I would do, when the time came,
With my body. The world leapt like the world
Driving nails, and the moon burned with the light it had when it split

From the earth. I slept and it was foretold
That I would live. My head came true
In a great smile. I reached for the bottle. It was dying and the moon
Writhed closer to be free; it could answer
My smile of foreknowledge. I forgot the mosquitoes that were going
Mad on my blood, of biting me once too often on the bites
Of bites. Had the Form in the moon come from the dead soldier
Of your bottle, Mother? Let down in blocked
Out light, a snakehead hung, its eyes putting into mine
Visions of a victory at sea. New Guinea froze. Midair was steady

Between. Snake-eyes needle-eyed   its
Lips halving its head
Stayed shut. I held up the last drop
In the bottle, and invited him

To sin   to celebrate
The Allied victory to come. He pulled back a little over
The evil of the thing I meant
To stand for brotherhood. Nightshining his scales on Detroit
Glass, he stayed on and on
My mind. I found out the angel
Of peace is limbless and the day will come
I said, when no difference is between
My skin and the great fleets
Delirious with survival. Mother, I was drunk enough on your birthday
Present, not to die there. I backed the jeep out
Of the Buna weeds
                              and, finally, where the sun struck
The side of the hill, there I was
                              back from the dark side
Of the mind, burning like a prism over the conquering Catherine
Wheel of the fleet. But ah, I turned

I sank I lay back dead
Drunk on a cold table   I had closed my eyes
And gone north   and lay to change
Colors all night. Out of the Nothing of occupation
Duty, I must have asked for the snake: I asked or the enemy told
Or my snakeskin told
Itself to be. Before I knew it in Yokahama, it was at my throat
Beginning with its tail, cutting through the world
wide Victory sign   moving under
My armpit like a sailor's, scale
By scale. Carbon-arc-light spat in the faces of the four
Men who bent over me, for the future lay brilliantly in
The needles of the enemy. Naked I lay on their zinc
Table, murmuring "I can't help it."
He coiled around me, yet

Headless   I turned with him side
To side, as the peaceful enemy
Designed   a spectrum of scales O yes
Mother I was in the tattoo parlor to this day
Not knowing how I got there as he grew,
Red scales sucking up color   blue
White with my skin running out of the world

Wide sun. Frothing with pinpricks, filling with ink
I lay and it lay
Now over my heart   limbless I fell and moved like moonlight
On the needles   moving to hang my head
In a drunk boy's face, and watch him while he dreamed
Of victory at sea. I retched but choked
It back, for he had crossed my breast, and I knew that many-
colored snakeskin was living with my heart   our hearts
Beat as one   port-of-call red   Yokahoma blue
O yes and now he lay low

On my belly, and gathered together the rainbow
Ships of Buckner Bay. I slumbered deep and he crossed the small
Of my back   increased
His patchwork hold on my hip   passed through the V between
My legs, and came
Around once more   all but the head   then I was turning   the snake
Coiled round my right thigh and crossed
Me with light hands   I felt myself opened
Just enough, where the serpent staggered on his last
Colors   needles gasping for air   jack-hammering
My right haunch burned by the hundreds
Of holes, as the snake shone on me complete   escaping
Forever   surviving   crushing   going home
To the bowels of the living,
His master, and the new prince of peace.

BOB KAUFMAN (1925–1986)

At the age of thirteen, Bob Kaufman ran away from home and joined the Merchant Marine; he survived four shipwrecks and circumnavigated the globe four times in the next twenty years. Closely identified with the Beat movement, Kaufman was often called the "Original Be-Bop Man." His books of poetry include Solitudes Crowded with Loneliness *and* Ancient Rain: 1956–1978.

War Memoir: Jazz, Don't Listen to It at Your Own Risk

In the beginning, in the wet
Warm dark place,
Straining to break out, clawing at strange cables
Hearing her screams, laughing
"Later we forgot ourselves, we didn't know"
Some secret jazz
Shouted, wait, don't go.
Impatient, we came running, innocent
Laughing blobs of blood and faith.
To this mother, father world
Where laughter seems out of place
So we learned to cry, pleased
They pronounced human.
The secret jazz blew a sigh
Some familiar sound shouted wait
Some are evil, some will hate.
"Just Jazz, blowing its top again"
So we rushed and laughed.
As we pushed and grabbed
While Jazz blew in the night
Suddenly we were too busy to hear a sound
We were busy shoving mud in men's mouths,
Who were busy dying on living ground
Busy earning medals, for killing children on deserted streetcorners
Occupying their fathers, raping their mothers, busy humans were
Busy burning Japanese in atomicolorcinescope
With stereophonic screams,
What one-hundred-percent red-blooded savage would waste precious time
Listening to Jazz, with so many important things going on
But even the fittest murderers must rest

So we sat down on our blood-soaked garments,
And listened to Jazz
                    lost, steeped in all our dreams
We were shocked at the sound of life, long gone from our own
Living sound, which mocked us, but let us feel sweet life again
We wept for it, hugged, kissed it, loved it, joined it, we drank it,
Smoked it, ate with it, slept with it
We made our girls wear it for lovemaking
Instead of silly lace gowns,
Now in those terrible moments, when the dark memories come
The secret moments to which we admit no one
When guiltily we crawl back in time, reaching away from ourselves
We hear a familiar sound,
Jazz, scratching, digging, bluing, swinging jazz,
And we listen
And we feel
And live.

KENNETH KOCH (1925–2002)

Kenneth Koch served in the Philippines with the 96th Infantry Division as a rifleman. For many years, he was an English professor at Columbia University. His collections of poetry include Thank You and Other Poems, The Art of Love, *and* On the Great Atlantic Railway.

To World War Two

Early on you introduced me to young women in bars
You were large, and with a large hand
You presented them in different cities,
Made me in San Luis Obispo, drunk
On French seventy-fives, in Los Angeles, on pousse-cafés.
It was a time of general confusion
Of being a body hurled at a wall.
I didn't do much fighting. I sat, rather I stood, in a foxhole.
I stood while the typhoon splashed us into morning.
It felt unusual
Even if for a good cause
To be part of a destructive force
With my rifle in my hands
And in my head
My serial number
The entire object of my existence
To eliminate Japanese soldiers
By killing them
With a rifle or with a grenade
And then, many years after that,
I could write poetry
Fall in love
And have a daughter
And think
About these things
From a great distance
If I survived
I was "paying my debt
To society" a paid
Killer. It wasn't
Like anything I'd done

Before, on the paved
Streets of Cincinnati
Or on the ballroom floor
At Mr. Vathé's dancing class
What would Anne Marie Goldsmith
Have thought of me
If instead of asking her to dance
I had put my BAR to my shoulder
And shot her in the face
I thought about her in my foxhole—
One, in a foxhole near me, has his throat cut during the night
We take more precautions but it is night and it is you.
The typhoon continues and so do you.
"I can't be killed—because of my poetry. I have to live on in order to write it."
I thought—even crazier thought, or just as crazy—
"If I'm killed while thinking of lines, it will be too corny
When it's reported" (I imagined it would be reported!)
So I kept thinking of lines of poetry. One that came to me on the beach on Leyte
Was "The surf comes in like masochistic lions."
I loved this terrible line. It was keeping me alive. My Uncle Leo wrote to me,
"You won't believe this, but some day you may wish
You were footloose and twenty on Leyte again." I have never wanted
To be on Leyte again,
With you, whispering into my ear,
"Go on and win me! Tomorrow you may not be alive,
So do it today!" How could anyone ever win you?
How many persons would I have had to kill
Even to begin to be a part of winning you?
You were too much for me, though I
Was older than you were and in camouflage. But for you
Who threw everything together, and had all the systems
Working for you all the time, this was trivial. If you could use me
You'd use me, and then forget. How else
Did I think you'd behave?
I'm glad you ended. I'm glad I didn't die. Or lose my mind.
As machines make ice
We made dead enemy soldiers, in
Dark jungle alleys, with weapons in our hands
That produced fire and kept going straight through
I was carrying one,
I who had gone about for years as a child

Praying God don't let there ever be another war
Or if there is, don't let me be in it. Well, I was in you.
All you cared about was existing and being won.
You died of a bomb blast in Nagasaki, and there were parades.

KOREAN WAR
(1950–1953)

At ease, gentlemen. Let's keep it brief. This map gives our share of the ridge: markings in blue, our howitzers and 8-inch pieces. Lacking radios the enemy's greater numbers are noise: bugle signals, hand-sirens, even bells. We own the air. That means night attacks, with only their first two waves coming armed. Their third and fourth waves may carry scythes, hooks, farm tools, sticks. Their fifth waves carry nothing. Remind your men Eighth Army is in full support if needed. Later today my G4 will have details on the R&R we're awarding every five kills confirmed.

FROM FLAG MEMOIR, REG SANER

Retreat! We're coming out of here as a Marine Division. We're bringing our equipment . . . our wounded . . . our dead. Retreat, hell! We're just fighting in another direction.

MAJOR GENERAL OLIVER PRINCE SMITH, ON WITHDRAWAL
FROM CHANGJIN (CHOSIN) RESERVOIR, DECEMBER 1950

HAYDEN CARRUTH (1921–   )

During World War II, Hayden Carruth served in the U.S. Army Air Corps in Italy in the public relations office of a heavy bomber group. He later served as poetry editor of Poetry *and* Harper's, *and he directed the creative writing program at Syracuse University. His many volumes of poetry include* The Crow and the Heart, The Sleeping Beauty, *and* Scrambled Eggs and Whiskey, *awarded the National Book Award.*

On a Certain Engagement South of Seoul

A long time, many years, we've had these wars.
When they were opened, one can scarcely say.
We were high school students, no more than sophomores,

When Italy broke her peace on a dark day,
And that was not the beginning. The following years
Grew crowded with destruction and dismay.

When I was nineteen, once the surprising tears
Stood in my eyes and stung me, for I saw
A soldier in a newsreel clutch his ears

To hold his face together. Those that paw
The public's bones to eat the public's heart
Said far too much, of course. The sight, so raw

And unbelievable, of people blown apart
Was enough to numb us without that bark and whine.
We grew disconsolate. Each had his chart

To mark on the kitchen wall the battle-line,
But many were out of date. The radio
Droned through the years, a faithful anodyne.

Yet the news of this slight encounter somewhere below
Seoul stirs my remembrance: we were a few,
Sprawled on the stiff grass of a small plateau,

Afraid. No one was dead. But we were new—
We did not know that probably none would die.
Slowly, then, all vision went askew.

My clothing was outlandish; earth and sky
Were metallic and horrible. We were unreal,
Strange bodies and alien minds; we could not cry

For even our eyes seemed to be made of steel;
Nor could we look at one another, for each
Was a sign of fear, and we could not conceal

Our hatred for our friends. There was no speech.
We sat alone, all of us, trying to wake
Some memory of the selves beyond our reach.

That place was conquered. The nations undertake
Another campaign now, in another land,
A stranger land perhaps. And we forsake

The miseries there that we can't understand
Just as we always have. And yet my glimpse
Of a scene on the distant field can make my hand

Tremble again. How quiet we are. One limps.
One cannot walk at all. Or one is all right.
But one owns this experience that crimps

Forgetfulness, especially at night.
Is this a bond? Does this make us brothers?
Or does it bring our hatred back? I might

Have known, but now I do not know. Others
May know. I know when I walk out-of-doors
I have a sorrow not wholly mine, but another's.

WILLIAM MEREDITH (1919–   )

William Meredith served as a navy aviator during World War II and the Korean War. He is the author of Love Letter from an Impossible Land, Partial Accounts, *and* Effort at Speech: New and Selected Poems, *winner of the National Book Award. He has taught at Princeton University, University of Hawaii, and Connecticut College.*

A Korean Woman Seated by a Wall

Suffering has settled like a sly disguise
On her cheerful old face. If she dreams beyond
Rice and a roof, now toward the end of winter,
Is it of four sons gone, the cries she has heard,
A square farm in the south, soured by tents?
Some alien and untranslatable loss
Is a mask she smiles through at the weak sun
That is moving north to invade the city again.

A poet penetrates a dark disguise
After his own conception, little or large.
Crossing the scaleless asia of trouble
Where it seems no one could give himself away,
He gives himself away, he sets a scale.
Hunger and pain and death, the sorts of loss,
Dispute our comforts like peninsulas
Of no particular value, places to fight.
And what is it in suffering dismays us more:
The capriciousness with which it is dispensed
Or the unflinching way we see it home?

She may be dreaming of her wedding gift;
A celadon bowl of a good dynasty
With cloud and heron cut in its green paste,
It sleeps in a hollow bed of pale blue silk.
The rice it bought was eaten the second winter.
And by what happier stove is it unwrapped
In the evening now and passed around like a meat,
Making a foliage in the firelight?

She shifts the crate she sits on as the March
Wind mounts from the sea. The sun moves down the sky
Perceptibly, like the hand of a public clock,
In increments of darkness though ablaze.
Ah, now she looks at me. We are unmasked
And exchange what roles we guess at for an instant.
The questions Who comes next and Why not me
Rage at and founder my philosophy.
Guilt beyond my error and a grace past her grief
Alter the coins I tender cowardly,
Shiver the porcelain fable to green shards.

DALE JACOBSEN (1950–   )

Dale Jacobsen is the author of Voices of the Communal Dark, Factories and Cities, *and* A Walk by the River. *Below, he writes of Pablo Picasso's* Massacre in Korea *(1951), inspired by the American intervention in South Korea in 1950 after armed forces of communist North Korea crossed the 38th Parallel and occupied the capital city of Seoul. As in Picasso's famous Spanish Civil War painting,* Guernica, Massacre in Korea *is a monochrome, showing innocent, resigned victims falling under fire.*

Viewing Picasso's *Massacre in Korea*

"Painting is an instrument of war for attack and defense against the enemy"

His are the human eyes of the world—
small child playing on the fields of death:

hands reaching toward breathing blossoms,
a shimmering room no one else sees.

But another child rushes through tunnels of terror,
away, a way out, the world is so wide!

A pregnant woman is tormented,
her pain twisted beyond the limits of a face.

Death is a gray river that opens
from their feet towards the valley.

There, like a wound, the brown chaotic strokes
slash the center of the landscape.

Another woman stares beyond the picture,
bride to all the dead, soldiers and civilians alike.

The eyes of another are sewn shut
against the terrible fact lodged in the rifle bores.

Perhaps a dog would call into the distance
on a day like this, but the dog shall be fed.

In bombed homes the smell of fear resides,
like a slaughter house thirsty for rain.

The victims are gathered against the hill,
which is the pillow of the afternoon.

American soldiers wear riveted helmets.
Something has made them into chrome machines.

Their bulbous eyes are drops of metal
from which the sun's glare blinds.

KEITH WILSON (1927–   )

After graduating from the United States Naval Academy, Keith Wilson served three tours of duty in Korean waters between 1950 and 1953. He has taught at the University of Nevada, University of Arizona, and New Mexico State University. His books include Graves Registry & Other Poems, Midwatch, *and* Warrior Song and Other Poems.

The Circle

U.S.S. Valley Forge, 1950

Out of the stirrings of the Yellow Sea,
20 miles off from Inchon Channel
we came to—blue leis
thrown on the water.

Sea, glassy. No wind.
I sat atop a 5" director, the ship
steamed on, no planes in sight:
a pleasant gunwatch, little excitement,
lost in quiet.

The first I knew we
were among them, circles of men
bound in faded blue lifejackets,
lashed together

Most of the men leaned
back, heads bobbing against
kapok collars, mouths open,
tongues swollen

—hundreds of them.
We steamed by, group after group,
for all my watch. I searched for
any sign of motion, any gesture
of any hand, but soon I just
watched as

bobbing gently, each circle
undulated, moved independently;
once or twice a hand did flop
& I caught the man's face in
my binoculars instantly,
slowly let them drop

We sailed on. I suppose that's all
there is to say: wartime commitments,
the necessity for being where you must
be & when

they were dead, hundreds
of them, a troopship gone down somewhere
—Korean, uncounted.

I remember one man, remember
him clearly. God knows why
but his ass was up instead
of his head; no pants left,
his buttocks glistened
grayish white in the clear sun.
the only one.

& we steamed on, routine patrol,
launched planes at 1800 for night
CAP, leaving the last of the circles
rocking gently in our darkening wake.

Memory of a Victory

Off the Korean Coast, beyond Wonsan
waiting for invasion soft winds blew
the scent of squid drying in the sun,
homely smells of rice paddies, cooking fires.

It was a picture world with low hills
much like New Mexico, except for water,
the strange smells. Little plumes of smoke.
Here & there, the glint of steel.

Under the waiting guns lay peachblossoms.
I could see them with my binoculars.
The planes still had not come, all eternity
waited beneath the sweep second hand.

Then the crackling radio commanded
"Fire!" and a distant world I could have loved
went up in shattering bursts, in greyblack explosions,
the strange trees that suddenly grew on the hillside.

They fired their rifles, light howitzers
back. After a while we sent boats into the silence.

ROLANDO HINOJOSA (1929–   )

In the Korean War, Rolando Hinojosa served as a tanker with a reconnaissance unit. He has taught and held administrative positions at a number of universities and currently teaches at the University of Texas. His books include Korean Love Songs, Klail City: A Novel, *and* The Useless Servants.

A Sheaf of Percussion Fire

(Moving North)

Death is alive and well in our zone;
Older, somewhat tired, yet up and around.

Early this morning, we opened up on Them;
Tit for tat, then,
They opened up on Us, and there was Death,
Out of breath,
Trying to keep the count. Death is badly in need of assistants,
But the young and able are busy for the moment.
So, resourceful Death makes do
With a Burroughs for Us and an abacus for Them.

No matter; it's totting the numbers right what counts
At this stage of affairs,
And Death is having one hell of a time:

    "You've no idea what I've been going through with these children;
    I mean, it's enough to make you cry;
    Hear them? They've been at it all day and half the night.
    And it's all I can do to keep up."

Eating on the run,
Twice chowtime's come and gone,
And we're still at it;
Pieces laid and relaid, sensings made and changed,
Lanyards pulled and the breechblocks clicking
Home towards the targets
Of opportunity.

There's some smoking white phosphorous.
Who the hell's firing that?
Alibi! Alibi! The gunners laugh;
The cooks and clerks are passing the ammo,
And they don't know H.E. from shit . . .

Death knows,
But did your mother,
That shrap from Heavy Explosive, at the instant of burst,
Leaves the case at an increased velocity
(and correct me if I'm wrong)
Of approximately 200 feet per sec?
And that if the One Gun doesn't get you,
The Two Gun will?

We're really laying it on now,
And Death, dragging ass,
Is being pushed to the limit.

It's so unfair.

REG SANER (1929–   )

Reg Saner served as a lieutenant in the U.S. Army from 1951 to 1953, including service as an infantry platoon leader in Korea in 1952 and 1953, where he was awarded a Bronze Star. He is Professor Emeritus of English at the University of Colorado at Boulder and the author of Climbing into the Roots, So This Is the Map, *and* Essay on Air, *among other books.*

Re-runs

All that flying iron was bound to hit something.
His odd nights re-visit a stare, let a torn head
trade looks with him, though the incoming whine
was only a power saw. If what's buried won't cry
and won't go away, if in some field on the world's
other side all crossfire tracers burn down
to old movies whose re-runs he's sick of,
who's to blame then for what's missing?
Odd nights, a clay pit or two may waken him
still, alone inside a nameless grief holding
nothing: their faces, grass shrapnel—which some field
on the world's other side bothers with. Like seed,
the shapes that won't go away without tears.
They just lie where they fell, and keep going.

WILLIAM CHILDRESS (1933–   )

William Childress served as an enlisted man in the army from 1951 to 1959, includ-
ing service in Korea in 1952 and 1953 as a demolitions expert and secret courier.
His books include Burning the Years, Lobo, *and* Out of the Ozarks.

Trying to Remember People I Never Really Knew

There was that guy
on that hill in Korea.
Exploding gasoline made him
a thousand candles bright.
We guided the Samaritan copter
in by flashlight
to a rookery of rocks,
a huge, fluttering nightbird
aiming at darting fireflies,
and one great firefly
rolling in charred black screams.

There was the R.O.K. soldier
lying in the paddy,
his lifted arms curved
as he stiffly embraced death,
a tiny dark tunnel over his heart.
Such a small door
for something as large as life
to escape through.

Later, between pages and chapters
of wars not yet written up
in Field Manuals or Orders of the Day,
there came shrieking down
from a blue Kentucky sky
a young paratrooper whom technology failed.
(I must correct two common errors:
they are never called *shroud lines,*
and paratroopers do not shoot *Geronimo.)*

I wish I could say
that all three men fathered sons,
that some part of them still lived.
But maybe I don't, for the children's ages
would now be such as to make them
ready for training as hunters of men,
to stalk dark forests
where leaden rains fall with a precision
that can quench a hunter's fire.

JAMES MAGNER, JR. (1928–2000)

James Magner, Jr. served in the infantry in the Korean War and was severely wounded. After his discharge in 1951, he spent five years in a Roman Catholic monastery. From 1962 to 1999, he taught at John Carroll University in Cleveland, Ohio. His books include Toiler of the Sea, The Dark Is Closest to the Moon, *and* The Temple of the Bell of Silence. *The port of Sasebo, mentioned in "Repository," lies on the southern island of Kyushu, the third largest of the major islands of Japan. During the Korean War, Sasebo acted as a base for American troops.*

Repository

> *"Be one on whom nothing is lost"*

A reader asked
The Sportsline
what college quarterback
named Adam
died
in The Korean War.
No record.
Even from the army and alma mater.

I remember an evening,
lit by lantern of a tent
in Jimungi of Kyushu,
before we sailed from Sasebo,
a second in silence
thirty-two years ago
in hills above Beppu
(strange, that I retain the face
of a man I never knew;
perhaps, in the secret of things,
a gift of him to you.)

I remember
a tall dark quick body,
alert dark-eyed gaze
(How can I see, now, so clearly!)
above his golden bars

caught in lantern
and the shadows
of what was to be
his austered and steely way
to memory.

Impossible to mind, impossible to heart
that one so quick,
who stepped so quick
in pocket
and rifled passes forty yards
for alma mater and the infantry
could die
and be forgotten
(even by his academy)
by all except me
who see
his face still,
dark eyes, dark hair—dark God
who disappeared
with him.
(How does heart, do eyes remember?)

Vanesca!
(Do I spell his name correctly?)
Vanesca!
(I say it again, so someone will remember.)
Vanesca!
(What is this repository that keeps the names,
the souls of men!)

HOWARD FAST (1915–2003)

Howard Fast was the author of over two dozen books, mostly historical novels of social justice. In 1951, after refusing a request from the House Un-American Activities Committee to provide information on an antifascist group, Fast, a member of the Communist Party from 1943 to 1956, was jailed for contempt and blacklisted. He turned the experience into Spartacus, *the story of a slave revolt in ancient Rome, which became a 1960 Oscar-winning film. Reminiscent of the poetic epitaphs of Edgar Lee Master's* Spoon River Anthology, *"Korean Litany" was first published during the Korean War as part of a fourteen-page pamphlet entitled* Korean Lullaby.

Korean Litany

Vernon Blake, Rifleman:

My name reads, as long as the wood lasts,
twenty-three, and read my name,
I, Vernon Blake, who died in action
from a sniper's bullet—and rests in peace,
or less than peace perhaps, in Korean soil.
And fortunate perhaps, for only one question
twists a little with the maggots.
You see, the American way of life
was all at one with me, ten generations on each side
all from this soil, and the house I lived in,
Chester, Vermont, white clapboard,
and easy with all those generations.
I ate, drank and slept and played,
studied a little, grew strong and tall and proud;
I saw it when my mother looked at me,
and my father's eyes were full of pride,
and I wrote to him, "I make a good soldier,
and all those days we tramped the fields
and brush together were not wasted—"
We went for rabbit and squirrel, and once a long shot
at a deer. How my mother loved us both!
"Two men," she said, "the Bible notwithstanding,
my own prescription for a happy home."
And I fought her when she wanted my college diploma,
framed in the livingroom—why didn't she

have four children, tall and strong and proud like me?
I would have answered her question eventually,
for I had no doubts and no questions.
It was in her that the doubts grew, like a cancer,
"Why, why, why, why? Why are you there, my son,
and not with me?" I would have framed the answer,
given time, framed it proudly for her to hang on the wall—
for there must be an answer.

Harry Morgan, Machine Gunner:

My old man never had much sense,
working on an assembly line all his life,
the candle burned at both ends, squeezed in the middle,
and always yapping of the pride of class
a worker has. "What future where the world is yours?"
I'd ask him. "You got only a past, old man,
and the smart money goes to the smart fingers.
Get smart, old man, get smart.
I'll take a buck and you—you keep your commie line."
He could have said a lot of things,
and talked of damn young punks,
but it wasn't easy for him to put in words
the things he felt, and the one letter he sent,
I never answered. "Only remember," he wrote,
"the men you fight are your brothers,
working with their own hands, as I work with mine,
and you with yours." Where are my hands,
old man? Both of them blown off by a mortar shell,
and me looking at the stumps as I bled to death.

Arthur Dembrowski, Chemical Warfare:

Dug up quickly, you would see,
snub nose, sandy hair and a broad face;
we never like what we see in our own mirror,
and I only started shaving three months before the service.
A girl would like or not like that face,
making a better judgment than mine—
but even love was postponed, this crazy kid
making a pal of a three year old, my brother,

sixteen years between him and me,
me the child of my mother's youth,
and he of her last bearing time.
The way it was, I never loved anything
the way I loved that kid,
and we were better friends than most brothers.
With his little fat hand in mine,
we'd walk on my furloughs, and they'd say,
"There's Dembrowski and his buddy."
I was a flame thrower, and out of one burning house
crawled a Korean child, blistered and singed
all over his skin. I picked him up
and cradled him in my arms, talking to him
when a bullet blew off the back of my head.

Al Carlton, Medic:

When I crawled up to a Korean wounded
to heal him, and got a bullet in my gut,
I hated for the first time in nine months,
dying wastefully and painfully, whimpering,
"Oh Jesus—what a lousy way!"
And he, with one arm torn off,
lay watching me and whispered,
"Hey, Yank—what for you come here?
Go home. Go home." And then we bled together,
blood mixing with blood,
and the last thing I thought of
was blood brothers, and then I died
by the side of the man who killed me.

Gerald Cartwheel, Tankman:

The day my tank rolled through a village,
flattening those flimsy houses,
I saw a woman caught under a beam,
screaming as the tank rolled over—
on that day, I wrote to my congressman,
my free and democractic right,
"Was I sent here to do this kind of thing,
or tell me why, or have I no right to know,

or do you know?" I sought no easy answer,
knowing—as others don't—
that things are not all black and white.
Others ribbed me, scoffed, and said,
"Tell it to the chaplain, bub."
I wonder what the answer would have been,
and whether I would have felt at ease,
cooking in a burning tank
and screaming for my mother.

Aaron Klein, Rifleman

I did what I did, and followed orders through,
and died with one hundred and sixteen men,
all together, brave men who fought and died,
and left a wife and child, and a mother
who will die too, this being too much pain
for her to take and live with,
and I was brave, and asked no questions,
and never asked to know what I,
a Jew and kin to those six million
whom Hitler slew, was doing here, in this strange land,
making a desert and a graveyard
of a sunny place where people lived and worked—
and never asked what good dead children did
in freedom's struggle. And if I thought,
am I or the man across the ridge and facing me,
fighting freedom's fight? I never changed
the thought to words or deeds—
then why do I rest so poorly,
in this strange soil?

Jamsie Anderson, Quartermaster:

I used to laugh and say,
"I got no future, but lots of past."
Well, take my past and put it you know where,
all of it, cleaning toilets and shining shoes—
not like them that sat and sighed
for a glass of beer at five o'clock,
just that to walk on them soft heaven clouds.

That ain't no heaven for me,
promoted to driving a half-track through Korean mud;
and then they'd say, "You're turning evil, Jamsie,
evil as all hell." Oh, no, never, not no evil
in me now, but just a little plain damned common sense.
"Then keep it to yourself," they said. "Black man's
got no business talking common sense."
But never was a man could take his common sense
and force it to behave, and mine kept plaguing me.
Oh, what a lot of questions I could ask
of them strange men who blew me all apart.
Not white men, boss men,
no southern accent there,
but colored men like me,
with eyes as full of pain—
lifted me tenderly,
and buried me in Korean soil. I'd ask them calm and gentle,
not evil, but just with common sense.

THOMAS MCGRATH (1916–1990)

"Ode for the American Dead in Asia" was first published in 1955 under the title "Ode for the American Dead in Korea." During the Vietnam War, Thomas McGrath changed the title to its present form. Casualties in the Korean War were heavy: U.S. losses were 33,629 dead and 103,000 wounded, while Chinese and Korean casualties were each at least ten times as high.

Ode for the American Dead in Asia

1.

God love you now, if no one else will ever,
Corpse in the paddy, or dead on a high hill
In the fine and ruinous summer of a war
You never wanted. All your false flags were
Of bravery and ignorance, like grade school maps;
Colors of countries you would never see—
Until that weekend in eternity
When, laughing, well armed, perfectly ready to kill
The world and your brother, the safe commanders sent
You into your future. Oh, dead on a hill,
Dead in a paddy, leeched and tumbled to
A tomb of footnotes. We mourn a changeling: you:
Handselled to poverty and drummed to war
By distinguished masters whom you never knew.

2.

The bee that spins his metal from the sun,
The shy mole drifting like a miner ghost
Through midnight earth—all happy creatures run
As strict as trains on rails the circuits of
Blind instinct. Happy in your summer follies,
You mined a culture that was mined for war:
The state to mold you, church to bless, and always
The elders to confirm you in your ignorance.
No scholar put your thinking cap on nor
Warned that in dead seas fishes died in schools
Before inventing legs to walk the land.
The rulers stuck a tennis racket in your hand,

An Ark against the flood. In time of change
Courage is not enough: the blind mole dies,
And you on your hill, who did not know the rules.

3.
Wet in the windy counties of the dawn
The lone crow skirls his draggled passage home:
And God (whose sparrows fall aslant his gaze,
Like grace or confetti) blinks and he is gone,
And you are gone. Your scarecrow valor grows
And rusts like early lilac while the rose
Blooms in Dakota and the stock exchange
Flowers. Roses, rents, all things conspire
To crown your death with wreaths of living fire.
And the public mourners come: the politic tear
Is cast in the Forum. But, in another year,
We will mourn you, whose fossil courage fills
The limestone histories: brave: ignorant: amazed:
Dead in the rice paddies, dead on the nameless hills.

VIETNAM WAR
(1964–1975)

I guess the things I remember most are massive wounds, primarily shrapnel wounds that had to be opened . . . There were a lot of amputations, multiple amputations, because there was so much mining. There were a lot of gunshot wounds, but in comparison it just seemed as though there were so many more of the distance kind of injuries, where you weren't face to face with the enemy when it happened.

Our major job in field hospitals was to keep these people alive; we didn't deal with the long-term psychological effect, like the medical people at the hospitals back in the States did. We were just part of the chain.

FIRST LIEUTENANT MARY REIS STOUT, NURSE,
2ND SURGICAL HOSPITAL (M.A.S.H.), 1967–1968

The soldiers are coming home,
they carry their sadness with them
like others carry groceries
or clothes in from the line.
There is no music in the parade;
the sound of their coming
waits at the bottoms of river,
stones rubbing against each other
in the current.

FROM "WAR STORY," GERALD MCCARTHY

DICK ALLEN (1939–   )

Dick Allen is the author of six volumes of poetry, including Ode to the Cold War: Poems New and Selected *and* The Day Before: New Poems. *The recipient of many honors and awards for his work, including the Academy of American Poets Prize, the Hart Crane Memorial Fellowship for Poetry, and the Union Arts and Civil League Prize, he has taught at the University of Bridgeport in Bridgeport, Connecticut.*

A Short History of the Vietnam War Years

Nothing was said until the house grew dark
And a fishnet of stars was cast upon its windows.
In the tall bedroom mirror, the door to Watergate
Opened again. A helicopter tiny as a moth
Flew across the lovers' flanks, its slow pinwheel blades
Making the sound of grief and churning rivers.

Placards lifted, the marchers of the Sixties
Stood in green meadows. Then folk songs began
Rising from their lips like blue leaves in summer
And time was a slipstream where a Phantom jet
Rolled in the sun. The lovers ran their hands
Over the rice fields and the panting oxen.

Deep in itself, the bedside clock unwound
By the edge of a pool, casting its minutes out
To a shoal of Destroyers. *Be still,* the lovers whispered.
In the room above the hall a mud-stained jeep
Backed up to a wooden brothel in Saigon,
An orange-robed monk knelt down in billowed flame.

The lovers grew sad. A soft rainy wind from Ohio
Brushed gunfire bursts and tear gas over them.
We will never love money, they said, clinging to each other,
Or dress like television, work like IBM.
We will grow flowers to slide into rifle barrels,
And we will dance barefoot on Wall Street's glass chin.

That was when hope was a temple bell, a bleeding eye,
A circle of books around the lovers' bed
As the soldiers looked on. Mai Lai fell half-asleep
Under the full thrust moon. On bruised hands and knees,
Tet advanced along the shadowed railroad ties
And the deltas awoke and flooded Washington.

We will drift to Cambodia, the lovers said,
Dance in People's Park, burn incense tapers
At Buddhist shrines. The house wrapped its black armband
Over the lovers as they lay entwined.
And if you listened, you could hear the mortar fire
Walking up the valleys like an old blind man.

ALLEN GINSBERG (1926–1997)

Allen Ginsberg was a leader of the Beat movement and the San Francisco Renaissance. He was the author of numerous volumes of poetry and prose, including Howl and Other Poems; Kaddish and Other Poems; The Fall of America: Poems of These States, 1965–1971; *and* Poems for the Nation.

War Profit Litany

To Ezra Pound

These are the names of the companies that have made money from this war
nineteenhundredsixtyeight Annodomini fourthousand eighty Hebraic
These are the Corporations who have profited by merchanising skinburning
    phosphorus or shells fragmented to thousands of fleshpiercing needles
and here listed money millions gained by each combine for manufacture
and here are gains numbered, index'd swelling a decade, set in order,
here named the Fathers in office in these industries, telephones directing
    finance,
names of directors, makers of fates, and the names of the stockholders of these
    destined Aggregates,
and here are the names of their ambassadors to the Capital, representatives to
    legislature, those who sit drinking in hotel lobbies to persuade,
and separate listing, those who drop Amphetamines with military, gossip,
    argue, and persuade,
suggesting policy naming language proposing strategy, this done for fee as
    ambassadors to Pentagon, consultants to military, paid by their industry:
and these are the names of the generals & captains military, who now thus
    work for war goods manufacturers;
and above these, listed, the names of the banks, combines, investment trusts
    that control these industries:
and these are the names of the newspapers owned by these banks
and these are the names of the airstations owned by these combines;
and these are the numbers of thousands of citizens employed by these
    businesses named;
and the beginning of this accounting is 1958 and the end 1968, that statistic be
    contained in orderly mind, coherent & definite,
and the first form of this litany begun first day December 1967 furthers this
    poem of these States.

ROBERT DUNCAN (1919–1988)

Robert Duncan taught at San Francisco State University, University of British Columbia, and Black Mountain College. He was the author of such books as The Opening of the Field, Roots and Branches, *and* Bending the Bow.

Up Rising

Now Johnson would go up to join the great simulacra of men,
    Hitler and Stalin, to work his fame
    with planes roaring out from Guam over Asia,
all America become a sea of toiling men
    stirrd at his will, which would be a bloated thing,
    drawing from the underbelly of the nation
    such blood and dreams as swell the idiot psyche
    out of its courses into an elemental thing
    until his name stinks with burning meat and heapt honors

And men wake to see that they are used like things
    spent in a great potlatch, this Texas barbeque
        of Asia, Africa, and all the Americas,
And the professional military behind him, thinking
    to use him as they thought to use Hitler
    without losing control of their business of war,

But the mania, the ravening eagle of America
    as Lawrence saw him "bird of men that are masters,
    lifting the rabbit-blood of the myriads up into—"
    into something terrible, gone beyond bounds, or
As Blake saw figures of fire and blood raging,
    —in what image? the ominous roar in the air,
the omnipotent wings, the all-American boy in the cockpit
    loosing his flow of napalm, below in the jungles
        "any life at all or sign of life" his target, drawing now
            not with crayons in his secret room
the burning of homes and the torture of mothers and fathers and children,
    their hair a-flame, screaming in agony, but
in the line of duty, for the might and enduring fame
    of Johnson, for the victory of American will over its victims,
    releasing his store of destruction over the enemy,

in terror and hatred of all communal things, of communion,
    of communism;

has raised from the private rooms of small-town bosses and business men,
from the council chambers of the gangs that run the great cities,
    swollen with the votes of millions,
from the fearful hearts of good people in the suburbs turning the savory
    meat over the charcoal burners and heaping their barbeque plates
    with more than they can eat,
from the closed meeting-rooms of regents of universities and sessions
    of profiteers—

back of the scene: the atomic stockpile; the vials of synthesized
    diseases eager biologists have developed over half a century
    dreaming of the bodies of mothers and fathers and children and
    hated rivals swollen with new plagues, measles grown enormous,
    influenzas perfected; and the gasses of despair, confusion of the
    senses, mania, inducing terror of the universe, coma, existential
    wounds, that chemists we have met at cocktail parties, passed daily
    and with a happy "Good day" on the way to classes or work, have
    workt to make war too terrible for men to wage.

raised this secret entity of America's hatred of Europe, of Africa, of Asia,
the deep hatred for the old world that had driven generations of America out
    of itself,
and for the alien world, the new world about him, that might have been Paradise
but was before his eyes already cleard back in a holocaust of burning Indians,
    trees and grasslands,
reduced to his real estate, his projects of exploitation and profitable wastes,

this specter that in the beginning Adams and Jefferson feard and knew
would corrupt the very body of the nation and all our sense of our common
    humanity,
this black bile of old evils arisen anew,
takes over the vanity of Johnson;
and the very glint of Satan's eyes from the pit of the hell of America's
    unacknowledged, unrepented crimes that I saw in Goldwater's eyes
now shines from the eyes of the President in the swollen head of the nation.

ROBERT PENN WARREN (1905–1989)

Robert Penn Warren published nine novels, eleven collections of poetry, a volume of short stories, a play, a collection of critical essays, a biography, two historical essays, and two studies of race relations in the United States. The recipient of nearly every honor and award for literature in America, including the Pulitzer Prize in both poetry and fiction, the National Book Award, and the National Medal for Literature, he was one of the twentieth century's most distinguished American writers.

Bad Year, Bad War: A New Year's Card, 1969

*And almost all things are by the law purged
with blood; and without shedding of blood
there is no remission.*
EPISTLE TO THE HEBREWS, 9:22

That was the year of the bad war. The others—
Wars, that is—had been virtuous. If blood

Was shed, it was, in a way, sacramental, redeeming
Even evil enemies from whose veins it flowed,

Into the benign logic of History; and some,
By common report even the most brutalized, died with a shy

And grateful smile on the face, as though they,
At the last, understood. Our own wounds were, of course, precious.

There is always imprecision in human affairs, and war
Is not exception, therefore the innocent—

Though innocence is, it should be remembered, a complex concept—
Must sometimes suffer. There is the blunt

Justice of the falling beam, the paw-flick of
The unselective flame. But happily,

If one's conscience attests to ultimate innocence,
Then the brief suffering of others, whose innocence is only incidental,

Can be regarded, with pity to be sure, as merely
The historical cost of the process by which

The larger innocence fulfills itself in
The realm of contingency. For conscience

Is, of innocence, the final criterion, and the fact that now we
Are troubled, and candidly admit it, simply proves

That in the past we, being then untroubled,
Were innocent. Dear God, we pray

To be restored to that purity of heart
That sanctifies the shedding of blood.

DANIEL BERRIGAN (1921–   )

Co-founder of the Catholic Peace Fellowship and the Clergy and Laity Concerned About Vietnam, Daniel Berrigan was first arrested at a Pentagon protest against the Vietnam War in 1967. In 1968, he traveled to North Vietnam to help arrange the release of three captured American airmen. That same year, Berrigan, his brother Philip, and seven other Roman Catholic activists burned draft files at the Selective Service office in Catonsville, Maryland. The Catonsville Nine, as the group was called, were found guilty and sentenced to three years in prison. The Berrigan brothers and two other defendants went underground and for several months were the focus of a massive manhunt. Captured in 1970, Berrigan served eighteen months of a reduced sentence in the federal prison in Danbury, Connecticut. "You Could Make a Song of It" appeared in Prison Poems, *written during Berrigan's incarceration.*

You Could Make a Song of It, A Dirge of It, A Heartbreaker of It

EVERYONE everyone in america
carries the war around with him
N. Mailer carries the war with him
2 inches on his waste line
B. Graham carries the war with him
at the root of his tongue   where the tongue forks out
left; turning a bible page
right; tasting the apples in the W. House garden
Bobby Seale carries the war with him
shackles to shoe laces.
The dying man in the cancer ward carries the war—
face to wall, kicked off the skids of the medicos.
The break-&-entry man   the acid freaks   the boy & girl
carry the war with them.   Making love
is mortal sin   the warmakers march
the lovemakers die
Cardinals carry the war around, a sign of the †
Jews carry the war   the yarmulke sits
on the classified head of Kissinger
                              The kids
toss a switchblade in the spring mud—
Territory!   they cry
carving the breathing earth like a turkey corpse.

HAYDEN CARRUTH (1921–   )

In "The Birds of Vietnam," Hayden Carruth employs elements of the traditional pastoral elegy to create a poem of outcry against the natural and human loss of the Vietnam War.

The Birds of Vietnam

O bright, O swift and bright,
you flashing among pandanus boughs
   (is that right? pandanus?)
under the great banyan, in and out
the dusky delicate bamboo groves
   (yes? banyan, bamboo?)
low, wide-winged, gliding
over the wetlands and drylands
   (but I have not seen you,
   I do not know your names,
   I do not know
   what I am talking about).

I have seen the road runner and the golden eagle,
the great white heron and the Kirtland's warbler,
   our own endangered species,
and I have worried about them. I have worried
about all our own, seen and unseen,
whooping cranes, condors, white-tailed kites,
and the ivory-bills (certainly gone, all gone!)
the ones we have harried, murdered, driven away
as if we were the Appointed Avengers,
   the Destroyers, the Wrathful Ones
out of our ancestors' offended hearts
at the cruel beginning of the world.
But for what? for whom? why?
   Nobody knows.

And why, in my image of that cindered country,
should I waste my mourning? I will never have
enough. Think of the children there,
insane little crusted kids at the beckoning fire,

think of the older ones, burned, crazy with fear,
sensible beings who can know hell, think
of their minds exploding, their hearts flaming.

I do think. But today,
O mindless, O heartless, in and out
the dusky delicate groves,
your hell becomes mine, simply
and without thought, you maimed, you
poisoned in your nests, starved
in the withered forests.
O mindless, heartless,
    you never invented hell.
We say flesh turns to dust, though more often
a man-corpse is a bloody pulp,
and a bird-corpse too, yet your feathers
    retain life's color
long afterward, even in the robes
    of barbarous kings,
still golden the trogon feather,
still bright the egret plume, and the crest
of the bower bird will endure forever
almost. You will always remind us of what
    the earth has been.

O bright, swift, gleaming
in dusky groves,
I mourn you.
O mindless, heartless, I can't
help it, I have so loved
    this world.

W. S. MERWIN (1927–   )

One of America's most distinguished poets, W. S. Merwin is the author of A Mask for Janus, The Drunk in the Furnace, The Lice, The Carrier of Ladders, *which was awarded the Pulitzer Prize, and* The River Sound, *among other volumes. He is also the translator of over twenty volumes of poetry and prose, including* The Poem of the Cid, The Song of Roland, *and* East Window: The Asian Translations. *He lives on Maui, Hawaii, where he raises rare palm trees.*

The Asians Dying

When the forests have been destroyed their darkness remains
The ash the great walker follows the possessors
Forever
Nothing they will come to is real
Nor for long
Over the watercourses
Like ducks in the time of the ducks
The ghosts of the villages trail in the sky
Making a new twilight
Rain falls into the open eyes of the dead
Again again with its pointless sound
When the moon finds them they are the color of everything

The nights disappear like bruises but nothing is healed
The dead go away like bruises
The blood vanishes into the poisoned farmlands
Pain the horizon
Remains
Overhead the seasons rock
They are paper bells
Calling to nothing living

The possessors move everywhere under Death their star
Like columns of smoke they advance into the shadows
Like thin flames with no light
They with no past
And fire their only future

GRACE PALEY (1922–   )

Poet, short-story writer, and activist Grace Paley is a member of the National Institute of Arts and Letters and the American Academy and Institute of Arts and Letters. She has taught at Columbia University, Syracuse University, and Sarah Lawrence College. Her books include New and Collected Poems, The Collected Stories, *and* Conversations with Grace Paley.

Two Villages

In Duc Ninh a village of 1,654 households
over 100 tons of rice and cassava were burned
18,138 cubic meters of dike were destroyed
There were 1,077 air attacks
There is a bomb crater that measures 150 feet across
It is 50 feet deep

Mr. Tat said: The land is more exhausted than the people
                 I mean to say that the poor earth
                 is tossed about
                 thrown into the air again and again
                 it knows no rest

                 whereas the people have dug tunnels
                 and trenches   they are able in this way
                 to lead normal family lives

In Trung Trach
a village of 850 households
a chart is hung in the House of Tradition

rockets	522
attacks	1,201
big bombs	6,998
napalm	1,383
time bombs	267
shells	12,291
pellet bombs	2,213

Mr. Tuong of the Fatherland Front
has a little book
In it he keeps the facts
carefully added

ROBERT BLY (1926–)

One of the most influential poets, translators, editors, and publishers of his genera-
tion, Robert Bly is the author of dozens of books, including Silence in the Snowy
Fields, The Light Around the Body, The Teeth Mother Naked at Last, *and* Eating
the Honey of Words: New and Selected Poems. *During the Vietnam War, he*
helped organize American Writers Against the Vietnam War.

Counting Small-Boned Bodies

Let's count the bodies over again.

If we could only make the bodies smaller,
The size of skulls,
We could make a whole plain white with skulls in the moonlight!

If we could only make the bodies smaller,
Maybe we could get
A whole year's kill in front of us on a desk!

If we could only make the bodies smaller,
We could fit
A body into a finger-ring, for a keepsake forever.

CLARENCE MAJOR (1936–   )

Clarence Major is the author of over ten collections of poetry, including Swallow the Lake *and* Configurations: New and Selected Poems, 1958–1998, *and nine novels. He teaches at the University of California at Davis.*

Vietnam #4

a cat said
on the corner

the other day
dig man

how come so many
of us
niggers

are dying over there
in that white
man's war

they say more of us
are dying

than them peckerwoods
& it just
   don't make sense

unless it's true
that the honkeys

are trying to kill us out
with the same stone

they killing them other cats
with

you know, he said
two birds with one stone

WALT MCDONALD (1934–)

Walt McDonald was an air force pilot, taught at the Air Force Academy, and also served in Vietnam. He was Texas Poet Laureate for 2001 and is currently the director of the creative writing program at Texas Tech University. His books include After the Noise of Saigon, Counting Survivors, *and* Climbing the Divide.

Christmas Bells, Saigon

Buses came late, each driver sullen,
head shaved above the ears. At the French
country club on base we nursed warm drinks
while French and their Viet Cong cousins
ignored us, strolling from room to room.

The maitre d' said wait, he'd find a place
for us. For hours, we stumbled around outside
trying to get drunk. After weeks of rockets
we needed to celebrate. Someone joked
the clerk who took our reservation

died in last night's rockets. People I knew
kept disappearing. I asked what's going on.
Vietnamese friends all looked at me
and shrugged. Men who'd been in Vietnam
for years kept dancing off with girls.

I listened for gunfire above the band's
loud brassy mist of Beatles and Japanese.
I studied guards buried in cages
ten feet above us in trees. Five minutes apart
they rattled bells to signal—what?—

We are alive? How could anyone believe
in bells dangled on barbed wires?

MICHAEL CASEY (1947–)

Drafted into the U.S. Army in 1968, Michael Casey graduated from the army's military police school at Fort Gordon, Georgia, and served in the American Division in Quang Ngai and Quang Tin provinces of Vietnam. His books include Obscenities, *winner of the Yale Series of Younger Poets Award,* Millrat, *and* The Million Dollar Hole.

AK–47

It was late
And we got stuck
Down the lurp range road
Bringing
You know whose
Girl friend back home
Krackkrackkrack
We heard and we started
Beating feet
Hauling ass
Scared shitless
I might say
I was driving
So I didn't have
That much time to think
The little people
In the back of the jeep
They fired back first
Long with his thirty-eight
And Hau with his M-sixteen
Bagley didn't do that cool
One of Hau's ejected rounds
Went down his neck
And he thought he was hit
He dropped his rifle
From the jeep
And we didn't even stop
To look for same
I hope he has to pay for it
Teach him some humility

He still thinks
He's war-wounded
From that sniper bullet
That graze-burned
His skin on the middle of his back
But didn't even leave no holes
In his shirt
I might believe that
But I kind of doubt it

For the Old Man

The old man was mumbling
And Albert was shouting at him
Im! Im! Im!
Until Booboo told Albert
To shut the fuck up
The old man was skinny
The old man had looked young
With the sand bag
Over his head
Without the bag
The man was old
There was a lump
The size of a grapefruit
On his head
When the bag was taken off
The man clasped his hands
In front of him
And bowed to us
Each in turn
To Booboo, Albert, and me
He kept it up too
He wouldn't stop
His whole body shaking
Shivering with fright
And somehow
With his hands
Clasped before him
It seemed as if

He was praying to us
It made all of us
Americans
Feel strange

Im: silence

DALE RITTERBUSCH (1946–   )

Author of Lessons Learned, *Dale Ritterbusch is Professor of Language and Literature at the University of Wisconsin, Whitewater. During the Vietnam War, he was a liaison officer responsible for coordinating classified shipments of anti-personnel mines used along the Ho Chi Minh Trail, a network of roads and trails stretching from North Vietnam, through Laos, to South Vietnam, used by North Vietnam to transport weapons, ammunition, and troops.*

Search and Destroy

They came out of the hootch
with their hands up—surrendered—
and we found all that rice
and a couple of weapons. They
were tagged and it all seemed so easy—
too easy, and someone started to torch
the hootch and I stopped him—something
was funny. We checked the hootch
a couple times more; I had them probe it
like we were searching for mines and
a lucky poke with a knife
got us the entrance to a tunnel.
We didn't wait for any damn
tunnel rats—we threw down
CS and smoke and maybe two hundred
yards to our right two gooks popped up
and we got 'em running across the field,
nailed 'em before they hit the trees.
We went to the other hole and popped more
gas and smoke and a fragmentation grenade
and three gooks came out coughing, tears
and red smoke pouring out of their eyes and
nose. We thought there were more
so we threw in another grenade and one of the
dinks brought down his arms, maybe he started
to sneeze with all that crap running out of his face,
maybe he had a weapon concealed, I didn't know,
so I greased him. Wasn't much else I could do.
A sudden move like that.

MICHAEL S. HARPER (1938–   )

Michael Harper has taught at Brown University since 1970. He has published ten volumes of poetry including Dear John, Dear Coltrane; Images of Kin: New and Selected Poems; *and* Songlines in Michaeltree. *"Caves" describes North Vietnam's Spring Offensive in April 1972. During the attack, the central highlands town of Dak To and several other strategic South Vietnamese outposts were overrun at a cost of many lives*

Caves

Four M-48 tank platoons ambushed
near Dak To, two destroyed:
the Ho Chi Minh Trail boils,
half my platoon rockets
into stars near Cambodia,
foot soldiers dance from highland woods
taxing our burning half:

there were no caves for them to hide.

We saw no action,
eleven months twenty-two days
in our old tank
burning sixty feet away:
I watch them burn inside out:
hoisting through heavy crossfire,
hoisting over turret hatches,
hoisting my last burning man
alive to the ground,
our tank artillery shells explode
killing all inside:
hoisting blown burned squad
in tank's bladder,
plug leaks with cave blood:

there were no caves for them to hide—

YUSEF KOMUNYAKAA (1947–   )

Yusef Komunyakaa served in Vietnam as correspondent and editor of The Southern Cross *and received a Bronze Star. For his poetry, he received the Thomas Forcade Award for Literature and Art Dedicated to the Healing of Vietnam in America, as well as the Pulitzer Prize for* Neon Vernacular: New and Selected Poems. *He is a professor in the Council of Humanities and Creative Writing Program at Princeton University.*

Communiqué

Bob Hope's on stage, but we want the Gold Diggers,
want a flash of legs

through the hemorrhage of vermilion, giving us
something to kill for.

We want our hearts wrung out like rags & ground down
to Georgia dust

while Cobras drag the perimeter, gliding along the sea,
swinging searchlights

through the trees. The assault & battery of hot pink
glitter erupts

as the rock 'n' roll band tears down the night—caught
in a safety net

of brightness, the Gold Diggers convulse. White legs
shimmer like strobes.

The lead guitarist's right foot's welded to his wah-wah.
"I thought you said

Aretha was gonna be here." "Man, I don't wanna see
no Miss America."

"There's Lola." The sky is blurred by magnesium flares
over the fishing boats.

"Shit, man, she looks awful white to me." We duck
when we hear the quick

metallic hiss of the mountain of amplifiers struck by
a flash of rain.

After the show's packed up & gone, after the choppers
have flown out backwards,

after the music & colors have died slowly in our heads,
& the downpour's picked up,

we sit holding our helmets like rain-polished skulls.

Thanks

Thanks for the tree
between me & a sniper's bullet.
I don't know what made the grass
sway seconds before the Viet Cong
raised his soundless rifle.
Some voice always followed,
telling me which foot
to put down first.
Thanks for deflecting the ricochet
against that anarchy of dusk.
I was back in San Francisco
wrapped up in a woman's wild colors,
causing some dark bird's love call
to be shattered by daylight
when my hands reached up
& pulled a branch away
from my face. Thanks
for the vague white flower
that pointed to the gleaming metal
reflecting how it is to be broken
like mist over the grass,
as we played some deadly
game for blind gods.
What made me spot the monarch

writing on a single thread
tied to a farmer's gate,
holding the day together
like an unfingered guitar string,
is beyond me. Maybe the hills
grew weary & leaned a little in the heat.
Again, thanks for the dud
hand grenade tossed at my feet
outside Chu Lai. I'm still
falling through its silence.
I don't know why the intrepid
sun touched the bayonet,
but I know that something
stood among those lost trees
& moved only when I moved.

BRUCE WEIGL (1949–)

Bruce Weigl is the author of seven collections of poetry, including A Romance, Song of Napalm, *and* Sweet Lorain. *He served in Vietnam with the First Air Cavalry, where he was awarded a Bronze Star. A recipient of many prizes and honors for his work, he teaches in the writing program at Pennsylvania State University. Napalm, to which Weigl refers in the following poem, is an incendiary material developed during World War II. Composed of a mixture of gasoline and naphthenic and palmitic acids, it creates a thick gelatin that sticks to targets as it burns.*

Song of Napalm

for my wife

After the storm, after the rain stopped pounding,
We stood in the doorway watching horses
Walk off lazily across the pasture's hill.
We stared through the black screen,
Our vision altered by the distance
So I thought I saw a mist
Kicked up around their hooves when they faded
Like cut-out horses
Away from us.
The grass was never more blue in that light, more
Scarlet; beyond the pasture
Trees scraped their voices into the wind, branches
Criss-crossed the sky like barbed wire
But you said they were only branches.

Okay. The storm stopped pounding.
I am trying to say this straight: for once
I was sane enough to pause and breathe
Outside my wild plans and after the hard rain
I turned my back on the old curses. I believed
They swung finally away from me . . .

But still the branches are wire
And thunder is the pounding mortar,
Still I close my eyes and see the girl
Running from her village, napalm

Stuck to her dress like jelly,
Her hands reaching for the no one
Who waits in waves of heat before her.

So I can keep on living,
So I can stay here beside you,
I try to imagine she runs down the road and wings
Beat inside her until she rises
Above the stinking jungle and her pain
Eases, and your pain, and mine.

But the lie swings back again.
The lie works only as long as it takes to speak
And the girl runs only as far
As the napalm allows
Until her burning tendons and crackling
Muscles draw her up
Into that final position
Burning bodies so perfectly assume. Nothing
Can change that; she is burned behind my eyes
And not your good love and not the rain-swept air
And not the jungle green
Pasture unfolding before us can deny it.

GALWAY KINNELL (1927–   )

Following a Fulbright Fellowship in Paris, Galway Kinnell served in the U.S. Navy and later as a field worker for the Congress of Racial Equality. He has taught at the universities of Grenoble and Nice and is presently the Erich Maria Remarque Professor of Creative Writing at New York University. His books include What a Kingdom It Was; Body Rags; The Book of Nightmares; Selected Poems, *winner of both the Pulitzer Prize and the National Book Award; and* New Selected Poems.

The Dead Shall Be Raised Incorruptible

1

A piece of flesh gives off
smoke in the field—

carrion,
caput mortuum,
orts,
pelf,
fenks,
sordes,
gurry dumped from hospital trashcans.

Lieutenant!
This corpse will not stop burning!

2

"That you Captain? Sure,
sure I remember—I still hear you
lecturing at me on the intercom, *Keep your guns up, Burnsie!*
and then screaming. *Stop shooting, for crissake, Burnsie,*
those are friendlies! But crissake, Captain,
I'd already started, burst
after burst, little black pajamas jumping
and falling . . . and remember that pilot
who'd bailed out over the North,
how I shredded him down to catgut on his strings?

one of his slant eyes, a piece
of his smile, sail past me
every night right after the sleeping pill . . .

"It was only
that I loved the *sound*
of them, I guess I just loved
the *feel* of them sparkin' off my hands . . . "

3

On the television screen:

Do you have a body that sweats?
Sweat that has odor?
False teeth clanging into your breakfast?
Case of the dread?
Headache so perpetual it may outlive you?
Armpits sprouting hair?
Piles so huge you don't need a chair to sit at a table?

We shall not all sleep, but we shall be changed . . .

4

In the Twentieth Century of my trespass on earth,
having exterminated one billion heathens,
heretics, Jews, Moslems, witches, mystical seekers,
black men, Asians, and Christian brothers,
every one of them for his own good,

a whole continent of red men for living in unnatural community
and at the same time having relations with the land,
one billion species of animals for being sub-human,
and ready to take on the bloodthirsty creatures from the other planets,
I, Christian man, groan out this testament of my last will.

I give my blood fifty parts polystyrene,
twenty-five parts benzene, twenty-five parts good old gasoline,
to the last bomber pilot aloft, that there shall be one acre
in the dull world where the kissing flower may bloom,
which kisses you so long your bones explode under its lips.

My tongue goes to the Secretary of the Dead
to tell the corpses, "I'm sorry, fellows,
the killing was just one of those things
difficult to pre-visualize—like a cow,
say, getting hit by lightning."

My stomach, which has digested
four hundred treaties giving the Indians
eternal right to their land, I give to the Indians,
I throw in my lungs which have spent four hundred years
sucking in good faith on peace pipes.

My soul I leave to the bee
that he may sting it and die, my brain
to the fly, his back the hysterical green color of slime,
that he may suck on it and die, my flesh to the advertising man,
the anti-prostitute, who loathes human flesh for money.

I assign my crooked backbone
to the dice maker, to chop up into dice,
for casting lots as to who shall see his own blood
on his shirt front and who his brother's,
for the race isn't to the swift but to the crooked.

To the last man surviving on earth
I give my eyelids worn out by fear, to wear
in his long nights of radiation and silence,
so that his eyes can't close, for regret
is like tears seeping through closed eyelids.

I give the emptiness my hand: the pinkie picks no more noses,
slag clings to the black stick of the ring finger,
a bit of flame jets from the tip of the fuck-you finger,
the first finger accuses the heart, which has vanished,
on the thumb stump wisps of smoke ask a ride into the emptiness.

In the Twentieth Century of my nightmare
on earth, I swear on my chromium testicles
to this testament
and last will
of my iron will, my fear of love, my itch for money, and my madness.

5

In the ditch
snakes crawl cool paths
over the rotted thigh, the toe bones
twitch in the smell of burnt rubber,
the belly
opens like a poison nightflower,
the tongue has evaporated,
the nostril
hairs sprinkle themselves with yellowish-white dust,
the five flames at the end
of each hand have gone out, a mosquito
sips a last meal from this plate of serenity.

And the fly,
the last nightmare, hatches himself.

6

I ran
my neck broken I ran
holding my head up with both hands I ran
thinking the flames
the flames may burn the oboe
but listen buddy boy they can't touch the notes!

7

A few bones
lie about in the smoke of bones.

Membranes,
effigies pressed into grass,
mummy windings,
desquamations,
sags incinerated mattresses gave back to the world,
memories left in mirrors on whorehouse ceilings,
angel's wings
flagged down into the snows of yesteryear,

kneel
on the scorched earth
in the shapes of men and animals:

do not let this last hour pass
do not remove this last, poison cup from our lips.

And a wind holding
the cries of love-making from all our nights and days
moves among the stones, hunting
for two twined skeletons to blow its last cry across.

Lieutenant!
This corpse will not stop burning!

KAREN SWENSON (1936–   )

Poet and journalist Karen Swenson is the author of five collections of poetry, including An Attic of Ideals, A Sense of Direction, *and* A Daughter's Latitude: New & Selected Poems. *She teaches at the City College of New York. "We" alludes to the March 16, 1968, massacre at the village of My Lai, in which American troops led by Second Lieutenant William Calley, Jr. of the 23rd Infantry Division killed 347 unarmed South Vietnamese civilians, including women, children, and infants. On September 29, 1971, Calley was found guilty of premeditated murder and sentenced to life imprisonment at hard labor. Calley's conviction was later overturned in Federal district court.*

We

In a museum of the city
once called Saigon, are snapshots. One's
been blown up so we can all see
it clearly. An American,

a young foot soldier, stands on battle
pocked land, his helmet at a jaunty
tilt, posed for buddies as the Model
Grunt. In his left hand he is dangling,

like Perseus, a head by its hair.
Though not Medusa's, it's his charm
for turning fear to stone. Its stare
will quiet, awhile, his throbbing chest.

The tattered flesh that once dressed collar
bones hangs rags from this Vietnamese
neck, captured with the soldier's scar
of grin by a friend's camera.

Is it enough to see it clearly?
We all know what to think. The whitewashed
walls of a second room show nearly
as many black-and-white shots of

Cambodian atrocities
against Vietnamese. No room's hung
with what was done to enemies
of Vietnam, just as there's no

American museum built
to show off snapshots of My Lai.
One pronoun keeps at bay our guilt
they they they they they they they they.

DENISE LEVERTOV (1923–1997)

Feminist and anti-war activist Denise Levertov traveled to North Vietnam in 1972 after a cease-fire had been declared. Driving south from Hanoi, she encountered what she called "a landscape of tender, moist shades of green, full of the 'water-mirrors' I had imagined in a poem, 'What Were They Like?,' written in 1966." She later compiled her impressions in "Glimpses of Vietnamese Life," an essay published in The Poet in the World.

What Were They Like?

1) Did the people of Viet Nam
   use lanterns of stone?
2) Did they hold ceremonies
   to reverence the opening of buds?
3) Were they inclined to quiet laughter?
4) Did they use bone and ivory,
   jade and silver, for ornament?
5) Had they an epic poem?
   Did they distinguish between speech and singing?

1) Sir, their light hearts turned to stone.
   It is not remembered whether in gardens
   stone lanterns illumined pleasant ways.
2) Perhaps they gathered once to delight in blossom,
   but after the children were killed
   there were no more buds.
3) Sir, laughter is bitter to the burned mouth.
4) A dream ago, perhaps. Ornament is for joy.
   All the bones were charred.
5) It is not remembered. Remember,
   most were peasants; their life
   was in rice and bamboo.
   When peaceful clouds were reflected in the paddies
   and the water buffalo stepped surely along terraces,
   maybe fathers told their sons old tales.
   When bombs smashed those mirrors
   there was time only to scream.
6) There is an echo yet
   of their speech which was like a song.

It was reported their singing resembled
the flight of moths in moonlight.
Who can say? It is silent now.

JOHN BALABAN (1943–)

John Balaban went to Vietnam in 1967 as a civilian conscientious objector with the International Voluntary Services and later as a field representative for the Committee of Responsibility to Save War-Injured Children. Recipient of the Lamont Poetry Prize and the William Carlos Williams Award, he is the author of eleven books of poetry and prose, including After Our War, Vietnam: The Land We Never Knew, Words for My Daughter, *and* Locusts at the Edge of Summer: New and Selected Poems. *He serves as Poet-in-Residence and Professor of English at North Carolina State University in Raleigh.*

News Update

> For Erhart, Gitelson, Flynn and Stone,
> happily dead and gone.

Well, here I am in the *Centre Daily Times*
back to back with the page one refugees
fleeing the crossfire, pirates, starvation.
Familiar faces. We followed them
through defoliated forests, cratered fields
past the blasted water buffalo,
the shredded tree lines, the human head
dropped on the dusty road, eyes open,
the dusty road which called you all to death.

One skims the memory like a moviola
editing out the candid shots: Sean Flynn
dropping his camera and grabbing a gun
to muster the charge and retake the hill.
"That boy," the black corporal said,
"do in real life what his daddy do in movies."
Dana Stone, in an odd moment of mercy,
sneaking off from Green Beret assassins
to the boy they left for dead in the jungle.
Afraid of the pistol's report, Stone shut his eyes
and collapsed the kid's throat with a bayonet.
Or, Erhart, sitting on his motorcycle
smiling and stoned in the Free Strike Zone
as he filmed the ammo explosion at Lai Khe.

It wasn't just a macho game. Marie-Laure de Decker
photographed the man aflame on the public lawn.
She wept and shook and cranked her Pentax
until a cop smashed it to the street. Then
there was the girl returned from captivity
with a steel comb fashioned from a melted-down tank,
or some such cliché, and engraved: "To Sandra
From the People's Fifth Battalion, Best Wishes."

Christ, most of them are long dead. Tim Page
wobbles around with a steel plate in his head.
Gitelson roamed the Delta in cut-away blue jeans
like a hippy Johnny Appleseed with a burlap sack
full of seeds and mimeographed tips for farmers
until we pulled him from the canal. His brains
leaked on my hands and knee. Or me, yours truly,
agape in the Burn Ward in Danang, a quonset hut,
a half a garbage can that smelled like Burger King,
listening to whimpers and nitrate fizzing on flesh
in a silence that simmered like a fly in a wound.

And here I am, ten years later,
written up in the local small town press
for popping a loud-mouth punk in the choppers.
Oh, big sighs. Windy sighs. And ghostly laughter.

W. D. EHRHART (1949–   )

*Poet, essayist, and editor W. D. Ehrhart enlisted in the U.S. Marines in 1966 and
served in Vietnam with the First Battalion, First Marines, receiving a Purple Heart
and two Presidential Unit Citations. Following his service, he became active in
Vietnam Veterans Against the War. His books include* To Those Who Have Gone
Home Tired: New & Selected Poems, In the Shadow of Vietnam: Essays
1977–1991, *and* Busted: A Vietnam Veteran in Nixon's America.

For a Coming Extinction

Vietnam. Not a day goes by
without that word on my lips.
I hear the rattle of small-arms fire
when I tuck my daughter in,
think of the stillborn dreams of other men
when I make love to my wife,
sharp snap of a flag in high wind—
blood, stars, an ocean of ignorance.
Sometimes I mumble the word to myself
like a bad dream, or a prayer:
Vietnam, Vietnam. Already
it's become what never was:
heroic, a noble cause. Opportunity
squandered, chance to learn turned
inside out by cheap politicians
and *China Beach.* So many so eager
so soon for others to die,
and the time's fast arriving
when Vietnam means only a distant
spot on the globe, only a name
on a dusty map, when no one alive
will understand what was or is,
what might been and was lost.

PHILIP BOOTH (1925–   )

A poet of New England, Philip Booth was born in Hanover, New Hampshire, and grew up on the Maine coast. The recipient of many awards and fellowships, including the Poets' Prize, the Lamont Prize, and the American Academy of Poets Fellowship, he has published a number of books, including Letter from a Distant Land, Before Sleep, *and* Lifelines: Selected Poems: 1950–1999. *He has taught at Bowdoin, Dartmouth, and Wellesley colleges, and served as Poet-in-Residence at Syracuse University.*

Places Without Names

Ilion: besieged ten years. Sung hundreds more, then
written down: how force makes corpses out of men.
Men whose spirits were, by war, undone: Salamis,

Shiloh, Crécy. Lives going places gone. Placenames
now, no faces. Sheepmen sent to Passchendaele:
ever after, none could sleep. Barely thirty years:

sons like fathers gone back to the Marne. Gone again to
Argonne Forest, where fathers they could not remember
blew the enemy apart, until they got themselves

dismembered. Sons, too, shot. Bull Run, Malvern Hill:
history tests. Boys who knew left foot from right
never made the grade. No rolls kept. Voices lost,

names on wooden crosses gone to rot. Abroad,
in rivers hard to say, men in living memory
bled their lives out, bodies bloating far downstream.

On Corregidor, an island rock of fortress caves,
tall men surrendered to small men: to each other
none could speak. Lake Ladoga, the Barents Sea, and Attu:

places millhands froze, for hours before they died.
To islands where men burned, papers gave black headlines:
Guadalcanal. Rabaul. Saipan. Iwo. Over which

men like torpedoes flew their lives down into the Pacific.
Tidal beaches. Mountain passes. Holy buildings
older than this country. Cities. Jungle riverbends.

Sealanes old as seawinds. Old villages where,
in some foreign language, country boys got laid.
Around the time the bands again start up, memory

shuts down, each patriot the prisoner of his own flag.
What gene demands old men command young men to die:
The young gone singing to Antietam, Aachen, Anzio.

To Bangladore, the Choisin Reservoir, Dien Bien Phu,
My Lai. Places in the heads of men who have no
mind left. Our fragile idiocy: inflamed five times

a century to take up crossbows, horsepower, warships,
planes, and rocketry. What matter what the weapons,
the dead could not care less. Beyond the homebound wounded

only women, sleepless women, know the holy names:
bed-names, church-names, placenames buried in their
sons' or lovers' heads. Stones without voices,

save the incised name. Poppies, stars, and crosses:
the poverty of history. A wealth of lives. Ours, always
ours: these holy names, these sacrilegious places.

ROBERT DANA (1929–)

Robert Dana has lived much of his life in Iowa, where he served as Poet-in-Residence at Cornell College. The recipient of many awards and honors, he is the author of Some Versions of Silence, In a Fugitive Season, *and* What I Think I Know: New & Selected Poems. *Authorized in 1980, the Vietnam Veterans Memorial lies on two acres of land near the Lincoln Memorial in Washington, D. C. It is comprised of two walls, each 200 feet long, of black granite inscribed with the names of the dead or missing.*

At the Vietnam War Memorial, Washington, D. C.

Today, everything takes
the color of the sun. The air
is filed and fine with it;
the dead leaves, lumped
and molten; flattened grass
taking it like platinum;
the mall, the simple, bare
plan of a tree standing
clothed and sudden in its
clean, explicable light.

And across the muddy
ground of Constitution
Gardens, we've come to find
your brother's name, etched
in the long black muster
of sixteen years of war—
the earth walked raw
this morning by workmen still
gravelling paths, and people
brought here by dreams
more solemn than grief.

A kid in a sweater hurries
past us, face clenched
against tears. And couples,
grey-haired, touching hands,
their midwestern faces calm,

plain as the stencilled names
ranked on the black marble
in order of casualty.
The 57,939 dead. Soldiers,
bag-boys, lost insurance
salesmen, low riders
to nowhere gone no place—
file after broken file
of this army standing at rest.

Were there roses? I can't
remember. I remember
your son playing in the sun,
light as a seed. Beside
him, the names of the dead
afloat in the darker light
of polished stone. Reo
Owens. Willie Lee Baker.
Your brother. The names
of those who believed and
those who didn't, who died
with a curse on their lips
for the mud, the pitiless sea,
mists of gasoline and rain.

In your photograph, it's
1967. June. On the pad
of a carrier, Donald squats
in fatigues, smoking, beside
a rescue chopper, a man
loneliness kept lean;
the sea behind him slurs
like waste metal. He looks
directly at the camera, and
his eyes offer the serious
light of one who's folded
the empty hands of his
life once too often.
Before nightfall, his bird
will go down aslant God's
gaze like a shattered

grasshopper, and the moons
in the rice-paddies cry
out in burning tongues.

All words are obscene
beside these names. In the
morning the polished stone
gives back, we see ourselves—
two men, a woman, a boy,
reflected in grey light,
a dying world among the dead,
the dead among the living.
Down the poisoned Chesapeake,
leaking freighters haul
salt or chemicals. In a grey
room, a child rises in her
soiled slip and pops the
shade on another day; blue,
streaked with high cloud.

These lives once theirs
are now ours. The silver
air whistles into our lungs.
And underfoot, the world
lurches toward noon and
anarchy—a future bright
with the vision of that
inconceivable, final fire-storm,
in which, for one dead second,
we shout our names, cut
them, like these, into air
deeper than any natural
shadow, darker than avenues
memoried in hidden trees.

GULF WAR
(1991)

According to U.S. strategy, if you never see the enemy, his destruction will be more acceptable ... so that when Iraqi soldiers surrendered, it was as if they emerged from a dream, a flash-back, a lost epoch—an epoch when the enemy still had a body and was still 'like us'.

SERGE DANEY, FRENCH FILM CRITIC, JULY 1992

WALT MCDONALD (1934–   )

On August 2, 1990, two years after the conclusion of its brutal war with Iran, Iraq invaded the neighboring country of Kuwait. After all diplomatic means of negotiating a withdrawal of Iraqi forces failed in the United Nations, Allied troops—American, British, French, and many others—liberated Kuwait in January 1991. The two-pronged Allied thrust into Kuwait and southern Iraq was labeled Operations Desert Storm and Desert Shield. The Gulf War was the last major military conflict of the twentieth century and was the first war in history to be televised live worldwide.

The Winter of Desert Storm

Our grandchild turned five on an Army post
under the roar of fighters training hard
for combat. My wife and I watched her coast,
granddaughter kicking wildly on a swing.
Before our son flew off to Desert Storm,
he drove us to posts of the Civil War,

past the prison cell of Jefferson Davis.
How safe it must have seemed in 1865, no war,
no killing anymore. Redcoats had dug pits
two centuries ago, and waited with muskets,
soldiers from Liverpool and Leeds on foreign soil.
In 1862 that Yorktown fort's stone walls

were blasted down by cannons. When I flew home
from Vietnam, how simple raising babies seemed,
our boy far from Desert Storm, boisterous in the hall,
inventing chaos in homeroom, his elbow
pumping a joyful noise with his palm
in an armpit till he and his teacher screamed.

On the post, with her daddy gone, I thought of wars
almost forgotten, the long black wall
in Washington, the names I touched last week.
Iraq on every channel, and our boy overseas.
What could we do but shove his daughter's swing,
the jets so loud she had to shout to sing.

CAROLYN KIZER (1925–   )

Carolyn Kizer is one of the most influential and recognizable figures in contemporary American poetry: as an early feminist, as a recipient of the Pulitzer Prize, as an editor, as the first director of the National Endowment for the Arts' literary program, and as Poet-in-Residence at a number of universities, including Columbia, Stanford, and Princeton. Her books include Knock upon Silence, Mermaids in the Basement: Poems for Women, *and* Cool, Calm & Collected: Poems 1960-2000.

On a Line from Valéry

Tout le ciel vert se meurt
Le dernier arbre brûle.

The whole green sky is dying. The last tree flares
With a great burst of supernatural rose
Under a canopy of poisonous airs.

Could we imagine our return to prayers
To end in time before time's final throes,
The green sky dying as the last tree flares?

But we were young in judgment, old in years
Who could make peace: but it was war we chose,
To spread its canopy of poisoning airs.

Not all our children's pleas and women's fears
Could steer us from this hell. And now God knows
His whole green sky is dying as it flares.

Our crops of wheat have turned to fields of tares.
This dreadful century staggers to its close
And the sky dies for us, its poisoned heirs.

All rain was dust. Its granules were our tears.
Throats burst as universal winter rose
To kill the whole green sky, the last tree bare
Beneath its canopy of poisoned air.

WILLIAM HEYEN (1940–   )

Part of a long book-length poem dealing with the Gulf War—America's "first war in the desert," as William Heyen writes—"The Heart" is essentially a catalogue of twentieth-century horrors set against the blind, bellicose patriotism of a young, innocent political science student who supports the American cause at all costs.

from Ribbons: The Gulf War

The Heart

One mid-century Long Island afternoon
I biked over for some schoolyard basketball.
My older brother Werner & his friends, that melting-pot gang:
Tony Routi, the Blumbergs, Ernie Olsen, Prez, Riley & the rest.
Later, they were just hanging around, smoking, telling dirty jokes,
when one of them—I've blocked out who—mentioned a movie
playing in Smithtown, a war movie. He said you saw
a Japanese soldier cut the heart out of an American prisoner.
He said the prisoner was still alive, & tied to a stake,
& the Jap had a razor-sharp sword, & cut the heart right out
of the prisoner's chest, right through bone, & held it in his hands.

I am fifty now & have heard, I guess, almost everything.
I have read Krafft-Ebing, true stories of genitals in soup,
& have followed serial murders on television, have witnessed
secondhand such lurid torture & dismemberment
that I am almost shock- and compassion-immune. I have seen
an American president's head blown apart, bits
of his brain & skull sticking to his wife's pink skirt,
& have been to Bergen-Belsen where Anne Frank died.
But I was only ten that afternoon when
for the first time in my mind a human body was cut open,

its heart removed, & I could not breathe well or sleep well
for a long time, & this morning, watching television news,
I heard a young political science major, one Randall Alden,
being interviewed at the University of California at Irvine
about this war in the Gulf, which he was for 100 percent,
& if it were not concluded very soon, he urged bombing civilians

& deployment of U.S. tactical nuclear weapons, & for him
the Iraqi people were not people, & our oil economy
was his religion, & I lost hope, for I knew, then, what had become
of the American whose heart had been cut out.

PAGE DOUGHERTY (1942–   )

Page Dougherty is author of No One with a Past is Safe. *She has received awards for her work from the New York Foundation for the Arts, the Mid-Atlantic States Arts Consortium, and the New York State Council on the Arts. She teaches at the Borough of Manhattan Community College in New York City.*

Ode to X

After TV I cannot shake the thought
of bombs dropping on Iraq, my desire off target.
In bed I know I will fail again,
incomplete, the body's explosion unworthy.
Oh, what rubble we grind through, brushing
wet from our lips, spittle of despair,
conspiracy of dark. Now they are flashing
stories so private, all stony. Hush.
Even the window shade flaps my country's role.
Too much TNT in the crook of an elbow,
tongues around the city needing to reproduce.
Nothing can remove this skin from grief.

In the spin of his hair I hear the bombs sing.
In the gyre of my hips I feel the graves being dug.

ALBERT GOLDBARTH (1948–   )

Albert Goldbarth has taught at Cornell, Syracuse, the University of Texas, and Wichita State University, where he is Distinguished Professor of the Humanities. He is the author of Original Light: New & Selected Poems 1973–1983; Marriage, and Other Science Fiction; *and* Troubled Lovers in History. *During the Gulf War, much of the conflict in southeastern Iraq occurred at the confluence of the Tigris and Euphrates rivers, in an area known as the Fertile Crescent, where the biblical Garden of Eden was said to have been located.*

Section Three

What's amazing isn't the war,
of course: the war has always been with us.
In Doré's engraving of Abel and Cain
the murdering brother stands in a pose we know
by now, the death-lust half burnt out of him
and still half-stiffening him in adrenaline readiness
—the other brother, centered in Doré's theatrical light,
is simply empty now of everything. And
on the ground, a muscular writhe of root
or cloth or fallen branch—something bunched
and darkened, to alleviate the undetailed middle plane—
is reminiscent of the serpent, yes, as if it
lashed its way here from the Garden, from that leafy, dim
pre-Neolithic haven, just to witness this and
make sure its mission would be carried on.
Pages later: "Joshua Committing the Town of Ai
to the Flames": and "The Slaying of the Midianites"
and . . . more, too much more, so much blood
that it becomes the medium of theme
the way the ink becomes the medium of place and person.
Bosch will show us these cruelties as well, and Goya.
It isn't a secret. The movies know it. Every
front-page photograph of bodies in Iraq
has been developed in a bath
of acid squeezed straight out of the rocks
on the slopes around Eden or Olduvai.
We've dreamed the poses of this dying
for a million years, and there they are again

at breakfast and then in the afternoon edition.
It's tragic, oh certainly tragic, and yet
as common as rust, a human rust, a walk
to buy the paper through the old corrosive air.

What's truly amazing is section three
—the newly-engaged are beaming out, unmarked
by anything other than promise; light's completion
seems to come in merely officiating over these smiles.
Just a page more, and the married are routinely making babies,
and the quilt fair, and the boat show, and the jello-wrestling contest
are announced. Who *are* they, going about their business in "Business,"
"Neighbors," "Entertainment"? Lollygaggers who have yet to catch up
with the pellmell armada of grief? or supramystics, who
have folded their torsos lotuswise, serenely closed their eyes, and
levitated above it all, as if on invisible garage-bay lifts? Are these
the loathsome?—the insufferably greedy, the complacent,
the morally blind, the ones whose small but daily fortune is a stink
inside the overriding aromas of human misery. Or are these
the blessed?—these, the next stage, here
already; these, the ones the planet was intended to accommodate
the first time, on the ur-green primocontinent, but something went
awry, and now they're here, again, in blurs of easeful waving
at the curbside. Aren't these lives unreal, leaking
of mirage-steam or of fogged narcotic landscape? Yes,
no, aren't these the fully-bodied dream-lives
we fight *for*, and would defend against bedevilment?
On any day, the questions spin
like a color wheel out of 5th grade science, until they make
a blankness we could funnel into. My friends are
writing their poems about daffodil country, writing
about some shattered hypodermics in the hall.
"Right now I'm working on a poem about oxymorons,"
she tells me, "you know: *jumbo shrimp* or when Thoreau writes
28 lbs. soft hardbread. Or THIS is amazing," she
unfolds today's paper. ACCIDENT (then, smaller type:)
Allies Die By Friendly Fire.

STEPHEN DOBYNS (1941–   )

Stephen Dobyns has taught at several universities and in the Masters of Fine Arts Program at Warren Wilson College. He is the author of Concurring Beasts; Black Dog, Red Dog; Cemetery Nights; *and* Pallbearers Envying the One Who Rides, *as well as over twenty novels.*

Favorite Iraqi Soldier

Into his kit when sent to the front he had tucked
his black three-piece suit and through night
after night of the frightful bombing, which
not only wiped out but pragmatically entombed

his luckless comrades in a marvel of technological
decadence, he had kept the suit protected
so that at the surrender he had stripped naked
and slipped it on. This is when the photographer

caught him, that among the thousands of defeated
there walked one Iraqi in a three-piece suit
who tried to express by his general indifference
that he had stumbled into all this carnage simply

by accident and was now intent on strolling away.
I am a modest banker tossed on the wrong bus.
I am a humble stockbroker who took a wrong turn.
And he passed through the American lines

and began hitchhiking south. Did he elect
to relocate in Kuwait? Fat chance! Did he
want the lovable Saudis as new neighbors?
Quite unlikely! What about the opportunities

offered by the Libyans, Tunisians, Egyptians?
Truly hilarious! Was there any place in Africa
where he hoped to lay his head? Decidedly
not! What about Europe where he could start

as a servant or chop vegetables in the back
of a restaurant but work his way up? Completely
crazy! Or North America where he could dig
a ditch but with the right breaks might buy

a used car? Too ludicrous! What about South
America where he could pick fruit or Asia where
he could toil in a sweatshop? You must be nuts!
In his black suit he is already dressed for the part

and hopes to hitchhike to one of those Antarctic
islands and stroll around with the penguins.
Good evening Mr. White, good evening Mrs. Black,
your children swim quite nicely, they look

so hardy and fit. No one to give him orders
but the weather. No one to terrify him
but the occasional shark. No one to be mean to
but the little fish, who were put into this ocean

to serve him and whom he praises with each bite.
Thank you, gray brother, for the honor you have bestowed
on my belly. May you have the opportunity
to devour me when my days on earth are done.

WILLIAM STAFFORD (1914–1993)

During World War II, William Stafford was a conscientious objector and worked on forestry and soil conservation projects in Arkansas and California. He was the author of numerous books, among them Traveling Through the Dark, Stories That Could Be True: New and Collected Poems, *and* The Way It Is: New and Selected Poems.

Old Glory

No flag touched ours this year.
Our flag ate theirs. Ours cried,
"Banner, banner," all over the sky—
the sky now ours, the sea this year
our pond. "Thus far," we said,
"no farther," and the storm advanced,
or stopped, or hovered, depending.

We won, they say. They say good came:
we live in the shadow of our flag.
We fear no evil. Salute, ye people.
That feeling you have, they call it glory.
We own it now, they say, under God,
in the sky, on earth, as it is in heaven.

ELEANOR WILNER (1937–   )

A lifelong activist for civil rights and peace, Eleanor Wilner has taught at many colleges and universities. Her awards include a MacArthur Foundation Fellowship and the Juniper Prize. She is the author of Maya, Shekhinah, *and* Reversing the Spell: New & Selected Poems.

Operations: Desert Shield, Desert Storm

1.

Who
are these two women, walking
through the great forum of the plain, walking
under the sun's blinded white eye,
under a hard, featureless sky, bright steel
without a trace of blue. Two women,
their shadows trailing them
like assassins.

What
are they speaking of,
so rapt in conversation they scarcely
seem to see the vacancy through which
they walk. One kicks reflexively at bits
of junk that litter the dry ground, raising
white spurts of dust that hover
at their feet like slavish hounds
of cloud, assiduous on the trail of
all lost things.
                    It is as if time itself
were a dry fountain, where the urn fills only
with pale ashes; where broken tablets
of illegible laws cobble the ground;
where church and court alike are built of bones,
a filigreed white latticework of chalk
through which the white sun casts
a black lace of shadows, widows' weeds;
where a small wind picks through debris,
an indigent in search of scraps; where,

in the desert of our god-drenched origins
the armies grow again, human beetles in
their masks, vague hatred with its poison
gas, the air itself a deadly trench
to these benighted boys, condemned
to fall again into the ranks
of what repeats: into the breach
once more, another city broken open like
a rotting fruit, the flies rising,
the delicate seeds exposed
to the sun, a book with a broken
spine, anything where enough
is left to name.

Antigone and Ismene,
or so we might call them,
these two women walking across this page
of history, this page that is not
a page, because no one can turn it, because
it extends and extends, the smoking cities
scattered like open lesions
to the periphery of sight, these wounds
that memory worries so they
cannot close, this sand
littered with the bodies of brothers.
These two women, whoever they might be,
have the look of those daughters
caught in the line of a self-blinded king
(a father who is also a brother)
debating again the choice
of terms—imprisoned in life, or death.
One is full of argument and heat,
an intellect who can face down a tyrant
with her tongue. The other has a downcast
face and sorrow even in the way her garments
hang, folds that hold the shadows deep
inside; though young, her soul
weighs like an ancient thing; Ismene
takes her sister's arm, to whom her life
is bound, for whose futility she feels
such a ravaged pity, and such

affection she agrees to lose
their argument, pretend to a weakness
she could never own, because she knows
the anger of Antigone must speak
although it end as an echo in a chamber
sealed in the granite hills, a tomb
whose stone is always rolled away
too late. Ismene, grieving,
lives, and walks the olive groves
alone, a lively shade for company.

Again, the dictator
in his empty boots
stalks the narrowing tunnels
of the streets, his little voice
widened by the megaphones of war,
death's echo amplified.
And then it is Ismene
recalls her sister to her side,
steels herself to animate
that shade, and lose her yet again,
if lose she must.

2.

What vicious agency of farce
recalled that ancient sister's act
of love, that wish for a brother's
burial? The stage darkens, the shadows
of the sisters merge, and deepen
to a common night:
                              the end of light
those young men, living, saw
(to think that horror stops the mind)
as the earthmovers pushed the tons of sand
up over them, and then rolled on.

And after the cheering crowds have gone
home, after the last yellow ribbon of sun
has faded in the west, where shall Ismene hide
when they open the cave where defiance

hangs, when those swaying sandals
brush her face, after they cut
the body down, where shall she turn
from all that is buried in the desert plot
made for headlines and parades,
a place too dry for even grief.
Yesterday's news.
Too topical for poems.
Welcome home, this is
America, welcome home.

WAR ON TERRORISM
(2001–   )

We cannot live in Eden anymore.
The wall is broken. The violence done.

We peer beyond the ruin of that day
and see . . . what do we see?

No enemy. Just smoke and rubble.
A vacancy terrible to behold . . .

FROM "THE BEAUTIFUL DAY," ELIZABETH SPIRES

Good afternoon. On my orders the United States military has begun strikes against Al-Qaida terrorist training camps and military installations of the Taliban regime in Afghanistan. . . . By destroying camps and disrupting communications we will make it more difficult for the terror network to train new recruits and coordinate their evil plans. . . . Today we focus on Afghanistan. But the battle is broader. Every nation has a choice to make. In this conflict there is no neutral ground. If any government sponsors the outlaws and killers of innocents, they have become outlaws and killers themselves. And they will take that lonely path at their own peril . . .

FROM PRESIDENT GEORGE W. BUSH'S ADDRESS
TO THE NATION, OCTOBER 7, 2001

JUDITH MINTY (1937–   )

Author of eight collections of poetry, Judith Minty teaches at Humboldt State University. "Loving This Earth" was written in response to the terrorist attacks of September 11, 2001. That morning, foreign terrorists hijacked four commercial American airplanes. Two of the planes were deliberately flown into the World Trade Center in New York City, crumbling the two 110-story steel and glass Twin Towers; the third plane was flown, also deliberately, into the Pentagon in Washington, D.C, demolishing a sizable portion of its west side; and the fourth plane crashed near Shanksville, Pennsylvania, brought down by passengers who had learned of the dev-astation already caused by the other planes. A total of 2,749 lives were lost. About "Loving This Earth," Minty has written: "I live in Michigan, in the center of these United States. . . . In times of sorrow or confusion, I am reassured by the cycle of liv-ing things. . . . It was not unusual then for me, on September 12th, to turn to Lake Michigan for answers in my grief, to walk miles along its beach trying to make sense of what has happened to us."

Loving This Earth

Lake Michigan: 9/12/01

—and we, here in the middle of this country, unable to watch any more
as the plane stabs the tower, as the TV film
reverses, the plane withdraws, no scar, then thrusts again and again
flames burst, smoke rises, the tower falling into itself, over and over; unable to
      listen any more to the stories of orderly evacuation, those stairs
that took more than 30 minutes to descend, people
lifting and leading each other, arms around shoulders, heads bowed, firemen
passing them on the way up; we, unable to imagine again what they have done
    to us:
the awful stench of jet fuel and electric fire, the bodies
falling from windows, cries from the rubble; unable to take in
any more stories of the electrician, the law clerk, the stockbroker,
the kids who looked all day for their father, the woman who at this moment is
    going
from hospital to hospital in search of her fiancé, the story of the shoe store that
gave sneakers to women who had to walk 100 blocks in high heels, the deli
that passed out free sandwiches to those trying to get home, to those
trying to find friends, lovers; we, in our own searching, in our own gloom and
    dread

and helplessness, quit the house and run down the stairs to the beach.
Here, a slight breeze plays dune grasses that twist and dip, their blades
drawing artful circles in the sand; here, waves roll frothy tongues toward land.
The tourists have gone—yesterday's rain washed their footprints away—
now sun glitters the sand. Miles from here, across the water in Wisconsin,
and beyond in the western half of this country, the sun
will set in beauty after it leaves Manhattan and sinks below this Michigan
     horizon.
We begin to walk the shoreline south, and everything speaks:
pieces of driftwood scattered like bones, deer tracks leading to water,
gull feathers along the shore, a dead carp the gulls are scavenging,
birthday balloon still tied with red and blue ribbons, a man's rubber sandal,
more gull feathers, another balloon—how old was that child?—
empty wine bottle with no message inside, a broken sand pail, crow feather,
zebra mussels stowed away in ballasts of foreign ships now
clustered in a sharp-edged fist, plastic glass from Red Lobster,
beer can from Milwaukee, lady bugs imported from Asia,
a tampax roll, a tennis shoe, more gull feathers, a baby bottle.
On our way back, we pass the carp. He is half-eaten now.
We begin to gather scattered feathers, wanting to put together what has been
lost and broken, those thousands of white papers fluttering down from the
     towers.

ROBERT CREELEY (1926–   )

At 9:59 A.M. on September 11, the north tower of the World Trade Center collapsed; twenty-nine minutes later, at 10:28 A.M., the south tower fell. The destructive energy of the towers coming down created earthquake-like after shocks that registered 2.5 on the Richter scale. The site where the World Trade Center stood, heaped with death and wreckage, is known as Ground Zero.

Ground Zero

What's after or before
seems a dull locus now
as if there ever could be more

or less of what there is,
a life lived just because
it is a life if nothing more.

The street goes by the door
just like it did before.
Years after I am dead,

there wlll be someone here instead
perhaps to open it,
look out to see what's there —

even if nothing is,
or ever was,
or somehow all got lost.

Persist, go on, believe.
Dreams may be all we have,
whatever one believes

of worlds wherever they are —
with people waiting there
will know us when we come

when all the strife is over,
all the sad battles lost or won,
all turned to dust.

MICHAEL WATERS (1949–   )

Born in Brooklyn, New York, Michael Waters is the author of numerous books, including The Burden Lifters, Bountiful, *and* Parthenopi: New and Selected Poems, *and editor of several others, including* Contemporary American Poetry *(with the late A. Poulin, Jr.). He is Professor of English at Salisbury University on the Eastern Shore of Maryland.*

Complicity

> *"I cross my fork and spoon / to ward off complicity"*
> —WILLIAM STAFFORD

Here in the new century,
   the new millennium, ash
      still rains on lower Manhattan—
   paper ash, human ash—
and we begin again, as we must,
   to reconstitute such debris
      into words, into language
   that will bear the burden
of becoming the appropriate
   gesture, the right response,
      not only to this tragedy,
   but to tragedies that await us.
In this mutilated world,
   flag-waving won't help
      locate such poetry.
   The transformation from grief
to articulation, from grief to art,
   might begin when we speak
      to our neighbors, when
   we cross our forks and spoons.

BILLY COLLINS (1941–)

Billy Collins was Poet Laureate of the United States for 2001–2002. He is the author of six collections of poetry, including Questions About Angels, The Art of Drowning, Sailing Around the World: New and Selected Poems, *and* Nine Horses. *He is Distinguished Professor of English at Lehman College of the City University of New York. Collins read "The Names" at a special joint session of Congress held in New York City on the second anniversary of the September 11th disaster.*

The Names

Yesterday, I lay awake in the palm of the night.
A soft rain stole in, unhelped by any breeze,
And when I saw the silver glaze on the windows,
I started with A, with Ackerman, as it happened,
Then Baxter and Calabro,
Davis and Eberling, names falling into place
As droplets fell through the dark.

Names printed on the ceiling of the night.
Names slipping around a watery bend.
Twenty-six willows on the banks of a stream.

In the morning, I walked out barefoot
Among thousands of flowers
Heavy with dew like the eyes of tears,
And each had a name—
Fiori inscribed on a yellow petal
Then Gonzalez and Han, Ishikawa and Jenkins.

Names written in the air
And stitched into the cloth of the day.
A name under a photograph taped to a mailbox.
Monogram on a torn shirt,
I see you spelled out on storefront windows
And on the bright unfurled awnings of this city.
I say the syllables as I turn a corner—
Kelly and Lee,
Medina, Nardella, and O'Connor.

When I peer into the woods,
I see a thick tangle where letters are hidden
As in a puzzle concocted for children.
Parker and Quigley in the twigs of an ash,
Rizzo, Schubert, Torres, and Upton,
Secrets in the boughs of an ancient maple.

Names written in the pale sky.
Names rising in the updraft amid buildings.
Names silent in stone
Or cried out behind a door.
Names blown over the earth and out to sea.

In the evening—weakening light, the last swallows.
A boy on a lake lifts his oars.
A woman by a window puts a match to a candle,
And the names are outlined on the rose clouds—
Vanacore and Wallace,
(let X stand, if it can, for the ones unfound)
Then Young and Ziminsky, the final jolt of Z.

Names etched on the head of a pin.
One name spanning a bridge, another undergoing a tunnel.
A blue name needled into the skin.
Names of citizens, workers, mothers and fathers,
The bright-eyed daughter, the quick son.
Alphabet of names in a green field.
Names in the small tracks of birds.
Names lifted from a hat
Or balanced on the tip of the tongue.
Names wheeled into the dim warehouse of memory.
So many names, there is barely room on the walls of the heart.

LAWRENCE FERLINGHETTI (1919–)

Lawrence Ferlinghetti was a lieutenant commander during World War II and was stationed in Nagasaki six weeks after its destruction. One of the leading figures of the San Francisco Renaissance and the Beat movement, he is the author of A Coney Island of the Mind, Starting from San Francisco, Landscapes of Living & Dying, *and* These Are My Rivers: New & Selected Poems 1955–1993. *"Speak Out" addresses America's reactions to the devastating destruction of the September 11th terrorist attacks, including references to the Patriot Act and the October 7, 2001 invasion of Afghanistan by combined American and British forces to destroy the Al-Qaida terrorist training camps of Osama bin Laden and the Taliban government of Afghanistan that protected them.*

Speak Out

And a vast paranoia sweeps across the land
And America turns the attack on its Twin Towers
Into the beginning of the Third World War
The war with the Third World

And the terrorists in Washington
Are drafting all the young men

And no one speaks

And they are rousting out
All the ones with turbans
And they are flushing out
All the strange immigrants

And they are shipping all the young men
To the killing fields again

And no one speaks

And when they come to round up
All the great writers and poets and painters
The National Endowment of the Arts of Complacency
Will not speak

While all the young men
Will be killing all the young men
In the killing fields again

So now is the time for you to speak
All you lovers of liberty
All you lovers of the pursuit of happiness
All you lovers and sleepers
Deep in your private dreams

Now is the time for you to speak
O silent majority
Before they come for you

TIMOTHY LIU (1965–   )

Timothy Liu is the author of five books of poetry, including Vox Angelica, Say Goodnight, *and* Of Thee I Sing. *He resides in Hoboken, New Jersey, and teaches at William Patterson University.*

For the New Year

What was America ever about
if not "Full Frontal Fashion"
if not McDonald's, Wendy's, and dropping rations
from a plane onto a war-torn landscape—
reports of Bin Laden smuggled out
in a head-to-floor-length burkah
across poppy fields fertilized with roadside corpses
overjacked on smack
on search & seizure / sneak & peak / whatever it takes
a hundred-thousand hits alone this week
on bushorchimp.com
lest we forget the sweet ache in our groins
after so much friction trying
to fuck in every room of the house
while B-52s carpet-bombed
Kabul, Kandahar, and Mazar-i-Sharif
till Afghanistan in its disgrace
like the faceless face of a Bamian Buddha
offered up its landmined limbs and amputated feet
to the God of Holy Law
underpants dangling on the chandelier
our wasted jizz enough to repopulate an entire nation
eager to fly those Friendly Skies again—
racial profiling ratcheted up
at security checks flanked by M-16s
and minimum wage
as anthraxed legions bulldozed through the lungs
of a child just getting born—

ROBERT BLY (1926–   )

*Arguing that Iraq was a terrorist threat to the world and that it had repeatedly vio-
lated U.N. sanctions imposed on the country following the Gulf War, America,
Britain, and other countries launched a pre-emptive strike on Iraq in March 2003.
Swept up in a wave of patriotism following the terrorist attacks of September 11,
many Americans supported the invasion and the subsequent toppling of President
Saddam Hussein's government. "Call and Answer" questions why there was such a
decided lack of dissent in the country over the invasion.*

Call and Answer

Tell me why it is we don't lift our voices these days
And cry over what is happening. Have you noticed
The plans are made for Iraq and the ice cap is melting?

I say to myself: "Go on, cry. What's the sense
Of being an adult and having no voice? Cry out!
See who will answer! This is Call and Answer!"

We will have to call especially loud to reach
Our angels, who are hard of hearing; they are hiding
In the jugs of silence filled during our wars.

Have we agreed to so many wars that we can't
Escape from silence? If we don't lift our voices, we allow
Others (who are ourselves) to rob the house.

How come we've listened to the great criers—Neruda,
Akhmatova, Thoreau, Frederick Douglass—and now
We're silent as sparrows in the little bushes?

Some masters say our life lasts only seven days.
Where are we in the week? Is it Thursday yet?
Hurry, cry now! Soon Sunday night will come.

ELEANOR WILNER (1937–   )

A poem of indictment, "Found in the Free Library" concerns Americans' fear of terrorism following the September 11th attacks. With references to the contested 2000 presidential election, the Patriot Act, and such corporate scandals as Enron, it accuses the Bush administration of manipulating that sense of vulnerability to justify the invasion of Iraq, promote its neo-conservative ideology at the expense of civil liberties, and indulge the financial interests of corporate America.

Found in the Free Library

"Write as if you lived in an occupied country."
EDWIN ROLFE

And we were made afraid, and being afraid
we made him bigger than he was, a little man
and ignorant, wrapped like a vase of glass
in bubble wrap all his life, who never felt
a single lurch or bump, carried over
the rough surface of other lives like
the spoiled children of the sultans of old
in sedan chairs, on the backs of slaves,
the gold curtains on the chair
pulled shut against the dust and shit
of the road on which the people walked,
over whose heads, he rode no more aware
than a wave that rattles pebbles on a beach.

And being afraid we forgot to notice
who pulled his golden strings, how
their banks overflowed while
the public coffers emptied, how
they stole our pensions, poured their smoke
into our lungs, how they beat our ploughshares
into swords, sold power to the lords of oil,
closed their fists to crush the children
of Iraq, took the future from our failing grasp
into their hoards, ignored our votes,
broke our treaties with the world,
and when our hungry children cried,

the doctors drugged them so they wouldn't fuss,
and prisons swelled enormously to hold
the desperate sons and daughters of the poor.
To us, they just said war, and war, and war.

For when they saw we were afraid,
how knowingly they played on every fear—
so conned, we scarcely saw their scorn,
hardly noticed as they took our funds, our rights,
and tapped our phones, turned back our clocks,
and then, to quell dissent, they sent. . . .

(but here the document is torn)

W. D. SNODGRASS (1926–   )

A strong denunciation of the American government and its motives for invading Iraq, "Talking Heads" charges that the invasion was a duplicitous act based on lies and greed, a neo-colonialist venture carried out not for the promotion of democracy in Iraq but to secure its oil and to fatten corporate America's coffers.

Talking Heads

TV's handpuppets don't ooze out one word
These days about Iraq's oil. That can be taken
For granted. Anyone tuned-in will have heard
Strongarm democracy brings home the bacon.
Once we've inflicted freedom and secured
Men's good will, we'll sleep sound, dream right, then wake

To heaped up platters. Nobody's been forbidden
To mention things that nobody dares think—
That's honor among thieves. Still, once hidden,
Loot can be sluiced off, quicker than a wink.
And where's your take gone then? Best check your eyelids:
Sly thieves and robber barons never blink.

Slick puppet masters have to keep track who's
Made a killing and who's been double-crossed
To bury it on the dark side of the news,
The brain's recycle bin. True recall might cost
Friends, income, or a life too good to lose.
Analysts sometimes ask how decent Germans,
Facing the sudden scarcity of Jews,
Could maintain ignorance of the Holocaust;
None mentions just how many we let squirm
And twist at rope's end for their predetermined,
Pre-emptive wars. But then, of course, they lost.

SHIRLEY KAUFMAN (1923–   )

Shirley Kaufman has published eight collections of poetry, including The Floor Keeps Turning, Claims, *and* Roots in the Air: New & Selected Poems, *as well as several volumes of translations of contemporary Hebrew poetry. Among her honors are fellowships from the National Endowment for the Arts and the Rockefeller Foundation, and the Shelley Memorial Award from the Poetry Society of America. She has made her home in Jerusalem since 1973.*

Cyclamen

And when it was claimed the war had ended, it had not ended

DENISE LEVERTOV

They are fragile, pale apparitions
among the stones after the heavy rains,
as if to tell us, "we're back,
you have to take notice."

Rosy and white like spun sugar wings
about to take off, we let these
tremblings alert us again
to possibility.

No more than that. While the planes
roar and practice over our heads,
and we dutifully buy bottled water,
tape for our sealed rooms,

and check our gas masks.
Caught in the same efficiency
that kills. How many marches
in the streets of peace?

How many wars?

C. K. WILLIAMS (1936–   )

C. K. Williams has worked as a group therapist for disturbed adolescents and as an editor and ghostwriter of articles and pamphlets in the areas of psychiatry and architecture, and he has taught at a number of colleges and universities, including Drexel, Columbia, George Mason, and Princeton. He has received the National Book Critics Circle Award and the Pulitzer Prize for Poetry. His books include A Day for Anne Frank, Tar, Selected Poems, *and* Repair.

War

I

I keep rereading an article I found recently about how Mayan scribes,
who also were historians, polemicists, and probably poets as well,
when their side lost a war—not a rare occurrence, apparently,

there having been a number of belligerent kingdoms
constantly struggling for supremacy—would be disgraced and tortured,
their fingers broken and the nails torn out, and then be sacrificed.

Poor things—the reproduction from a glyph shows three:
one sprawls in slack despair, gingerly cradling his left hand with his right,
another gazes at his injuries with furious incomprehension,

while the last lifts his mutilated fingers to the conquering warriors
as though to elicit compassion for what's been done to him: they,
elaborately armored, glowering at one another, don't bother to look.

II

Like bomber pilots in our day, one might think, with their radar
and their infallible infrared, who soar, unheard, unseen, over generalized,
digital targets that mystically ignite, billowing out from vaporized cores.

or like the Greek and Trojan gods, when they'd tire of their creatures,
"flesh ripped by the ruthless bronze," and wander off, or like the god
we think of as ours, who found mouths for him to speak, then left.

They fought until nothing remained but rock and dust and shattered bone,
Troy's walls a waste, the stupendous Meso-American cities abandoned
to devouring jungle, tumbling on themselves like children's blocks.

And we, alone again under an oblivious sky, were quick to learn
how our best construals of divinity, our "Do unto, Love, Don't kill,"
could easily be garbled to canticles of vengeance and battle prayers.

III

Fall's first freshness, strange: the season's ceaseless wheel,
starlings starting south, the leaves annealing, ready to release,
yet still those columns of nothingness rise from their own ruins,

their twisted carcasses of steel and ash still fume, and still,
one by one, tacked up by hopeful lovers, husbands, wives, on walls,
in hospitals, the absent faces wait, already tattering, fading, going out.

These things that happen in the particle of time we have to be alive,
these violations which almost more than any altar, ark, or mosque
embody sanctity by enacting so precisely sanctity's desecration.

These broken voices of bereavement asking of us what isn't to be given.
These suddenly smudged images of consonance and piece.
These fearful burdens to be borne, complicity, contrition, grief.

ADRIENNE RICH (1929–   )

Adrienne Rich has taught at a number of colleges and universities, including Brandeis, Swarthmore, Harvard, and Columbia. Her many honors include the Dorothea Tanning Prize from the Academy of American Poets and the Ruth Lilly Poetry Prize. In 1974, she shared the National Book Award with Allen Ginsberg. Her collections of poetry and prose include Necessities of Life, Diving into the Wreck, The Dream of a Common Language, An Atlas of a Difficult World, *and* Blood, Bread, and Poetry: Selected Prose 1979–1985.

The School Among the Ruins

Beirut. Baghdad. Sarajevo. Bethlehem. Kabul. Not of course here.

1.
Teaching the first lesson and the last
—great falling light of summer will you last
longer than schooltime?

When children flow
in columns at the doors
BOYS GIRLS and the busy teachers

open or close high windows
with hooked poles drawing darkgreen shades

closets unlocked, locked
questions unasked, asked, when

love of the fresh impeccable
sharp-pencilled yes
order without cruelty

a street on earth neither heaven nor hell
busy with commerce and worship
young teachers walking to school

fresh bread and early-open foodstalls

2.

When the offensive rocks the sky when nightglare
misconstrues day and night when lived-in

rooms from the upper city
tumble cratering lower streets

cornices of olden ornament human debris
when fear vacuums out the streets

When the whole town flinches
blood on the undersole thickening to glass

Whoever crosses hunched knees bent a contested zone
knows why she does this suicidal thing

School's now in session day and night
children sleep
in the classrooms teachers rolled close

3.

How the good teacher loved
his school the students
the lunchroom with fresh sandwiches

lemonade and milk
the classroom glass cages
of moss and turtles
teaching responsibility

A morning breaks without bread or fresh-poured milk
parents or lesson-plans
diarrhea first question of the day
children shivering it's September
Second question: where is my mother?

4.

One: I don't know where your mother
is Two: I don't know
why they are trying to hurt us
Three: or the latitude and longitude

of their hatred Four: I don't know if we
hate them as much I think there's more toilet paper
in the supply closet I'm going to break it open

Today this is your lesson:
write as clearly as you can
your name home street and number
down on this page
No you can't go home yet
but you aren't lost
this is our school

I'm not sure what we'll eat
we'll look for healthy roots and greens
searching for water though the pipes are broken

5.
There's a young cat sticking
her head through window bars
she's hungry like us
but can feed on mice
her bronze erupting fur
speaks of a life already wild

her golden eyes
don't give quarter She'll teach us Let's call her
Sister
when we get milk we'll give her some

6.
I've told you, let's try to sleep in this funny camp
All night pitiless pilotless things go shrieking
above us to somewhere

Don't let your faces turn to stone
Don't stop asking me why
Let's pay attention to our cat she needs us

Maybe tomorrow the bakers can fix their ovens

7.
"We sang them to naps told stories made
shadow-animals with our hands

washed human debris off boots and coats
sat learning by heart the names
some were too young to write
some had forgotten how"

QUINCY TROUPE (1943–   )

Quincy Troupe is the author of seven volumes of poetry, including Embryo, Skulls Along the River, Avalanche, *and* Transcircularities: New & Selected Poems. *He has also written two best-selling books about jazz legend Miles Davis. Among his many awards and honors are American Book Awards for both poetry and nonfiction, as well as the Peabody Award for radio. He has taught at the University of California at San Diego.*

Transcircularities

across, beyond, moving toward the soon other coast,
transcending a change of appearance, as when
transfigurating a moment that is circular,
as the O of a dead man's mouth is a circle
sometimes after his last deep breath has been sucked in,
becomes the shape of a spinning snake chasing, or swallowing
its own tail, can be a sign, an omen, perhaps, of what has been
forgotten, erased from the circular thought-waves
history provides, the highway of metaphors:
bombs & bullets & flag-waving guiding the way into madness
drunk on power, the hypocrisy of slaughter bombastic
with language rooted in opposing religious fervors, greed,
the sad war dead made over into blood-dripping saints,
converted to propaganda-iconography,

now we find ourselves once again here, as yesterday,
our speech a copy of a copy of a copy,
our histories located in roots, clues underground, bleached
bones, skulls without vanity marking the spots where
ancestral voices once swelled & grew colorful as bright flowers
were there, rhythmic, beautiful, full of surprises, bold with the new
twists inside language grown fresh in an instant,
then suddenly gone, erased in a blink,
as history quickly removes those who lose wars of iconography,
even as music of their speech echoes choices they made
when they stood visible, unbroken, inside their own loved skins,
their heartbeats thumping drumbeats in time with their spirits,
their voices musical instruments, they sang & shaped
a language they danced to then, even now you still hear
echoes of its rhythms on our own tongues here

now the faces of those ghosts are invisible as death
coming in the dark, after midnight when most eyes shut down,
close themselves off to light, live only inside shifting dreams,
it is a roundabout way that we have brought ourselves here,
shrouded in this moment of looping shadows,
whispering in this graveyard of rundown tombstones,
whispering to the memory of what could have been, like autumn,
brown leaves scattered across asphalt, or dirt, or stone,
after the chill of coming winter's tongue sentenced them here
to the fate of dried corpses rotting on a battlefield,

the eyes of owls, their whooping language of mystery
our only companions here, as time tick-tocks down,
our eyes rotate upward toward where we think heaven is,
as if looking for a sign, hoping for a savior

SELECTED BIBLIOGRAPHY
OF RELATED TITLES

GENERAL

Eberhart, Richard and Rodman, Seldon, eds. *War and the Poet.* New York: The Devin-Adair Company, 1945.

Eggleston, George Cary, ed. *American War Ballads and Lyrics: A Collection of the Songs and Ballads of the Colonial Wars, the Revolution, the War of 1812–15, the War with Mexico, and the Civil War.* New York: G. P. Putnam's Sons, 1889.

Forché, Carolyn, ed. *Against Forgetting: Twentieth Century Poetry of Witness.* New York: W. W. Norton, 1993.

Foss, Michael, ed. *Poetry of the World Wars.* New York: Peter Bedrick Books, 1990.

Fussell, Paul, ed. *The Norton Book of Modern War.* New York: W. W. Norton, 1991.

Giddings, Robert, ed. *Echoes of War: Portraits of War from the Fall of Troy to the Gulf.* London: Bloomsbury Publishing, Ltd., 1992.

Keegan, John. *Fields of Battle: The Wars for North America.* New York: Alfred A. Knopf, 1996.

Nalty, Bernard C. *Strength for the Fight: A History of Black Americans in the Military.* New York: Free Press, 1986.

Philip, Neil, ed. *War and the Pity of War.* New York: Clarion Books, 1998.

Stallworthy, Jon, ed. *The Oxford Book of War Poetry.* New York: Oxford University Press, 1984.

REVOLUTIONARY WAR

Barlow, Joel. *The Vision of Columbus: A Poem in Nine Books.* Hartford: Hudson and Goodwin, 1787.

Freneau, Philip. *Poems Written and Published During the Revolutionary War.* Delmar, New York: Scholars' Facsimiles & Reprints, 1976.

_____. *Poems,* edited by Harry Hayden Clark. New York: Harcourt Brace, 1929.

Gaston, James C. *London Poets and the American Revolution.* Troy, New York: Whitson Publishing Company, 1979.

Moore, Frank. *Songs and Ballads of the American Revolution.* New York: New York Times, 1856, 1969.

Patterson, Samuel White. *The Spirit of the American Revolution: A Study of American Patriotic Verse from 1760–1783* [Ph.D. dissertation]. Boston: R. G. Badger, 1915.

Wheatley, Phillis. *The Collected Works of Phillis Wheatley,* edited by John Shields. New York: Oxford University Press, 1988.

WAR OF 1812

Mahon, John K. *The War of 1812.* Gainesville: University of Florida Press, 1972.

Molotsky, Irvin. *The Flag, The Poet & The Song: The Story of the Star-Spangled Banner.* New York: Dutton, 2001.

Roosevelt, Theodore. *The Naval War of 1812.* Annapolis: Naval Institute Press, 1987.

Whitman, Benjamin. *The Heroes of the North, or, the Battles of Lake Erie and Champlain.* Boston: Barber Badger, 1816.

Willey, Eli B. *The Soldier's Companion: Being Six Poems.* Boston: N. Coverly, 1814.

MEXICAN-AMERICAN WAR

Goetzmann, William F., ed. "Our First Foreign War," *American Heritage.* New York: American Heritage Publishing Company, XVII (1966): 18–27.

Palmer, John Williamson. "The Fight at the San Jacinto," *Poems of American History,* edited by Burton Egbert Stevenson. New York: Houghton Mifflin, 1922.

Simms, William Gilmore. *Lays of the Palmetto: A Tribute to the South Carolina Regiment, in the War with Mexico.* Charleston: John Russell, 1848.

CIVIL WAR

Aaron, Daniel. *The Unwritten War: American Writers and the Civil War.* Madison: University of Wisconsin Press, 1987.

Bénet, Stephen Vincent. *John Brown's Body.* New York: Henry Holt & Company, 1928.

Cox, James M. "Walt Whitman, Mark Twain, and the Civil War," *Sewanee Review,* LXIX (1961): 187–193.

Hudgins, Andrew. *After the Lost War.* New York: Houghton Mifflin, 1988.

Marius, Richard, ed. *The Columbia Book of Civil War Poetry.* New York: Columbia University Press, 1994.

Melville, Herman. *Battle-Pieces and Aspects of War,* edited by Sidney Kaplan. Gainesville, Florida: Scholars' Facsimiles & Reprints, 1960.

_____. _Selected Poems of Herman Melville,_ edited by Robert Penn Warren. New York: Random House, 1970.

Negri, Paul, ed. _Civil War Poetry._ New York: Dover Publications, Inc., 1997.

Sweet, Timothy. _Traces of War: Poetry, Photography, and the Crisis of the Union._ Baltimore: The Johns Hopkins University Press, 1972.

Whitman, Walt. _Complete Poetry and Collected Prose,_ edited by Justin Kaplan. New York: Library of America, 1982.

INDIAN WARS

Astrov, Margot, ed. _American Indian Prose & Poetry._ New York: The John Day Company, 1972.

Bierhorst, John, ed. _In the Trail of the Wind: American Indian Poems and Ritual Orations._ New York: The Noonday Press, 1971.

Brown, Dee. _Bury My Heart at Wounded Knee._ New York: Holt, Rinehart & Winston, 1970.

Cronyn, George W., ed. _American Indian Poetry._ New York: Ballantine Books, 1962.

Day, Grove A. _The Sky Clears._ Lincoln: University of Nebraska Press, 1951.

Densmore, Frances. _Teton Sioux Music._ Bureau of American Ethnology, Bulletin 61. Washington, 1918.

Heyen, William. _Crazy Horse in Stillness._ Brockport, New York: BOA Editions, 1996.

Meyer, Roy. _History of the Santee Sioux._ Lincoln: University of Nebraska Press, 1967.

Momaday, N. Scott. _The Way to Rainy Mountain._ Albuquerque: The University of New Mexico Press, 1969.

_____. _House Made of Dawn._ New York: Harper & Row, 1977.

Mooney, James. _The Ghost Dance Religion and the Sioux Outbreak of 1890._ Fourteenth Annual Report of the Bureau of American Ethnology. Washington, 1896.

Neihardt, John G. _Black Elk Speaks._ New York: Pocket Books, 1959.

_____. _The Twilight of the Sioux._ Lincoln: University of Nebraska Press, 1971.

Niatum, Duane, ed. _Carriers of the Dream Wheel._ New York: Harper & Row, 1975.

_____. ed. _Harper's Anthology of 20th Century Native American Poetry._ New York: Harper & Row, 1988.

Swann, Brian. _Smoothing the Ground: Essays on Native American Oral American Indian Literature._ Berkeley: University of California Press, 1983.

Utley, Robert, ed. _The American Heritage History of the Indian Wars._ New York: American Heritage Publishing Company, 1977.

Warren, Robert Penn. _Chief Joseph of the Nez Percé._ New York: Random House, 1982.

SPANISH-AMERICAN WAR

Cashin, Hershel V. *Under Fire With the Tenth U.S. Cavalry.* New York: Arno Press, 1969.

Crane, Stephen. *The War Dispatches of Stephen Crane,* edited by R. W. Stallman and E. R. Hagemann. New York: New York University Press, 1964.

Katz, Joseph, ed. *The Poems of Stephen Crane: A Critical Edition.* New York: Cooper Square Publishers, 1966.

Moody, William Vaughn. *Gloucester Moors and Other Poems.* New York: Houghton Mifflin, 1910.

Sandburg, Carl. "Soldier," *Always the Young Strangers.* New York: Harcourt, Brace and Company, 1952.

Waller, Effie. *Songs of the Months.* New York: Broadway Publishing Company, 1904.

FIRST WORLD WAR

Clark, George Herbert, ed. *A Treasury of War Poetry: British and American Poems of the World War, 1914–1919.* Boston: Houghton Mifflin, 1919.

Cornebise, Alfred E., ed. *Doughboy Doggerel: Verse of the American Expeditionary Force, 1918–1919.* Athens: Ohio University Press, 1985.

Cross, Tim. *The Lost Voices of World War I: An International Anthology of Writers, Poets, & Playwrights.* Iowa City: University of Iowa Press, 1988.

Fussell, Paul. *The Great War and Modern Memory.* New York: Oxford University Press, 1975.

Khan, Nosheen. *Women's Poetry of the First World War.* Lexington: The University Press of Kentucky, 1988.

Reilly, Catherine W., ed. *Scars Upon My Heart: Women's Poetry and Verse of the First World War.* London: Virago, 1982.

Seeger, Alan. *Poems.* New York: Scribner's, 1916.

Silkin, Jon, ed. *The Penguin Book of First World War Poetry.* London: Oxford University Press, 1984.

Untermeyer, Louis. *From Another World.* New York: Harcourt Brace, 1939.

Van Wienen, Mark W., ed. *Rendezvous With Death: American Poems of the Great War.* Urbana: University of Illinois Press, 2002.

Wheeler, W. Reginald. *A Book of Verse of the Great War.* New Haven: Yale University Press, 1917.

SECOND WORLD WAR

Aiken, Conrad. *The Soldier.* New York: New Directions, 1944.

Ciardi, John. *The War Diary of John Ciardi.* Fayetteville: University of Arkansas Press, 1988.

Des Pres, Terrence. *Praises and Dispraises: Poetry and Politics, The Twentieth Century.* New York: Viking, 1988.

Fussell, Paul. *Wartime.* New York: Oxford University Press, 1989.

Gubar, Susan. *Poetry After Auschwitz.* Bloomington: Indiana University Press, 2003.

Heyen, William. *Ericka: Poems of the Holocaust.* New York: Vanguard Press, 1984.

Meredith, William. *Love Letter from an Impossible Land.* New Haven: Yale University Press, 1944.

Nemerov, Howard. *War Stories: Poems about Long Ago and Now.* Chicago: University of Chicago Press, 1987.

Reznikoff, Charles. *Holocaust.* Los Angeles: Black Sparrow Press, 1975.

Richler, Mordecai, ed. *Writers on World War II: An Anthology.* New York: Alfred A. Knopf, 1991.

Schiff, Hilda. *Holocaust Poetry.* New York: St. Martin's Griffin, 1995.

Schweik, Susan M. *A Gulf So Deeply Cut: American Women Poets and the Second World War.* Madison: University of Wisconsin Press, 1991.

Shapiro, Harvey, ed. *Poets of World War II.* New York: The Library of America, 2003.

Snodgrass, W. D. *The Führer Bunker: A Cycle of Poems in Progress.* Brockport, New York: BOA Editions, 1977.

Stokesbury, Leon, ed. *Articles of War: A Collection of American Poetry about World War II.* Fayetteville: University of Arkansas Press, 1990.

Williams, Oscar, ed. *The War Poets.* New York: John Day Company, 1945.

KOREAN WAR

Edwards, Paul M. *The Hermit Kingdom: Poems of the Korean War.* Dubuque, Iowa: Kendall/Hunt Publishing Company, 1995.

Ehrhart, W. D. "I Remember: Soldier-Poets of the Korean War," *War, Literature & the Arts* 9, no. 2 (1997): 1–241.

_____. *Back Where The Past Is Mined: American War Poetry of the Korean War* [Ph.D. dissertation]. 2002.

_____. and Jason, Philip, eds. *Retrieving Bones: Stories and Poems of the Korean War.* New Brunswick, New Jersey: Rutgers University Press, 1999.

Fast, Howard. *Korean Lullaby.* New York: American Peace Crusade, n.d.

Fehrenbach, T. R. *This Kind of War.* New York: Bantam, 1991.

Rizzo, Victor P., ed. *The Korean War Anthology: Korea, The Forgotten War.* Mount Holly, New Jersey: PPS Publishing, 2001.

So, Chi-mun and Perkins, James A. *Brother Enemy: Poems of the Korean War*. Buffalo, New York: White Pine Press, 2002.

Wantling, William. *The Source*. El Cerrito, California: Dustbooks, 1966.

VIETNAM WAR

Anisfield, Nancy, ed. *Vietnam Anthology: American War Literature*. Bowling Green, Ohio: Bowling Green State Popular Press, 1987.

Biedler, Charles. *Rewriting America: Vietnam Authors in Their Generation*. Athens: University of Georgia, 1991.

Ehrhart, W. D., ed. *Carrying the Darkness: The Poetry of the Vietnam War*. Lubbock: Texas Tech University Press, 1985.

_____, ed. *Unaccustomed Mercy: Soldier-Poets of the Vietnam War*. Lubbock: Texas Tech University Press, 1989.

Franklin, Bruce H. *The Vietnam War in Songs, Poems, and Stories*. Boston: Bedford Books of St. Martin's Press, 1995.

Gotera, Vince. *Radical Visions: Poetry by Vietnam Veterans*. Athens: University of Georgia Press, 1993.

Lowenfels, Walter. *Where Is Vietnam?* New York: Doubleday Anchor, 1967.

Mahony, Phillip, ed. *From Both Sides Now: The Poetry of the Vietnam War and Its Aftermath*. New York: Scribner, 1998.

Robertssen, Lowell. *Remembering the Women of the Vietnam War*. Eden Prairie, Minnesota: Tessera Publishing Company, 1990.

Terry, Wallace. *Bloods: An Oral History by Black Veterans of the Vietnam War*. New York: Ballantine Books, 1984.

Van Devanter, Lynda and Furey, Joan A., eds. *Visions of War, Dreams of Peace: Writings of Women in the Vietnam War*. New York: Warner Books, 1991.

GULF WAR

Heyen, William. *Ribbons: The Gulf War*. St. Louis, Missouri: Time Being Books, 1991.

Meek, Jay and Reeve, F. D., eds. *After the Storm: Poems on the Persian Gulf War*. Washington, D. C.: Maisonneuve Press, 1992.

WAR ON TERRORISM

Cohen, Allen and Matson, Clive, eds. *An Eye for an Eye Makes the Whole World Blind: Poets on 9/11*. Oakland, California: Regent Press, 2002.

Hamill, Sam, ed. *Poets Against the War*. New York: Thunder's Mouth Press, 2003.

Heyen, William, ed. *September 11, 2001: American Writers Respond.* Silver Springs, Maryland: Etruscan Press, 2002.

Johnson, Dennis Loy and Merians, Valerie, eds. *Poetry After 9/11: An Anthology of New York Poets.* Hoboken, New Jersey: Melville House, 2002.

PERMISSIONS AND ACKNOWLEDGMENTS

IN ORDER TO OBTAIN CURRENT COPYRIGHT INFORMATION, I have attempted in every instance to contact the author, publisher, or copyright holder of the material included in this collection. In some cases, such information may still be incomplete. The copyright to each individual work remains with the author or other copyright holder as designated by the author.

"The Wars and the Unknown Soldier" by Conrad Aiken. Copyright © 1944, 1972 by Conrad Aiken. Reprinted by permission of Brandt & Hochman Literary Agents, Inc.

"A Short History of the Vietnam War Years" from *Ode to the Cold War: Poems New and Selected* by Dick Allen, published by Sarabande Books. Copyright © 1997. Reprinted by permission of Sarabande Books and the author.

"News Update" by John Balaban is reprinted by permission of the author.

"You Could Make a Song of It, A Dirge of It, A Heartbreaker of It" by Daniel Berrigan is reprinted by permission of the author.

'The Moon and the Night and the Men" from *Collected Poems* by John Berryman. Copyright © 1989 by Kate Donahue Berryman. Reprinted by permission of Farrar, Straus & Giroux.

"Roosters" from *The Complete Poems: 1927–1979* by Elizabeth Bishop. Copyright © 1979, 1983 by Alice Helen Methfessel. Reprinted by permission of Farrar, Straus & Giroux.

"In the Dordogne" and excerpt from "They Should Have Gone Forth With Banners" from *The Collected Poems of John Peale Bishop*, edited by Allen Tate. Copyright © 1933 by Charles Scribner's Sons; copyright renewed © 1961 by Margaret G. A. Bronson. Reprinted by permission of Scribner, an imprint of Simon & Schuster Adult Publishing Group.

"Call and Answer" by Robert Bly is reprinted by permission of the author.

"Counting the Small-Boned Bodies" from *Eating the Honey of Words: New and Selected Poems* by Robert Bly, published by HarperCollins. Copyright © 1999 by Robert Bly. Reprinted by permission of the author.

"To My Brother Killed: Haumont Wood: October, 1918" from *Blue Estuaries* by Louise Bogan. Copyright © 1968 by Louise Bogan. Copyright renewed 1996 by Ruth Limmer. Reprinted by permission of Farrar, Straus and Giroux, LLC.

"Places Without Names" from *Lifelines* by Philip Booth. Copyright © 1999 by Philip Booth. Used by permission of Viking Penguin, a division of Penguin Group (USA) Inc.

"Mothers" and "The People Cry" from *Collected Poems* by Kay Boyle. Copyright © 1991 by Kay Boyle. Reprinted by permission of Copper Canyon Press, P.O. Box 271, Port Townsend, Washington, 98368-0271.

"The Birds of Vietnam" from *From Snow and Rock, From Chaos* by Hayden Carruth. Copyright © 1973 by New Directions Publishing Corp. Reprinted by permission of New Directions Publishing Corp.

"On a Certain Engagement South of Seoul" from *Collected Shorter Poems 1938–1988* by Hayden Carruth. Copyright © 1959, 1992 by Hayden Carruth. Reprinted by permission of Copper Canyon Press, P.O. Box 271, Port Townsend, Washington, 98368-0271.

"AK-47" and "For the Old Man" by Michael Casey are reprinted by permission of the author.

"Trying to Remember People I Never Really Knew" by William Childress is reprinted by permission of the author.

"A Box Comes Home" and "V-J Day" by John Ciardi are reprinted by permission of the Ciardi Family Trust.

"The Names" by Billy Collins is reprinted by permission of the author.

"Chateau de Soupir: 1917" from *Blue Juniata: A Life* by Malcolm Cowley. Copyright © 1985 by Malcolm Cowley. Used by permission of Viking Penguin, a division of Penguin Group (USA) Inc.

"Ground Zero" from *If I Were Writing This* by Robert Creeley. Copyright © 2003 by Robert Creeley. Reprinted by permission of New Directions Publishing Corp.

"Return" from *Collected Poems of Robert Creeley, 1945–1975*. Copyright © 1982 by the University of California Press. Reprinted by permission of the University of California Press and the author.

"i sing of Olaf glad and big." Copyright © 1931, 1959, 1991 by Trustees for the E. E. Cummings Trust. Copyright © 1979 by George James Firmage, "my sweet old etcetera." Copyright © 1926, 1954, 1991 by the Trustees for the E. E. Cummings Trust. Copyright © 1985 by George James Firmage, from *Complete Poems: 1904–1962* by E. E. Cummings, edited by George J. Firmage. Reprinted by permission of Liveright Publishing Corp.

"At the Vietnam War Memorial, Washington, D.C." by Robert Dana is reprinted by permission of the author.

"Hunting Civil War Relics at Nimblewill Creek" from *Poems 1957–1967* by James Dickey. Copyright © 1967 by James Dickey. Reprinted by permission of Wesleyan University Press.

"Victory" from *The Eye-Beaters, Blood, Victory, Madness, Buckhead* by James Dickey. Copyright © 1968, 1969, 1970 by James Dickey. Reprinted by permission of Doubleday, a division of Random House, Inc.

"Champs d'Honneur" and "Killed Piave—July 8—1918" from *88 Poems* by Ernest Hemingway. Copyright © 1979 by The Ernest Hemingway Foundation and Nicholas Gerogiannis. Reprinted by permission of Harcourt, Inc.

"The Heart" from *Ribbons: The Gulf War—A Poem* by William Heyen. Copyright © 1991 by Time Being Books. Reprinted by permission of Time Being Books.

"Unknown" from *Crazy Horse in Stillness* by William Heyen, published by BOA Editions, 1996. Reprinted by permission of the author.

"A Sheaf of Percussion Fire" by Rolando Hinojosa is reprinted by permission of the author.

"Jim Crow's Last Stand" from *The Collected Poems of Langston Hughes* by Langston Hughes. Copyright © 1994 by the Estate of Langston Hughes. Used by permission of Alfred A. Knopf, a division of Random House, Inc.

"Letter to Simic from Boulder" from *Making Certain It Goes On: Collected Poems of Richard Hugo* by Richard Hugo. Copyright © 1984 by The Estate of Richard Hugo. Reprinted by permission of W. W. Norton & Company, Inc.

"Viewing Picasso's *Massacre in Korea*" by Dale Jacobson is printed by permission of the author.

"The Death of the Ball Turret Gunner" and "Losses" from *The Complete Poems* by Randall Jarrell. Copyright © 1969, renewed 1997 by Mary von S. Jarrell. Reprinted by permission of Farrar, Straus & Giroux.

"War Memoir: Jazz, Don't Listen to It at Your Own Risk" from *The Ancient Rain: Poems 1956–1978.* Copyright © 1981 by Bob Kaufman. Reprinted by permission of New Directions Publishing Corp.

"Cyclamen" by Shirley Kaufman is reprinted by permission of the author.

"The Dead Shall Be Raised Incorruptible" from *The Book of Nightmares* by Galway Kinnell. Copyright © 1971 by Galway Kinnell. Reprinted by permission of Houghton Mifflin Co. All rights reserved.

"Vaudeville" from *Rhymes and More Rhymes of a PFC* by Lincoln Kirstein. Copyright © 1964, 1966 by Lincoln Kirstein. Reprinted by permission of New Directions Publishing Corp.

"On a Line from Valéry" from *Cool, Calm & Collected: Poems 1960–2000* by Carolyn Kizer. Copyright © 2001 by Carolyn Kizer. Reprinted by permission of Copper Canyon Press, P.O. Box 271, Port Townsend, Washington, 98368-0271.

"To World War Two" by Kenneth Koch is reprinted by permission of The Kenneth Koch Literary Estate and Karen Koch.

"Communique" and "Thanks" from *Neon Vernacular: New and Selected Poems* by Yusef Komunyakaa. Copyright © 1993 by Yusef Komunyakaa. Reprinted by permission of Wesleyan University Press.

"The Last Picnic" from *The Collected Poems* by Stanley Kunitz. Copyright © 2000 by Stanley Kunitz. Reprinted by permission of W. W. Norton & Company, Inc.

"Buchenwald, Near Weimar" from *Selected Poems* by Joseph Langland. Copyright © 1991 by Joseph Langland. Reprinted by permission of the University of Massachusetts Press.

"Christmas 1944" from *Collected Earlier Poems 1940–1960* by Denise Levertov. Copyright © 1957, 1958, 1959, 1960, 1961, 1979 by Denise Levertov. Reprinted by permission of New Directions Publishing Corp.

"What Were They Like" from *Poems 1960–1967* by Denise Levertov. Copyright © 1966 by Denise Levertov. Reprinted by permission of New Directions Publishing Corp.

"Trophy, W. W. I" from *The Selected Poems of Janet Lewis* by Janet Lewis, edited by R. L. Barth (Swallow Press/Ohio University Press, 2000). Reprinted by permission of Swallow Press/Ohio University Press, Athens, Ohio.

"Abraham Lincoln Walks at Midnight" from *Collected Poems, Revised Edition* by Vachel Lindsay (New York: Macmillan, 1925). Reprinted by permission of Scribner, an imprint of Simon & Schuster Adult Publishing Group.

"For the New Year" by Timothy Liu is printed by permission of the author.

"Patterns" from *The Complete Poetical Works of Amy Lowell.* Copyright © 1955 by Houghton Mifflin Co. Copyright © renewed 1983 by Houghton Mifflin Co., Brinton P. Roberts, and G. D'Andelot Belin, Esquire.

"For the Union Dead," "Memories of West Street and Lepke," and "Verdun" from *Complete Poems* by Robert Lowell. Copyright © 2003 by Harriet Lowell and Sheridan Lowell. Reprinted by permission of Farrar, Straus & Giroux.

"Memorial Rain" and "Wildwest" from *Collected Poems, 1917–1982* by Archibald MacLeish. Copyright © 1985 by The Estate of Archibald MacLeish. Reprinted by permission of Houghton Mifflin Co. All rights reserved.

"Repository" by James Magner, Jr. is reprinted by permission of Maureen M. Sylak.

"Harry Wilmans" from *Spoon River Anthology* by Edgar Lee Masters, originally published by Macmillan Company, 1966. Reprinted by permission of Hilary Masters.

"Vietnam #4" by Clarence Major is reprinted by permission of the author.

Excerpt from "War Story," from *War Story* by Gerald McCarthy, published by The Crossing Press. Copyright © 1977 by Gerald McCarthy. Reprinted by permission of the author.

"Christmas Bells, Saigon" from *After the Noise of Saigon* by Walt McDonald. Copyright © 1988 by the University of Massachusetts Press. Reprinted by permission of the University of Massachusetts Press.

"The Winter of Desert Storm" from *Climbing the Divide* by Walt McDonald. Copyright © 2003 by Walt McDonald. Reprinted by permission of the University of Notre Dame Press and the author.

"We" from *A Daughter's Latitude* by Karen Swenson. Copyright © 1999 by Karen Swenson. Reprinted by permission of Copper Canyon Press, P.O. Box 271, Port Townsend, Washington, 98368-0271.

"Ode to the Confederate Dead" from *Collected Poems: 1919–1976* by Allen Tate. Copyright © 1977 by Allen Tate. Reprinted by permission of Farrar, Straus & Giroux.

"There Will Come Soft Rains" from *Collected Poems, Revised Edition* by Sara Teasdale (New York: Macmillan, 1937). Reprinted by permission of Scribner, an imprint of Simon & Schuster Adult Publishing Group.

"Transcircularities" from *Transcircularities; New and Selected Poems* by Quincy Troupe. Copyright © 2001 by Quincy Troupe. Reprinted by permission of Coffee House Press, Minneapolis, Minnesota, www.coffeehousepress.com.

"Bad Year, Bad War: A New Year's Card, 1969" from *New and Selected Poems* by Robert Penn Warren. Copyright © 1985 by Robert Penn Warren. Reprinted by permission of William Morris Agency, Inc., on behalf of the author.

"Complicity" by Michael Waters is printed by permission of the author.

"Song of Napalm" by Bruce Weigl is reprinted by permission of the author.

"First Snow in Alsace" from *The Beautiful Changes and Other Poems*. Copyright © 1947 and renewed 1975 by Richard Wilbur. Reprinted by permission of Harcourt, Inc.

"War" from *Singing* by C. K. Williams. Copyright 2003 by C. K. Williams. Reprinted by permission of Farrar, Straus & Giroux.

"War, the Destroyer!" from *Collected Poems 1939–1962, vol. II* by William Carlos Williams. Copyright © 1942 by William Carlos Williams. Reprinted by permission of New Directions Publishing Corp.

"Found in the Free Library" and "Operations: Desert Shield, Desert Storm" from *Reversing the Spell: New and Selected Poems* by Eleanor Wilner. Copyright © 1997 by Eleanor Wilner. Reprinted by permission of Copper Canyon Press, P.O. Box 271, Port Townsend, Washington, 98368-0271.

"The Circle" and "Memory of a Victory" from *Graves Registry* by Keith Wilson, originally published by Clark City Press. Reprinted by permission of the author.

INDEX OF AUTHORS, TITLES, AND FIRST LINES

ABOUT THE EDITOR

Rᴏʙᴇʀᴛ Hᴇᴅɪɴ is the author, translator, and editor of seventeen volumes of poetry and prose. Awards for his work include three National Endowment for the Arts Fellowships, a Bush Foundation Fellowship, a Minnesota State Arts Board Fellowship, a North Carolina State Arts Council Fellowship, a Minnesota State Book Award, and the 2000 McKnight Artist Fellowship, Loft Award of Distinction in Poetry. He has taught at Sheldon Jackson College in Sitka, Alaska; the Anchorage and Fairbanks campuses of the University of Alaska; St. Olaf College, Wake Forest University, and the University of Minnesota. He serves as director of the Anderson Center for Interdisciplinary Studies in Red Wing, Minnesota.